I stared. as if the
curtain enough
for us to glimpse a vague, dark shape detaching itself from a
rhododendron bush.

Lauren squeaked in terror as the blur of shadow edged
horribly into focus. Now you could see the wide-brimmed
hat, which Delilah had described as 'funky'. There, too, was
that stick she'd talked about. It was more of a staff really, the
kind that weary pilgrims lean on in biblical pictures. Only this
was crook-shaped. Evil.

The Creep! With a sick lurch of my stomach I knew this
was the source of that shameful, cringing feeling. Whoever the
Creep was, he had reason to hate us.

Delilah was mumbling, '*Go away*. Just go away, Creep, and
mind your own.'

'Delilah, what does he want?' I whispered.

Other titles by Susan Davis and available from Corgi Books:

The Henry Game

DELILAH AND THE
DARK STUFF

DELILAH AND THE DARK STUFF
A CORGI BOOK: 0552 547948

Published in Great Britain by Corgi Books,
an imprint of Random House Children's Books

This edition published 2003

1 3 5 7 9 10 8 6 4 2

Papers used by Random House Children's Books are natural,
recyclable products made from wood grown in sustainable
forests. The manufacturing processes conform to the
environmental regulations of the country of origin.

Set in 12/14 pt Bembo by Falcon Oast Graphic Art Ltd.

Corgi Books are published by Random House Children's Books,
61–63 Uxbridge Road, London W5 5SA,
a division of The Random House Group Ltd,
in Australia by Random House Australia (Pty) Ltd,
20 Alfred Street, Milsons Point, Sydney, NSW 2061, Australia,
in New Zealand by Random House New Zealand Ltd,
18 Poland Road, Glenfield, Auckland 10, New Zealand
and in South Africa by Random House (Pty) Ltd,
Endulini, 5a Jubilee Road, Parktown 2193, South Africa

THE RANDOM HOUSE GROUP Limited Reg. No. 954009

A CIP catalogue record for this book is available from the British Library.

Printed and bound in Great Britain by
Bookmarque Ltd, Croydon, Surrey

Delilah
and the
Dark Stuff

SUSAN DAVIS

CORGI BOOKS

For Isobel and William

ACKNOWLEDGEMENTS:

Thanks to Naiad of The Awareness Shop for her demonstration of Casting the Circle.

Thanks as always to Mary Pachnos at Gillon Aitken Associates.

Also to the team at Random House Children's Books: Annie Eaton, Charlie Sheppard and especially Harriet Wilson for her professionalism and patience with my endless queries.

Chapter One

Trouble

I once heard my mother say about a neighbour of ours that 'Wherever that girl goes, Trouble's never far behind.' Like Trouble was some kind of tangible thing you could touch. If you touched trouble it would feel like a bony cat with its hackles up. Trouble had a shape to it. It slunk like a rat at Delilah's heels; it squatted on her shoulder like a dirty great crow. It squawked with laughter when Phil Humphries, our English teacher, nervously suggested that 'Perhaps you'd like to tell us a bit about yourself, Delilah?'

The new girl at Bromfield High just shrugged and stood up slowly like it was a real effort. Then she scraped her tongue-ring across her front teeth, which was kind of a statement in itself, like when boys drag a stick along iron railings.

'Yeah, well, I'm Delilah. What else d'you want to know?'

Lauren passed me a note that said, 'Where did she get a name like Delilah?'

I scribbled back, 'From the Bible, you ignoramus.'

At least her parents had imagination, I reckoned, naming their daughter after that mad woman who chopped off her bloke Samson's hair while he slept, and reduced him to a wimpy bullet-head.

Talking of heads, Phil Humphries was waggling *his*

1

like his collar was too tight, and suggesting that perhaps Delilah had some hobbies or interests she'd like to tell us about?

'Dunno. Would you call having the sight a hobby?'

This was too much for the Fionas, who sat just in front of me and Lauren. They began nudging each other and coughing. 'Did she say *having* the sight or *being* one?' Fiona Fitzgerald wondered aloud.

'The sight?' Humphries cleared his throat. He wasn't sure if this counted as a hobby exactly, but the class would love to hear more.

'I see things other people don't.' Delilah stifled a yawn. 'Y'know – dead people, ghosts, whatever you want to call them. Oh yeah, and I'm a Scorpio, so that makes Pluto my, like, ruling planet. Pluto –' she studied her bitten fingernails as if she were bored witless – 'that's the Lord of the Underworld for those of you who don't know.'

She said this as if she didn't expect anyone in our group to have the faintest idea who Pluto was, which was kind of an insult seeing as astrology and the planets and everything are my personal thing.

Or *were*. I keep forgetting. Just the other month Lauren and I had sworn to give up all that stuff, hadn't we? No more stargazing, fortune-telling, Ouija boards or messages from beyond of any kind. From now on Lauren and I were your typical everyday teenage girls, concerned only with logos, labels, navel piercings and, er, boys. Oh yes.

'That's, er . . . very interesting, Delilah.' Phil Humphries, privately referred to as Uncle Phil, sat there nodding as if Delilah were yacking on about origami and

2

cake-decorating. He liked to give the impression that he was one of us – bomb-proof, unshockable. Yet I could see that he'd gone kind of pale beneath his right-on stubble.

It was hardly surprising: Delilah's appearance alone was enough to scare anyone. Her hair, for a start. Part-shaved, part-dreadlocks, it looked like a piece of unfinished crochet unravelling down her back. Her monkey-brown eyes glinted beneath thick brows – eyes that apparently saw things the rest of us didn't: the insides of people's heads, rainbow explosions of auras, spirits flitting like moths. She was completely upfront about these skills of hers, as if they were absolutely nothing to be embarrassed about.

'So you believe in ghosts then, Delilah?' Phil said, nervously shuffling his papers around.

'I didn't say I *believed* in them. We've just got one at home.'

'Um, is it the ghost of anyone in particular?'

'I don't know. Just some creep.'

'Ah,' said Phil, nodding like he was suddenly enlightened. Then, more feebly, 'Ah. Well, thank you, er, Delilah,' before turning with some relief to the poet William Blake, who apparently saw angels all the time, and was practically locked up in an asylum because of it.

Anyway, I reckoned good old Phil asked for that. Imagine having to stand up in front of your new class and talk about yourself! I mean, what would I have said?

'Hi, my name's Abbie. I've got no brothers and sisters, and I live in this tiny little flat that you can hardly swing a cat in with my chiropodist mum and my ambulance-driver dad. I used to read palms and stuff, but after some unfortunate business with a poltergeist last term I gave

3

that up. I've also given up men, after some other un-fortunate business with a Greek sex-god, but that's another story. Suffice it to say, I'm still a virgin, and work-ing on being a prime swot, and that's about it . . .'

Oh, sad! You had to hand it to Delilah. At least she'd come up with something different.

'It takes bottle to stand up in front of strangers like that,' I said to Lauren later. We were getting ready to go home, and I was pulling at my tights, where my big toe poked through a hole. 'Especially with Uncle Phil nodding away like a glove puppet and the three Fionas giving you their famous withering looks.'

'Huh,' Lauren said. 'I'll bet her ghost isn't half as scary as ours was. I think she was just showing off, trying to be different. Like with the tongue-ring.'

'Maybe. But if she's into astrology, she can't be all bad. Damn it! Tell me, Lauren, what is it about my toes always poking through my tights?'

'Maybe they're deformed,' Lauren suggested. Considering she was such a hypochondriac herself, she was very unsympathetic to other people's problems, I sometimes felt.

'Wait for me then!' I hobbled after her down Bromfield's chestnut-lined drive, my bag bulging with textbooks, weighing me down. When I got home, I'd be writing up two hours of notes on Blake. 'Genius or Madman?' Uncle Phil wanted to know.

'Hey, look at that,' I called softly to Lauren. Just ahead of us, Delilah was stomping towards the gates, the three Fionas twittering around her like a flock of killer canaries.

4

'I wouldn't have thought she was their type,' Lauren said.

'She's not. Didn't you hear them in class, when she got up to talk, coughing and making those puking noises?'

I should explain about the Fionas. Only one of them is actually called Fiona. The other two are Cressida Hampshire and Tamsin French. It was just that they all looked like Fionas, with sleek blonde hair that looks like it's been steam-ironed every morning along with their brains. All three had rich daddies and designer clothes, and got through more blokes in a year than I got through tights, which was saying something.

I bent down to yank off my boot – the hole had wiggled in line with my toe again. As I did so, Cressida's voice came trilling through the smutty November air at me.

'Dee-lilah? Is that your real name? Can we call you Del?'

'Call me whatever you like.' Delilah paid no more attention to the Fionas than an elephant pays to flies on its backside.

'I really *love* your hair!' Tamsin cooed. 'Dreadlocks used to be banned at Bromfield. That was before the grungy look became so, like, passé. Did they let you wear it like that at your last school?'

'Did you say where your last school was, Delilah?' Fiona sweetly enquired. 'Was it up north somewhere?'

'Do tell us about your ghost.' Cressida swished back her honeyed mane. 'Does it, like, rattle its chains and everything? You know, you should talk to Abigail.' She nodded at me, as Lauren and I drew level with them.

5

'She's a bit of a sight too – oh, silly me, I mean she's *got* the sight.'

I glared at her. Word had got around, of course. How Lauren and Marina and me conjured up the spirit of Henry VIII with an Ouija board, and how Henry turned out to be more spirited than we'd bargained for. With the result that Marina's parents had sent her to another sixth-form college to do her A levels. The Fionas might never have got to hear of all this, but Mr Bullet, our dipstick head, had been informed by Marina's parents, and arranged for some priest to give the whole school a talk on the dangers of 'dabbling with the occult'.

'That was ages ago,' I said in my sneeriest voice.

'Yes,' Lauren confirmed. 'We don't talk about it now.'

Fiona was distracted for a moment by her own re-flection. A quick on-the-hoof mirror-check revealed that her eyebrows were due a waxing. Then she said, 'Oh come on, Abbie, I'm just letting Delilah know she's not the only freak in the world. You know very well, you and Lauren and that other girl who went loopy – can't recall her name – but you lot used to commune with the spirits on a regular basis.'

'Yeah, well. Better than communing with you lot. The conversation's more interesting.'

'And she reads palms.' Tamsin had to break into a jog to keep up with the totally uninterested Delilah. 'Whatever happened to that disgusting smelly old book you used to hump around with you, Abbie?'

Cheiro's Book of the Hand, she meant. Actually I'd given it to my mum for the Scouts' jumble sale. God knows what the Scouts were making of it.

'I don't know,' I said. 'What happened to that book of

yours, *The Famous Five Go Fishing* way, excuse me – this conversation is have a bus to catch. Come on, Lauren.'

The Fionas had already had their fun case. Now they were piling into a ho Porsche that was waiting outside the gate whisking them off to do a spot of late-night sh Kensington.

As for Delilah, Lauren and I just caught a glimpse of her disappearing up the street that ran alongside Bromfield Park.

'She must live close by,' I murmured. 'I wonder where exactly?'

'Does it matter?' Lauren was jealously watching the Fiona-packed Porsche roar away from the school gates. She pushed up her Peruvian knitted helmet, exposing a brow positively dimpled with worry lines, not helped by those little plaits she'd taken to braiding on either side of her head. 'You heard what she said,' she reminded me in her 'end is nigh' voice. 'She said that she'd changed schools about fifty times, and that her family were always moving around. She probably won't be here five minutes, anyway.'

'Probably not. I just wondered where she lived, that's all.'

'Well, don't wonder. Just remember what we decided on after the summer. We swore an oath, remember, on our grandmothers' lives, never to get involved with – well, you know, any more *weird* stuff. And if you want my opinion, that girl is into weird stuff up to her pierced eyebrows.'

'OK, OK,' I said impatiently. 'So she's a bit of a freak.

ou think I'm going to do – chase after her and
..e her home to my place for a spot of devil-worship?
Honestly, Lauren, just keep your plaits on, will you? And
– oh, there's my bus anyway . . .' I began to run towards
the stop, glad to escape her mithering. 'I'll see you
tomorrow, yeah?'

Lauren was right, of course. Only Delilah was more than
just weird. Not only did she see things other people
didn't; not only did she look like she could kick ass for
England. There was more to it than that – the shadow
that she carried around with her, like some dark force
field you couldn't penetrate. Like she was holding up a
sign telling you to KEEP OUT for your own good. If only
I'd known then, if only I'd known what – or rather, who
– Delilah was about to unleash on us, maybe I'd never
have marched straight up to her in the cloakroom. If I'd
had the sight like she had, maybe I'd have seen him there,
lurking in the shadows, watching, scratching endless
incriminating notes with his quill pen: the Devil's List.

But all I could think of when I saw Delilah the
following afternoon was how she knew about the stars
and planets and that, and how she was new and – no
matter how tough she looked – probably lonely. She was
in the cloakroom, yanking her army greatcoat from the
hook, ready to go home, when I caught her.

'Sorry about yesterday, but you have to ignore the
Fionas,' I told her. 'I mean, don't take anything they say
personally. They're snot-bags. Most people just treat them
as a joke.'

'Yesterday?' At first Delilah looked suspicious. She
looked like she hadn't the faintest idea what I was on

8

about. 'Fionas? Oh, you mean those fluff-heads?' She snorted dismissively. 'Don't worry. I can handle their sort.'

With that she shouldered her bag. She might have been straight out of there, if Lauren hadn't showed up. Not that Lauren is more interesting than me, or has a magnetic personality or anything. It was just her hand-creaming ritual with the stinky old marigold ointment – it seemed to fascinate the new girl.

'What's that stuff you're using?' Delilah demanded.

'This?' Lauren, looking vaguely terrified, showed her the pot. 'It's for my rash.'

'Let me see.' Before Lauren could whip on her gloves, Delilah had dumped her bag and grabbed hold of Lauren's scaly hand, taking it in her own heavily ringed paw. She began turning her hand this way and that, inspecting it in a medical kind of way beneath the glare of the strip lights.

'It's just my eczema.' Lauren glowered accusingly at me over Delilah's head, as if I'd delivered her into the hands of Dracula's daughter.

'Looks bloody painful,' Delilah remarked, as Lauren snatched back her hand. 'Is it always like that?'

Lauren shrugged, but I could see Delilah was winning her over. There was nothing Lauren relished more than a good chat about her medical condition. 'It's worse in the cold weather, and my skin starts to crack. It's an allergy, but no one can find out what I'm allergic to exactly. Except for cheese and the house-dust mite.'

'And Life on Earth As We Know It,' I finished for her. I didn't want Lauren boring Delilah to tears with her health problems.

But strangely, Delilah didn't seem bored at all. 'I can get rid of that for you, no problem,' she said.

Now hundreds of people had told Lauren they could cure her eczema. She'd done the rounds – Chinese herbs, dairy-free diet, enough lotions to make a crocodile as smooth as a baby's bum – so you could hardly blame her for her lack of enthusiasm. 'Thanks,' she said. 'But really, I've tried everything.'

'She has,' I backed her up. 'You name it, she's tried it.'

'She hasn't tried *my* stuff though. It works. Trust me.'

'Stuff?' Lauren began blinking like she had a speck of grit in her eye.

'It's more of an essence really,' Delilah explained. 'You can't get it in the shops or anything. It's my own recipe. Unique. Well, it's up to you.' She shrugged. 'If you both want to come back to my place tonight, I'll sort it for you.'

'Well . . ' I could see Lauren was torn. Usually she'd jump at any kind of bizarre miracle cure that came along – and I mean *anything*: dragon-snot, the blood of virgins . . .

'It's quite safe,' Delilah snarled impatiently. 'I mean, I'm not going to give you poisonous toad-spit or anything. It's up to you. D'you want to get rid of your cracked skin or don't you?'

Even while excuses formed on Lauren's tongue, Delilah was growing bored with us, I could see. Hoicking her bag over her shoulder, she turned towards the door.

I decided to go for it. 'Yeah,' I called after her. 'Thanks. That'd be great. For Lauren, I mean. Wouldn't it, Lauren?' And I stared hard at Lauren until she had no choice but to agree.

'Yeah,' she said. 'That's, like, really kind of you — thanks.'

So that was the start of it. Me and Lauren, scurrying along behind Delilah as she stomped through the school gates into a Northgate night smelling of damp and leaf mould and traffic fumes. Lauren hissing in my ear, 'Thanks a bunch. Actually, I had other plans for tonight.'

'Yeah? Like what? Don't tell me — a fun night in with your medical dictionary?'

I didn't admit to Lauren that I had misgivings too. It wasn't Delilah herself who worried me; it wasn't the studs, or having the sight, or the way she paused to spit out gum *splat* on the kerb before snarling, 'Are you two coming then, or what?'

Even as we fell into step with her, the back of my neck was prickling. I couldn't figure out why. I thought it must be something to do with that invisible shadow I'd sensed hovering around her. I turned, but there was no one behind us. Nothing. Yet what I heard — or rather, what I *thought* I heard — made me shiver. The leisurely crunch of boots on gravel, stalking us into the night.

Chapter Two

Life Line

Delilah lived on Bromfield Avenue, on the far side of the park where the houses were huge, with ivy-clad porches and crumbly old balconies you wouldn't dare stand on. The kind of house I hoped my parents would have the sense to buy if they won the lottery. Although, knowing them, they'd probably say something like, 'Ten million pounds won't change *our* lives, oh no! Number sixty-two Smedhurst Road is good enough for us, thank you very much.'

'You're safe tonight.' Delilah pushed the front gate so hard she practically swung it off its hinges. 'The Loathsome Verne is out of town, thank God.'

'The Loathsome Worm?' Lauren loitered on the pavement, twisting the fingers of her woolly gloves. 'That's not the ghost you were talking about, is it?' From the look on her face you'd think we were about to enter the dark portals of Dracula's castle, never to be seen again.

'Nah, not him. And I said, V-E-R-N-E, not Worm.' Delilah rattled her key in the lock. 'Short for Vernon, my mother's partner. She has this disgusting taste in men. And yeah, "worm" isn't far off the mark, since you mention it. Hey, Sid! How's my baby?' She scooped up an evil-looking black cat and planted a slurpy kiss on its snout. This was toe-curling to watch, because Sid had globs of pus in the corners of his yellow eyes. 'He's a bit knackered-looking,' Delilah explained. 'But so would you be if you were a hundred and ten.'

I gasped admiringly. 'He's a hundred and ten?'

'In cat years she means,' Lauren said in withering tones, standing well back because animal fur was a major allergy-trigger.

With Sid slung over her shoulder like a moth-eaten stole, Delilah led us across a dim hall crowded with boxes and packing cases. 'Ignore the mess – we haven't unpacked properly yet. We're only renting this place, because Verne gets itchy feet. Poor old Sid.' Delilah planted another 'mwah mwah' on the cat's nose. 'By the time he's beaten off the neighbourhood competition and marked his territory, we're off again.'

She pushed open a door at the end of the hall, and a warm yeasty smell whooshed out at us. 'You're not baking again, Mum?' Delilah said in a disgusted voice.

A woman with tumbling brown hair was pummelling a chunk of dough on a marble slab. As she kneaded, tiny bells jingled from the waist of her Indian cotton skirt. She looked like one of those old-fashioned folk singers who sing about trees and men going to war and that.

It wasn't fair. Somewhere in this world was a girl with a mother older and frumpier than mine, but I'd yet to find her. Still, having a mum who looked like the original hippy could have its embarrassing moments, I supposed. Plus she had this really sad, melodious voice that sounded like she was on the verge of tears.

'You know how Verne feels about shop bread, Lilah,' she said. 'You can never be sure what kind of raising agent they use.'

'Sod how Verne feels. This is Abbie and Lauren, by the way. They're in my English group.'

Delilah's mother wiped floury hands on her skirt. 'Would you girls like some shortbread? A hot drink?'

'No thanks, they're fine,' Delilah answered for us unfortunately, because the smell of baking was giving me major hunger pangs. She grabbed three Cokes from the fridge. 'We'll take these upstairs. Verne's not back to-morrow, is he? Please tell me he's not.'

'I don't know, love – he––'

'Don't tell me: he wants to surprise us, like always. So he can catch us in some unspeakably evil act, like eating shop bread.'

Leaving her mum bread-bashing, Delilah led us back into the hall and up two flights of stairs. I began to change my mind. About my parents winning the lottery, I mean, and moving to a house near the park. Well, I wouldn't want to live in *this* house, anyway. Despite the bland, creamy walls, the coir matting stair carpet, the house was as gloomy as brown paint. Away from the kitchen with its warm baking-fug, it was also freezing. There was something else, too, that I couldn't put my finger on – more of a feeling than anything; something that made me glance back over my shoulder more than once.

Only Lauren was behind me, of course, making her 'I don't want to be here' faces, whispering in her hissy voice, 'I am *not* taking any home-made potions. You have to test these things first, in a laboratory. You realize this is a complete waste of time?' And so on. I mean! As if she had anything better to do!

'You want to get rid of your eczema, don't you?' I hissed back at her. 'Anything's worth a try.'

'We don't even *know* her.' Lauren lifted an accusing finger from the banister rail. 'See that?'

'What?'

'Dust. Ugh.' She brushed it from her fingers. 'Thick white dust. I won't be able to breathe tonight, thanks to you.'

'You two need a stair-lift or something?' On the landing above us, Delilah was heaving her shoulder sideways at one of the doors. 'It always bloody sticks. Just like all the dumps Verne chooses to live in.'

Why was it that other girls' mothers, clothes, rooms were always a zillion times more interesting than my own? I stood taking in the sloping ceiling, the churchy-shaped window, the dark granny furniture looming monster-like in the half-light, with seizures of green envy. Delilah's room was big and messy and mad, like she was. Everywhere you looked were stones, crystals, feathers, candles, bits of twig and seashells. Clothes were flung about, leather and furs and lycra contorted into strange animal shapes as if they had a life of their own. There was a smell of earth and joss sticks and charity shops, which sent Lauren into a frenzy of sneezing.

Delilah flung herself on the bed, Doc Marts crossed at the ankles. 'It's a tip, right, but that's how I like it. It's like a nomadic thing. Wherever we go, my nest goes with me, every stick, stone and feather, which drives Verne up the stinking walls. You can sit down, by the way – just watch out for my altar.'

The altar was actually a table draped with an old blue curtain and wedged in front of the fairy-tale window. On it, pebbles glowed like pink sugar lumps alongside a tawny owl's wing and something that looked like a paperknife, which Delilah called an 'athame'. The two fat candles were for the god and goddess, Delilah said. The god squatting next to the candles might have been the Indian elephant god Ganesh, because he had a trunk like a particularly ugly teapot. There was also a statuette of a goddess with more than her fair share of boobs stuck all over her.

'That's Artemis,' Delilah explained when I asked. 'She rules the new moon.'

'What's it for – the altar?' Lauren enquired dubiously.

Delilah punched a cushion into shape behind her head. 'For sacrificing chickens on – what d'you think?' When she laughed, it was like a surprised kind of roar, husky and unused, as if she didn't laugh that often. 'Chickens, virgins, goats, whatever I can get hold of. Oh God, your faces! It's all right. That was a joke. I don't do dark stuff. Dark stuff comes back on you three times over.'

'Dark stuff? You mean, like, spells and that?' Clearing some old *Prediction* magazines off a chair, I sat down. Did Delilah fancy herself as a witch then? Too many girls fancied themselves as witches, just so they could ponce about looking like a cross between Cher and Morticia Addams. Like the occult was a style-thing. Lauren and I knew different, of course.

'I don't wave my magic wand and say "Abracadabra", if that's what you mean.' Delilah yanked at the neck of her sweater to scratch her shoulder, like she was bored. As she did so I noticed a tattoo, an elongated eye that seemed to be staring at me. Noticing my look, she yanked her sweater down further to show it off. 'Like it? It's the Eye of Horus.'

16

'Didn't it hurt?' Lauren asked anxiously. 'I'd never have a tattoo myself. They can get infected. You can be scarred for life – I read about it.'

'Not if you go to a kosher tattooist,' Delilah said. 'I had it done when we lived in Crawley. The beautician woman nearly freaked out when I showed her what I wanted. I think she was used to doing nice little pink hearts, and TRACY LOVES BRIAN and all that crap.'

'Why an eye though?' I said, my admiration growing by the second. One girl I knew had a butterfly on her bum, but compared to Delilah's eye that seemed totally last year.

Delilah explained that it was an ancient form of protection against the evil eye. 'The two eyes, see, they stare each other out.' Her small brown eyes fixed beadily on mine.

'Protection? Protection from whose evil eye?' Lauren glanced nervously over her shoulder.

'She means that ghost, of course – don't you, Delilah?' I said, although this really wasn't a subject I wanted to get onto. 'You told Phil Humphries about it. Some kind of creep, you said.'

'Did I? Oh yeah, I did.' Delilah looked away and began fiddling with her bootlaces. 'Anyway, I got the eye done well before the Creep turned up.'

'But who is this Creep?' Lauren persisted.

'No idea. He didn't exactly introduce himself. He's just like I say, some creepy geezer hanging around. I hear his boots sometimes, creaking on the landing and that, usually when I'm doing a ritual. And I get this smell –' Delilah wrinkled her nose – 'like this really strong tobacco smell, mixed with leather and animals and sweat.

God knows who he is. He probably comes with the house, y'know, like bats in the attic.'

'But have you actually *seen* him?' I was certain Delilah's ghost would be pathetically tame compared to the one Lauren and I had to deal with over the summer. I mean, a smell, a bit of boot-creaking . . . What was that, compared to the stuff *we'd* been through?

But it seemed she *had* seen him. 'I've caught sight of him a few times, usually on the corner of the stairs. I see this cloak swirling, out of the corner of my eye. Oh, and he's got this funky hat I wouldn't mind myself.' She screwed up her eyes, as if he was actually appearing to her this moment. 'Then there's the stick.'

'Stick?'

'I hear it tapping on the banisters sometimes, like he's beating out a tune with it on the wood. It's like he's really trying to scare me when he does that. Y'know, tapping a warning – like, "Here I *co-ome* . . . !"' She said this last bit mockingly, like it would take a lot more than a stick tapping to scare her.

'Oh, but that's horrible.' Lauren was shooting me 'let's leave *now*' messages with her aerobic eyebrows. I might have taken the hint if not for Delilah's sudden change of mood.

'Listen, I don't just see dead things, y'know. I see good things too. Like auras, for instance. I can see your auras right now.'

Lauren brightened visibly. 'You can see mine? Oh, what colour is it? Tell me, please, Delilah.'

Delilah's monkey eyes glinted, like she'd been counting on this reaction. 'Tell you what, we'll do a deal. Abbie can read my palm, and I'll read both your auras.'

'Oh no.' I shook my head. 'Sorry, I can't. I gave my Cheiro book to the Scouts. Plus I'm, like, out of practice.'

Lauren glared at me. 'Go on, you don't need the book. You've been reading palms since primary school. Go on, Abbie, just this once. I really really want to know what colour my aura is.'

Outnumbered, I sighed. 'OK then. Who's going first?'

Delilah said *she* would. 'Just relax. Be normal,' she growled at us, as we sat stiffly, posing as if for a photo. Her bright eyes burrowed into Lauren, as if she could see beyond the surface Lauren with her snivelly nose and plaits and lizardy skin-patches. Lauren seemed to preen herself, waiting to be told she exuded a heavenly blue mist.

Unluckily for her, it was more dirty great rain cloud than blue mist.

'Not a dirty old sludge-type grey,' Delilah said, as if to soften the blow. 'It's got a blueish tone. You know – pigeon-coloured.'

'Pigeon-coloured!' Lauren looked crestfallen. 'But . . . are you sure?'

Delilah said this was most likely due to Lauren's allergies. 'It's like your aura is sick too, so it gets all dingy. If you think yours is bad you should see Verne's. Dog-shit brown, right. I tried telling my mum, but she wasn't having it. When it comes to Verne she's got rose-tinted glasses.'

Talking of her stepdad had a similar effect on her, I noticed. The very mention of his name was like some kind of dimmer switch, turning Delilah on and off, taking the shine out of her.

'Your turn.' Delilah turned her beady gaze on me. I

19

imagined the worst, as her eyes searched the air around my head. What colour would my aura be? Mushroom-brown? Puke-green? Anything seemed possible after the past few months, losing my best friend, my lover – and practically my marbles along with them. So, when Delilah said it was orange, I nearly fell off my chair.

'Orange? You're kidding! Not orange as in orange-squash orange?'

'Well what other kind is there? What's wrong with orange, anyway?'

'It's just so . . . so . . . *bright*.'

Delilah groaned. 'This is your *aura* we're talking about, not the latest cat-walk collection. Orange is about energy and creativity. You should be well chuffed to be orange.'

'Yes, well, I am. Chuffed, I mean. Thanks.'

'Don't mention it. Just tell me about my great future.' She thrust her palm eagerly beneath my nose – a squarish, rough hand scarred with inkblots, sparkly black polish flaking from bitten nails. 'It has to be great because my present is shit, frankly.'

Oh dear. I felt a bit nervous about reading Delilah's palm. I mean, she wasn't just anybody. I couldn't give her any old waffle like I'd done with some of the girls in my class. All they wanted to know about was their love line: would they be rich, famous, eternally gorgeous? That kind of guff. But Delilah wasn't that stupid.

'Get on with it then!' she growled impatiently. 'It's not that bad, is it?'

What could I say? Actually it *was* that bad. The first thing that jumped out at me was Delilah's life line – that line that curves down from between the thumb and

20

forefinger to the wrist. Except in her case it *didn't* curve to the wrist. Not nearly that far.

I couldn't tell her this, of course. Instead I went on about the impressive fate line, the star upon the Mount of Saturn, the sturdy thumb. 'That means you've got attitude, in spade-loads. Sorry, but that's the best I can do. It's like I've got this mental block right now. I'm not sure I have a future as a fortune-teller, to be honest. I used to think I did.'

Delilah withdrew her hand from my grasp. Did she know I was lying? She seemed disappointed in me. But how could I tell her that, judging from her life line, she'd be lucky to see her seventeenth birthday?

Lauren began mumbling excuses about getting home. 'My mother may be late, and I promised to walk the dog.'

'You've got a dog?' Delilah said. 'Doesn't that affect your allergy or something?'

'Oh, this one is hairless,' Lauren explained. 'It's just got skin. It came with Harv-wit, and frankly you'd think he'd take more responsibility for it. I think he has an after-school meeting tonight, and Mum'll go crazy if it pees on the carpet.'

I shot Lauren a sceptical look. This was the first I'd heard about her pet-care duties. She just wanted out, I guessed, because she was miffed about her pigeon-grey aura.

'Hang on a minute. I promised to get rid of that rash for you, didn't I?' Delilah suddenly remembered.

'Oh no, that's OK,' Lauren said quickly. 'I don't want to put you to any bother on my account.' She was already ramming her Peruvian helmet over her plaits. She had lost faith in Delilah, I could see.

'*Bother? On my account?*' Delilah, on her hands and knees to rummage beneath her bed, imitated Lauren's mimsy voice good-naturedly. She looked at me. 'Is she for real? Listen, I said I'd help you and I will, if I can just find it among all this junk.' She dragged out a box; it was like a shoe box, only with a pentagram drawn on the lid. 'Yes! Knew it was lurking here somewhere.' The box contained various bottles, one of which Delilah drew out. She gave it a little shake. 'This,' she announced with a hint of pride, 'is moon-dew.'

The small glass phial appeared to contain ordinary, colourless tap water. 'Use it sparingly, right?' She deposited it in Lauren's palm. 'It doesn't go far, and it takes bloody ages to collect.'

Lauren stared at it like it was dog poo. 'What am I supposed to do with it exactly? Drink it, or—?'

Delilah laughed her rare, snorty laugh. 'No, you divvy. You anoint yourself with it all over. If you do it without your togs on, the power is stronger. By the light of the full moon is even better.'

Consulting the poster-sized moon chart which hung over the bed, she added that the moon would not be full till next week. 'But if you can't wait, just give it a go tonight.'

Lauren looked aghast because she didn't do naked, and especially not in the great outdoors of her Highgate garden, full moon or no full moon. 'Thanks,' she said, with about as much enthusiasm as if she'd just opened a Christmas present from her great-aunt and found a pair of pink elephant-sized knickers inside. 'Thanks. Maybe I will.'

★ ★ ★

As we walked back down Bromfield Avenue towards the high street, I told her off.

'You might have acted a bit more grateful. How do you know that stuff isn't really a miracle cure?'

'Because I just do, all right? I mean, telling me my aura is *grey*. Hah! Nobody has a grey aura. There's no such thing as a grey aura. The trouble with you, Abbie, is you're so gullible. You'd believe her if she said the moon was made of green cheese.'

'No I wouldn't. And anyway, since when did Harv-wit own a dog?'

'Since today.'

'Lauren,' I said sternly, 'you can be a heartless, ungrateful cow sometimes – you know that?'

'So? Better than being a gullible idiot.'

'Yeah, well, this gullible idiot knows a thing or two you don't. If I tell you something about Delilah's palm, promise not to say anything?'

'On my honour. Does she have hard skin or something?'

'No, Lauren, she doesn't. Hard skin is the least of her problems. If my reading is right, then Delilah won't be sticking around long enough to *get* hard skin.'

'What do you mean, she won't be sticking around long enough?' Lauren said. She could be really dumb sometimes.

'I mean, Lauren, that she won't be around long enough on this earth. She may not even see her next birthday because she may be dead, OK?'

But Lauren wasn't convinced. If anyone was going to die before her next birthday, she said, it would be her. 'I can just feel it,' she said mournfully. 'My grey aura wrapped round me like a shroud.'

23

★ ★ ★

When I got home, at first – oh horrible thought – I imagined I'd walked in on my parents in the act of you-know-what. Which would have been gross, seeing as how they were ancient enough to be my grandparents. But no, my mother was rubbing some yellowish ointment into my father's back with vigorous circular motions like she was cleaning the windows. Why they couldn't perform this disgusting ritual in the privacy of the bathroom, I couldn't imagine. Except that some hospital soap was on – a type of programme to which they were truly addicted.

'All right, Abbie love?' Dad murmured automatically.

'Yeah, OK, thanks, Dad. Does your back hurt?'

Mum retorted that *my* back would hurt if I'd just had to carry a hundred-kilo woman on a stretcher. 'People should have more consideration. They stuff themselves with cream doughnuts with no thought for the poor ambulance driver who has to pick them up off the floor when they collapse.'

I sighed. Why were my parents so frumpily devoted to each other, so super-uncool? I tried to imagine Lauren's mum, the belly-dancing Izzie, rubbing ointment into her partner Harv-wit's back, and failed. Or maybe Delilah's homespun hippy mum did stuff like this for the Loathsome Verne? If this was what marriage was all about, then count me out!

I left my parents to it and went to my room, which seemed about the size of a walk-in wardrobe compared to Delilah's. Tonight everything seemed to be wrong with it. It was too lilac, too prissy, too boring. I was just looking around, trying to figure out where I might

24

squeeze in an altar like Delilah's, when my mobile beeped with a text message. I read the words:

DELS A FAKE. MOON–DEW USELESS. LAUREN.

Uh-oh. Poor Lauren, stuck with her scaly skin. Poor Delilah too, with her hardly-there lifeline. I couldn't help wondering what terrible accident awaited her. Maybe it had something to do with that Creep of hers? Whatever it was, maybe I could save her? Could you change your fate like that – re-route the lines on your hands like some kind of road-improvement scheme?

I decided to text Lauren back.

Y DONT U WAIT TIL FUL MOON? ABBIE.

Chapter Three

Moon Maidens

Was Delilah really a fake? Lauren reckoned she was. Lauren swore blind that the moon-dew was actually tap water and that Delilah was a deluded screwball, and if we had any sense we'd have nothing more whatsoever to do with her.

So how come we were watching the moon rising over the rooftops of Northgate like a pink grapefruit, preparing for a ritual that, Lilah maintained, would banish Lauren's eczema for good? I mean, what kind of imbeciles would strip down to their undies on a freezing November night, all because of a full moon in Scorpio?

I must admit, Lauren had taken some persuasion to go through with this. But as I explained to her, we had to give Delilah a chance. 'I mean, if I'm right and she hasn't got – you know, much longer, like, on this earth, she needs friends at least. Doesn't she?' I whispered to Lauren behind Delilah's back, as she stomped about the grubby glass lean-to at the back of the house, plonking candles on saucers.

'If. If you want my opinion, she's tough as old boots. She'll probably live to be a hundred and two, whereas I am very likely to die of pneumonia after tonight.' Lauren adjusted the veil that was part of her mum's belly-dancing costume. It came down to her feet. Beneath this – never one to take chances with her health – she was wearing some special heat-sensing, thermal undies.

'You're sure about your stepfather?' Lauren asked Delilah for the third time. 'Supposing he comes home unexpectedly?'

Delilah said there was no chance of this happening. 'They've gone to one of Verne's boring old lectures, haven't they? It's their idea of a great night out, listening to a bunch of maniacs raving about the end of the world. They won't be back until gone eleven.'

'But is this undressing thing really necessary?' Lauren whinged.

Delilah stood, thoughtfully scratching the Eye of Horus. She admitted that stripping off was something of an experiment. 'Going sky-clad is traditional. It's about energy-flow and the elements and that. It's not like a pervy thing.'

She herself was wearing a pair of frayed denim shorts and a big, fearsome, no-nonsense bra that had an armoured look about it. Sky-clad or not, what with the boots and tattoos and body piercings, Delilah seemed far less exposed than Lauren and me. Even without clothes she was warrior-like, a force to be reckoned with.

'What kind of a lecture have they gone to anyway?' I asked her.

'You don't want to know. It's a religious sect – the Puritan Brethren. It's like a sinister version of Friends of the Earth. How he ever persuaded my mum into it I'll never know. She's not as dippy as she looks. She's got a psychology degree and everything. And now she's like . . . she's like—'

Delilah broke off and held her middle fingers to her temples, as if she were trying to clear her head of family

27

problems. 'Listen, how did we get onto Verne? I'm supposed to be focusing on the ritual.'

Lauren and I followed her warily into the garden, the chill air forcing us to jiggle about like a pair of demented lap dancers to keep from freezing.

'I c-c-can't believe it,' Lauren muttered through chattering teeth. 'I can't believe I've let you talk me into this.'

'Listen, if anyone's moaning it should be me. I'm risking hypothermia for the sake of your skin problem, you realize. I mean, what am I going to get out of this? Nothing, that's what?'

There was the sound of a door banging from somewhere behind us. We turned. The house loomed tall and silent. The only light was from the kitchen, a faint yellowish glow flooding the patio.

'Must have been next door,' I said to Lauren.

We looked ahead to the tangle of fruit trees with moon-pearled trunks. All along the garden boundaries rhododendrons huddled, dark and disapproving like ancient aunts. I sniffed. There was a smell of dead leaves, and that fusty smell you get from old stockings, a scent my mother often brought home from work with her.

'Are you ready then?' Now we were outside, Delilah's manner seemed to change. Her monkey eyes were bright and feverish as she gazed up at the moon. 'You've got the dew?'

'Right here.' Lauren held the phial between finger and thumb. 'Can we make it snappy, please, before I *freeze*?'

'Make it snappy?' Delilah frowned, taking the moon-dew from her. 'What d'you think this is, some kind of party game? This is serious, Lauren. This is real, OK? The real thing.'

'That's what I kept telling her,' I put in. 'She's got no sense of ceremony, that's the trouble.'

'Yeah, well, remember – when I call upon the goddess, you must anoint yourself, right? Just smear yourself all over with that stuff, concentrating on where your eczema is worst. Course, if we were being really kosher, me and Abbie would do the smearing, what with us being your handmaidens, but that would be—'

'Completely gross!' I said quickly, holding up my palms. 'Sorry, but there's no way I'm anointing Lauren on her bare skin.'

Delilah sighed. 'Just make yourself useful and help me, will you?'

While Lauren jiggled and shivered in her veil like a jilted bride, I did as I was told and helped Delilah drag three plastic chairs across the grass. Using the chairs and an old tree stump, she began to position candles at all points of the compass. 'You can do the honours, OK?' She tossed me the box of matches. 'You light them one at a time, as I call up the elements.'

'OK,' I agreed, wondering what calling up the elements had to do with it. Still, we wouldn't have long to find out.

Delilah stood for a moment, legs astride, holding her *athame* in her outstretched arm. She didn't look particularly witch-like, I have to say; more like a champion darts player, psyching herself up to hit the bull's eye. Only the *athame* itself, glinting in the moonlight, seemed charged with a strange kind of energy. For an instant I thought I could see it, a flash of white light zizzing torch-like across the grass.

As if she too sensed the light, Delilah lifted her arm. Using the point of the *athame* she began sketching a shape in the air. You couldn't see what shape exactly. You could sense it, though, as if the *athame* had left a sizzling vapour trail behind it. A pentagram. My heart quickened. Delilah had sketched a massive pentagram. The ceremony had begun.

Now words began rolling off Delilah's tongue like a well-rehearsed poem. Her voice sounded older as she called up the Ancient One of Air. 'I ask that you attend this circle and witness these rites. So mote it be.'

Maybe it was the words, or the way she spoke them, or the Ancient One of the Air looking on, I don't know, but my hand trembled as I struck the first match to light the candle to the east. The flame flickered, fragile, as if the slightest breeze would snuff it out. Yet somehow it held. There was a hiss of melting wax, a faint scent of lavender wafting in the night air.

Delilah went on calling up the elements as if they were personal mates of hers, dropping in for a chat. As the fourth candle was lit, I felt a sense of relief. This was *it* then. Ritual over, let the smearing begin. But we hadn't even got started yet.

'*Now*,' Delilah said, as if this was the moment she'd been waiting for. 'Now we draw the circle.'

Arm outstretched, she pointed the *athame* to the east. It was no longer just a tool, I noticed; not merely some strange paperknife she kept on her altar. It was more an extension of Delilah herself, as it began to scratch an invisible circle about us, moving from east to west in a smooth clockwise motion. As it did so, Delilah intoned the words in her odd, un-Delilah-ish voice.

'This is the boundary of the circle of magic,' she told the Northgate night. 'Let naught but love enter in, let naught but love emerge from within.'

Naught but love. I held my breath, feeling as if I were in the presence of something special, marvellous. These weren't silly words she'd just made up for the hell of it, you could tell. You just knew that witches had been using these words since the dawn of time. The circle too. You couldn't *see* the circle she'd drawn about us, but you could feel it, like a cradle rocking you, holding you safe.

'Hail to thee! Hail to thee, Levannah! We ask that your rays fill this essence with light and heal our sister, Lauren.'

The dew-cum-tap water shimmered. It had a honeyed tinge as Delilah held it up to the moon. Passing it back to Lauren, she nodded. Her signal. Her signal for Lauren to get stuck in.

Oh dear. You would think that after all that hailing and stuff Lauren would at least try to get into the spirit of the thing. I'd expected a bit of ceremonial dabbing, like one of those girls in the perfume ads. Then a quick turn in the moonlight, arms held aloft to the silver disc, to the great Levannah, whoever she might be. Instead of which she began slathering the stuff on like it was cheap suntan lotion, as if she couldn't wait to get it over with. I almost winced to see her slapping it on her legs, feet tangling in the veil.

'Oooh! Oh God, it's cold! Ouch, ooh, it stings,' Lauren moaned.

Forgetting about the Ancient Ones looking on for a minute, I suggested, 'Make sure you get all the crusty bits.'

She glared at me. 'I don't have "crusty bits", thank you ver—'

'*Shhh!*' Delilah waved the *athame* at us, as if to turn us to stone. At first I thought she was just annoyed with us for talking during the ceremony. But she was staring past us, towards the house. Staring and staring, like something terrible was going to emerge from it any minute.

Not Verne. 'Please not Verne,' I muttered under my breath.

'Arse!' Delilah cursed softly. 'We've got company. Can you feel it?'

'Feel what?' Lauren stopped slapping her legs and dropped the moon-dew on the grass. She gathered the veil around her, as if a man in a dirty raincoat were about to leap out of the bushes any minute.

Somehow I knew this wasn't what Delilah meant. 'Can you *feel* it?' she'd said. It. *It* wasn't something you could see, or run from, or reason with. *It* wasn't even human. *It* was a feeling, that was all. An indescribable hatred. An ill-wish. A poisonous gas of loathing.

Feebly, I tried to cover myself with my arms. Whatever it was radiating this evil stuff, I wanted to curl up into a ball, to disappear. It was like one of those dreams where you find yourself sashaying down the high street with your most disgusting granny-type knickers showing, or even no knickers at all. Only worse. I was ashamed, not just of my shrunken bikini and my blue-dimpled thighs, but of myself. *Me*. The person I was inside, beneath the skin.

Even to whisper to Delilah took all my courage. 'What is it?'

Delilah was standing bolt upright, holding her *athame*

like a knife, pointing it at the shadows. 'It's *him*. I thought it might be. I thought he might stick his nose in.'

'But you said he was at a meeting, you promised . . .' Lauren mumbled through her veil.

'It's the Creep, not Verne,' Delilah said quietly.

'Oh . . . not *that* Creep?' I felt numb suddenly, as if the moonlight had turned me to stone.

Delilah gazed defiantly into the darkness of the shrubbery. 'You mustn't let him see you're scared, OK? Just ignore him. He can't hurt us as long as we stay in the circle. We go on with the ritual.'

But the ritual was over, thanks to Lauren. 'Ohmigod, look . . . Look, Abbie – there's someone there!'

I stared. It was one of those lightning-flash moments, as if the curtain dividing this world from the next fluttered just enough for us to glimpse a vague, dark shape detaching itself from a rhododendron bush.

Lauren squeaked in terror as the blur of shadow edged horribly into focus. Now you could see the wide-brimmed hat, which Delilah had described as 'funky'. There, too, was that stick she'd talked about. It was more of a staff really, the kind that weary pilgrims lean on in biblical pictures. Only this was crook-shaped. Evil.

The Creep! With a sick lurch of my stomach I knew this was the source of that shameful, cringing feeling. Whoever the Creep was, he had reason to hate us.

Delilah was mumbling, '*Go away*. Just go away, Creep, and mind your own.'

'Delilah, what does he want?' I whispered.

'Dunno. I just know he's an evil sod, and he's got something against me. But you know what? I'm not scared. I'm not . . .'

Who did she think she was fooling? Our eyes were fixed on the stick. The shadowy figure seemed to toss it lightly into the air, then catch it like a baton, so that the crook-end pointed straight at us. I stared at the polished curve of wood. There was something horrible about the way it pointed at us. It might have been some great hook. It might at any minute shoot out and haul us in, all three of us, squirming and helpless as a catch of fish.

Would he speak? Would the Creep actually speak to us? I clapped my hands to my ears in case he did. Closing my eyes tight, I held my breath. At first there was only my heart doing a kind of clog dance in my ear. Then, after what seemed like half a lifetime but was probably only a second or two, Delilah's unexpected roar of pleasure nearly blasted my eardrums.

'Joel! You total low-life. It's bloody you!'

At first I thought she'd lost it, the way she started muttering and rushing round the invisible circle anti-clockwise, the *athame* stroking the air as if slicing it into segments. 'Be on your way in peace and power, be on your way in peace and power, and thank you for coming!' she gabbled all in one breath, explaining to me and Lauren, 'Got to close the circle first. Can't just leave it. Never never never . . .'

She didn't have time to say why this was such a total no-no. Someone was crossing the lawn towards us. Not the Loathsome Verne. Not a shadowy, stick-waving phantom. A real, living, breathing, fit-type bloke dressed in an old flying jacket and combats. The next thing I knew, Delilah was hurling herself at this hapless stranger like a human cannonball. The way she was screeching, this had to be someone special.

As she began whirling him around the lawn, I realized that the feeling of self-loathing which had gripped me earlier had vanished. It was like a curtain lifting. Now I just felt stupid in an everyday way, like anyone caught bulging out of their bikini in a moonlit suburban garden.

'For Christ's sake, Lilah!' Delilah's bloke was half groaning, half laughing. 'Put me down, you mad tart. You nearly broke my bloody back.'

Delilah was dragging him over to where Lauren and I stood, gormless as a pair of garden gnomes. 'Hey, you two, meet my big bruv, Joel.'

Bruv! Delilah's brother, who was supposed to be abroad somewhere – Europe, I thought she'd said. As far away as he could get from the Loathsome Verne. Now here he was, flicking coils of dark, snaking hair from his eyes and nodding vaguely in our direction.

'Did I, er, interrupt something?' He looked as embarrassed as we felt, as his glance registered the fact that we had hardly any clothes on.

'Yeah, you big bozo, you did. Why didn't you ring first? You just gate-crashed our private ceremony, but never mind, we'll forgive you. We were about finished anyway. Come on, let's go inside.' Taking her brother's arm, Delilah began tugging him towards the house.

As Lauren and I tagged on foolishly behind, I couldn't resist a backward glance at the shadowy garden. But all I could see were the motionless trees and the silvered specks of mist whirling like plagues of insects.

Chapter Four

Joel

For once Lauren and I were of the same mind. All we wanted was to get our kit back on as quickly as possible and leg it out of there.

While Delilah and Joel were doing all that embarrassing huggy stuff in the kitchen, we raced up the three flights of stairs to her room and yanked on our woolly winter layers as if the house were on fire.

Lauren moaned that she was 'utterly mortified'. 'You realize I've made a complete exhibition of myself tonight. I mean, how could I be so stupid as to fall for that stuff? And all the time that brother of hers was ogling us from—'

'*He* wasn't ogling us.'

'Well, who else was it, lurking around in the bushes?'

'It wasn't her brother is all I'm saying. Her brother was coming from the direction of the house. That —' I paused to yank my sweater over my head — 'that "shadow" you screamed at was nothing to do with her brother. It was the Creep. It was Delilah's ghost. You saw it, didn't you? You saw the hat, that hideous shepherd's crook thing, pointing at us . . . ?'

Lauren turned away. She was re-plaiting one of her braids, which had become loose during the ceremony. 'If you don't mind, I'd rather not discuss it,' she said frostily.

36

'Suit yourself, but it was hardly one of the neighbours popping in to borrow a cup of sugar, was it?'

'Maybe it was. Maybe Delilah has weird neighbours.'

'Come on, Lauren. It was some kind of *entity*. I could *feel* it. You must've felt it too. The air was just thick with this terrible hatred. You could hardly move for it. Her brother must've scared it off, thank God.'

Catching sight of the statuette of Artemis on Delilah's altar, I shuddered. Was she on our side or not? It seemed somehow wrong to be in her presence without Delilah here with us.

Lauren continued to fuss with her hair in stubborn silence. I turned towards the door. 'Lauren, if you plait it any tighter, you'll give yourself a premature face-lift. Anyway, we ought to go down. Are you decent yet?'

Just to make sure, Lauren wound her favourite scarf, hand-knitted by Bolivian peasant women, several times around her neck. Practically all you could now see of her bare flesh was her nose poking over the top and the tips of her fingers dangling beneath her sleeves. 'I'm ready,' she decided. 'And listen, Abbie, we just say goodbye and then we leave, OK?'

'Suits me.' I shrugged, because frankly I was still feeling somewhat faint after our encounter with the shepherd from hell. 'Whatever you say.'

But Delilah wasn't letting us off that lightly. 'You can't just bugger off straight after the ceremony.' Delilah, now wearing a shaggy sweater over her shorts, sloshed boiling water onto tea bags. 'Don't let Joel scare you off.'

Joel didn't say anything. He stood leaning against the dresser, eating a slice of some grainy-looking cake that Lilah's mother had made. Taking a sneak glance, I saw that he had Lilah's strong features, the same strong nose and wonky mouth, except they looked better on him.

'He's quite safe, aren't you, Joel?' Delilah slid mugs of pale tea across the table to Lauren and me.

'Yeah yeah,' Joel said, mouth twitching into a smile. His eyes met Lilah's, then flickered to the door. 'When's the old man get back then?'

'Not for a couple of hours. Relax. Forget him.'

'Actually, we ought to be going,' Lauren said, nudging me so that my tea slopped over the rim.

Delilah sat at the table. 'What's the hurry? Got a bus to catch?'

'No, but, well yes – we—'

'Have a slice?' Lilah began hacking wedges of the teabread thing like there was no tomorrow. 'We're celebrating – we're celebrating my big bruv's home-coming, aren't we, bruv?'

Joel was licking crumbs from his fingers like he hadn't eaten for a week. 'Think yourself lucky it was me and not Verne who caught you at it back there. You were taking a chance, Lilah. I was beginning to think you'd lost it altogether, flitting about like a bunch of fairies.'

He didn't say this in a nasty way; it was more a brotherly kind of teasing. Not that I'd know much about it, not having a brother. I wouldn't have minded one like Joel though.

Delilah didn't like the 'fairies' bit: she began lecturing him about how it was serious stuff, medicinal, a healing ceremony and all that. 'Lauren's got a bit of a problem,' she said in her blunt, tactless way. I could feel Lauren cringing with shame. 'Did you use all that stuff I gave you, by the way, Lauren?'

'Stuff? Er, yes. Every drop. Thanks. I'm sure I'll be fine now.' Lauren tugged the sleeves of her sweater further down over her hands until even the tips of her fingers disappeared. I knew she was worried that Delilah would want to check her skin condition in front of the well-fit bruv, and that would be, like, so humiliating. But luckily for Lauren, the talk turned back to Joel – how he'd been staying with a mate since he got home from his travels.

'Tell Mum I'm OK, but I'm not going back to uni. I'm working for the council to earn a few quid, then I'm off again – probably Australia somewhere.'

'Australia somewhere? Great,' Delilah snapped. 'Mum'll be over the moon to hear that. Anyway, what's this council job all about?'

Joel folded his arms. 'Maintenance.' He mumbled the word as if he were ashamed of it.

'Maintenance?'

'Yeah, I maintain things.'

'What things?' Lilah persisted.

He sighed. 'What is this, an interrogation or something? Vandals rip up a park bench, I fix it. Not exactly rocket science, but I get plenty of fresh air. And no one bothers me.'

Joel looked as if this was all that mattered – no one bothering him. I couldn't imagine anyone daring to bother him. He had this kind of nervy, brooding look, like some invisible shield stood between him and the rest of the world. I couldn't figure out why this struck me as sexy. It just was. I became horribly aware of myself slurping my tea. I tried to swallow quietly. If only I'd been wearing a more flattering bikini, was my one thought now. Not that it mattered. Joel had probably written off Lauren and me as the dippy schoolfriends of his crazy sister, not worth a second thought.

'Tell Mum I'll call and see her soon,' he was saying. 'But only when Verne's out of the way.'

Delilah began to explain to us how Joel had had this terrific row with their stepfather. 'He came home late a few times, a bit laced, didn't you, Joel? No big deal, y'know? But in Verne's book, anything stronger than Appletize is a mortal sin. Verne's favourite tipple is Adam's Ale.'

'Adam's Ale?' Lauren looked blank.

'Water, you clot,' I told her.

Delilah laughed. 'I'll have some of your finest Adam's Ale, landlord – that's Verne.'

All this talk of Verne made me uneasy, especially as Lauren and I were sitting with our backs to the door. Supposing he came crashing in on us now?

'So what's the latest?' Joel looked like he was pulling a splinter from his knuckle, probably from the vandalized park bench. 'What's he up to now?'

Delilah looked depressed suddenly. She rested her chin in her hand and said thoughtfully, 'Oh, you know, he gets worse. He's got Mum baking all our bread, and she can't replace the washing machine we left at the last house – seems he'd like her to go down to the river and beat the hell out of the washing on the stones. And he's getting totally paranoid about the lecky. Goes round switching lights off all the time because it's a waste of world resources, so we have to blunder around like bats in the pitch bloody dark. That's not all – I could give you a whole list: too many covers on the bed isn't healthy, mattresses are too soft, and, like, do we really need

40

cushions to plonk our bums on? No, says Verne, I think not. All the usual Brethren crap. Well, I don't need to tell you – you know.'

'So who *are* the Brethren anyway?' I couldn't help asking.

'The Brothers?' Joel laughed drily. Obviously quoting Verne, he added in a mock priest-like tone, '*They are the Righteous Ones. Halleluiah and praise the Lord!*' He didn't look at us when he spoke. His mouth tightened, and his face had a clenched, pale look.

'Basically,' Delilah said, 'they're a bunch of sad losers who want everyone to be as miserable as they are. They can't get enough of pain and suffering; if it hurts it's doing you good – oh, you get the idea. Sorry, it gets me down just talking about it. Can't we change the subject, please, Joel? I mean, I have to live with Verne; I don't want to sit around talking about him all night.' She grinned wickedly. 'So tell me about your adventures in sunny España. How many señoritas did you manage to pull?'

This time, when Lauren kicked my ankle, I got up to go. Partly because I really didn't want to stick around and hear about Joel's pulling power. Not that he was likely to tell, the face he was making at Lilah. I had a feeling that when we left, they would go on discussing the Loathsome Verne. That they had serious family stuff to talk about.

Lilah didn't bother to stop us this time; she didn't even see us to the door. She just called out to Lauren something about not having a bath tonight. 'You've got to let the moon-dew soak in and do its work. I'll see you at school tomorrow, OK?'

41

As for Joel, he barely acknowledged the fact that we were leaving, beyond a curt nod in our direction.

'See you then,' I said to the room in general.

'Yeah. See you,' in a voice that implied: Not if he saw me first.

I hurried to catch Lauren up. 'Hey, wait a minute, Lauren.'

'What now?' She stopped beneath a streetlamp, well out of sight of Delilah's house.

'Hang on a minute. I just wanted to see your arm, to see if it's worked.'

'Perhaps you'd like me to strip off in the street and give you a twirl?'

'Lauren, that stuff could have worked miracles for all you know.'

'Oh yes, tap water is well known for its healing properties.'

'Delilah says it's moon-dew, it *is* moon-dew.'

'So? And what is moon-dew exactly?'

'Well, I suppose it's . . . it's . . .'

'Yes?' Lauren snapped impatiently.

'Well, it's dew, isn't it? Lilah must go out and collect it from leaves and that by the light of the moon.'

'Yes, well, it could be sulphuric acid for all we know.'

'O ye of little faith.' I sighed because this was a saying my mother came out with from time to time. 'Think about it, Lauren: if it was some chemical your skin would be peeling off like wallpaper. Anyway, it was a bit of a laugh, wasn't it? God knows, we don't get many laughs these days. Or it was until . . .' I stopped, thinking of the apparition in the garden, the terrible force field of hatred, the sense of humiliation that had held me in its grip. I couldn't believe Lauren hadn't felt it too, but I decided not to say anything more about it. No sense in putting her off Delilah altogether; not when things were getting interesting.

'I knew she was weird when she stood up in class,' Lauren was griping as we neared the bus stop. 'Why can't we make a normal friend? Why do we have to get involved with loonies all the time?'

'Delilah's not a loony. Anyway, what do you reckon on her brother?'

'Not much.' Lauren squinted into the distance for signs of her bus. 'No doubt he set *your* pulses racing,' she added nastily. 'Knowing you.'

'What d'you mean, *knowing me*?'

'Just, knowing you,' Lauren said.

Dad was on late shift when I got home, and my mother was already in her quilted dressing gown, boiling milk for her cocoa. Maybe it was thinking of Lilah and Joel, I don't know, but it seemed a good time to enquire why Mum had never had any more children. I expected her to say something about how she wasn't 'blessed', but would be everlastingly grateful for the miracle of having me at the advanced age of forty-seven.

But all she said was, 'One was quite enough, thank you, Abigail. Quite frankly, having you drained all my energy.'

'Oh. Well. It would have been nice to have a brother or something.'

'Babies don't come to order, dear.' She sighed, snatching at the milk saucepan. 'They're a gift. You have to be grateful for what you get.'

Charming. I retired to my yucky lavender, last-season room and flopped onto my bed. It wasn't fair. Think what an advantage an older brother would have been. All those mates hanging around the house, the air a-buzz with testosterone, while your big bro looked out for you, like Joel watched out for Lilah. But then, having Joel as a brother would be a bit of a waste, I suppose . . .

My mobile bleeped, and there was the usual mad scrabble to fish it out of my bag.

'Hello?'

I can't think why I expected it to be Joel, when he'd shown zero interest in me back at Delilah's. Still, Lauren's voice, gushing excitedly at the other end, caused my poor romantic heart to plunge in disappointment.

Wait a minute. Lauren? Gushing excitedly?

'Abbie, you'll never guess what.'

'What?'

'My eczema. I just checked myself from head to foot – I mean, absolutely all over – and it's gone.'

'Gone? Are you sure?'

'Positive. I'm standing right under the spotlight, with Mum's magnifying mirror trained on me. My skin is smoooooooooth, Abbie! It even feels different, like it's totally healed. I don't itch. Not anywhere. I'm cured, Abbie. I'm cured!'

'Wow. Well, good – I mean, congratulations.' It was hard to know what to say. Despite my assurances, I'd never really expected the moon-dew to work the miracles Delilah claimed. How could it, when Lauren had tried every cure known to woman, and the scaly patches still cropped up like mushrooms at the slightest provocation? 'That moon-dew must be powerful stuff,' I murmured.

'Powerful? It's magic, it's an absolute miracle. You realize this could change everything? My whole life.'

'I take it that means you're still friends with Delilah then?' I said carefully.

'*Naturellement.* I shall be for ever in her debt. I owe her, Abbie. From now on,' Lauren gushed in a completely uncharacteristic way, 'from this day forth, I am Delilah's devoted slave.'

Chapter Five
Imelda's Web

The day after the moon-ritual thing, I woke up feeling BAD. Not sick-bad. Just mean-bad. So mean, I couldn't even stand my *own* company, let alone anyone else's. Just the sight of myself in the mirror, scrunching lavish dollops of mousse into my mop, made me want to gag. I felt like that boy in the fairy tale with the niggly splinter of ice lodged in his heart. Rotten. Naff. No good to anyone.

Throughout the day the bad feeling intensified. It was all very well for Lauren, now entirely eczema-free and skipping about the New Age shop in the mall like a born-again flower fairy, but what had her blessed moon-dew done for me?

In a word: nothing.

Something was missing from my life, and the goods on display in Imelda's Web seemed only too keen to tell me what this was. Everywhere I looked, my eyes hit upon Cupid crystals, Venus bracelets, and teetering piles of books entitled *Pulling Potions*, which guaranteed to pep up your love life in minutes.

It was Delilah who brought us here after school, of course. She was looking for a tiger's-eye stone for her mojo bag, she said, among other things. 'I need tools,' she told us mysteriously, marching ahead of us in her Doc Marts, hair whipping around like the hanging gardens of

Babylon. 'I need tools of the trade. You two coming, or what?'

We were.

Funny, I'd never bothered much with this place before. Imelda's Web was on the bottom level of Northgate's indoor shopping mall, otherwise known as The Gates. There wasn't much else on this level – just the loos and a bicycle parts shop that never seemed to be open. A quarter of an hour before closing we three were the only shoppers down here. Through the window I could see only a flickery yellow emptiness, and the escalator. No wonder the owner watched us so avidly, like she didn't want to let us go.

'We've got a special offer on these at the moment, dear.' She teetered over to Delilah, click-clack on heels that would give you vertigo just to look at. Flicking a dream-catcher into a spin, she said, 'They're end of line. Nothing wrong with them, just the odd feather missing – if you're interested.'

We looked up into a blur of flamingo-pink feathers. The woman's tinny voice seemed to convey some deeper message that had nothing to do with special offer dream-catchers.

Delilah stuck out her chin and said, 'We're just looking, thanks.'

'I have them specially made, between you and me,' the woman confided. 'Know what I'm saying, dear? The secret's in the webbing.'

I tried to guess how old she was behind the make-up. Forty? Fifty? Hard to tell. A leather mini showed off amazing fish-net legs and a spider-shaped talisman dangled in her cleavage. Obviously she had a thing about spiders. Imelda's Web had taken its name from its unusual range of mirrors, each of them set in a bronze and silver web frame, decorated with tiny metallic spiders.

As she clacked back to the counter, Delilah murmured darkly, 'See her – she works with the dark side.'

'The dark side?'

'She doesn't work in the light. You can tell.'

'You can?' I took a sneaky glance, as the woman, annoyed by our lack of response to her sales pitch, flicked moodily at some wind chimes with a black feather duster.

'Dream-catchers, my arse!' Delilah snorted. 'Buy one of them and we're talking the nightmare-zone.'

'Huh,' I murmured. 'So what's new?'

Lauren looked me over, as if she'd only just noticed me. 'What's wrong with you today? Did you have a row with your mum or something?'

'No. Should I have done?'

'Well, something's wrong.'

'Nothing's wrong.'

'Then why aren't you buying anything? How can you resist these beautiful crystals?' Lauren caressed the chunk of quartz nestling in her palm.

'Quite easily,' I snapped, 'when I've got two quid to last till the weekend.'

Delilah's monkey eyes pierced mine, so I had to blink and look away. I didn't want her to see the meanness inside me, all brooding and bubbling like poison. But there was no fooling Delilah. 'What's happened to your aura?' she wanted to know.

I clutched at my head in mock panic. 'Dunno. Isn't it there?'

Delilah gave me an appraising look, the way your friends do when your eye-shadow's the wrong shade. 'Abbie, your aura is seriously bogging. What have you done to it? Looks like it fell in a puddle or something.'

'I thought it was orange,' I said, beginning to worry now.

'It was. Now it's more of a rust.'

'Oooh, you've gone rusty, Abbie.' Lauren, she of the pigeon-grey aura, smiled smugly.

'Yeah, well, it could be the atmosphere in this place,' Delilah said. 'Let's get out of here, shall we?'

She headed for the till, basket loaded with what she called tricks of the trade, while Lauren followed with the entire rainbow spectrum of crystals. I was the only one leaving the shop empty-handed. Perhaps that was why the web-woman singled me out.

'I could let you have that dream-catcher for two pounds,' she said slyly. 'I saw you looking at it just now.'

Two pounds! How did she know that that was exactly the amount I had in my purse? But even as I hesitated, Delilah spoke for me.

'Thanks, but she'll pass. Doesn't go with her décor, does it, Abbie? Flamingo-pink and lilac – it's a bit harsh on the eyes. Know what I mean?'

'How did you know I've got lilac walls?' I asked her, as we dashed for the escalator.

'I didn't. Have you?'

'Sort of. Lilac's the same as lavender, isn't it?'

'*Yes!*' Delilah yelled, punching the air. 'My powers are getting stronger by the day.'

We piled onto the escalator, giggling. That is, until I glanced over my shoulder and saw the web-woman scowling at us as she put up her CLOSED sign. 'Look. She's staring at us, that woman.'

'What did I tell you, she's got the evil eye.' Lilah tripped off the escalator onto level two, where the big department stores were somehow reassuring. 'Did you know the evil eye can . . .' She paused, leering, and continued in a mock-spooky voice, 'Turn milk sour and sink ships at will.'

Then she stopped laughing and sobered instantly. 'That's the truth, in fact. What's the time?'

Lauren rolled up her sleeve to consult her watch. Any excuse to show off her marble-smooth skin. 'Five-twenty. Are you going straight home, Lilah?'

Shutters were rattling down. A voice droned out of the loudspeaker that the mall was closing in ten minutes. Would everyone make their way to the exit, please?

'Home?' Delilah's face clouded. 'Verne'll have a fit if he sees this lot. False gods and all that. Idols. Pieces of the precious planet. He goes on and on; he spoils everything. Anyway, don't let's think about him. You know, Abbie —' she scrutinized my face again, or rather, around it — 'your aura still looks like a dog's breakfast. Something's bugging you. What's up, then? Is it school?'

'It's probably her love life,' Lauren chirruped, betraying my weak spot. 'Or lack of it.'

'What would you know about it?' I flung back at her.

'Yes, we're getting there,' Delilah said. 'You fancy someone, but he doesn't fancy you — is that it?'

I shrugged. 'Yeah. I mean, no. I don't know.'

Delilah's eyes gleamed with sly triumph. She'd got me. She had me sussed. My miserable, non-existent love life was out in the open, exposed, up for discussion.

'Listen –' she grabbed hold of my elbow – 'we did that spell for Lauren yesterday, but we didn't do anything for *you*, did we?' With a look of sudden resolve, she half dragged me towards the entrance to Woolworths. 'Quick, move it! We've got five minutes.'

Five minutes? It would take more than five minutes to sort my love life. We followed her anyway, as she clumped purposefully towards the kitchenware department.

'What's she doing now?' I grumbled to Lauren. 'I don't need saucepans or bread bins. And thanks a bunch for discussing my most personal affairs.'

'Don't mention it. Anyway, it's not saucepans she's after. Quick – she's gone to the gardening section.' Lauren pointed. 'Over there by the fertilizer bags.'

We found Lilah contemplating the string bags of autumn bulbs. Her bright eyes drilled into me. 'There's a man, right? A boy? A male person of the opposite sex?'

'Not really,' I mumbled.

'Come on, there must be someone.' For some inexplicable reason, Lilah had grabbed a bag of gladiolus bulbs.

'What are you doing? Lilah, I don't like gladioli. I haven't got the dosh anyway . . . Lilah?'

But she was already at the till, thrusting a scrunched-up fiver at the weary-looking assistant. 'Shut up,' she snapped before I could protest. 'It's an early birthday present, OK?'

We followed her out to the street, where shutters were rattling down and cars and lorries snorted their way through the evening rush hour.

'Is this your stop then?' Delilah demanded of me, as we

reached the bus stop outside the school gates. 'Is this where we get the bus to your house?'

'My house?'

Delilah dangled the bulb bag in front of me. 'Bulbs, remember? You have to plant one, you know – in soil, like the stuff you have in your back garden, right? Then you watch it grow.'

Lauren looked as confused as I did. 'Sorry, Lilah, but what has that got to do with Abbie's non-existent love life?'

'It's a ritual, you twerps,' Lilah groaned. 'What d'you think? You think I want to give Abbie's garden a make-over or something?'

'You can't,' I said quickly. 'I mean, I live in an upstairs flat. I haven't got a garden. Well, there's a strip of earth out the back with a few roses, but we share that with our neighbour, Mrs Croop. Also, my mother has a weird-goings-on radar alert system. If she sees us digging by moonlight she'll think the worst: drugs, dead bodies – really, you name it.'

'OK, OK. Look, it doesn't matter where we plant the thing anyway, as long as it's not in my garden, because Verne's at home. I know what . . .' Her eyes lit on the railings of the park across the street. 'The park. We'll plant it in the park.'

'But the park's already closed,' Lauren protested. 'It closes at dusk.'

A waste of breath, because Delilah was already weaving her way perilously through the evening traffic. It seemed we had no choice but to follow her.

Five minutes later we were in the dank, smelly alleyway

that divided the Bromfield Avenue gardens from the park. Delilah showed us the place where there was a gap in the railings just wide enough to squeeze through. Just. The question was, did we want to squeeze through it?

'Actually, er, Lilah,' I began, 'can we put my love life on, like, hold, please? I'm not that desperate. Really.'

'Yes you are,' Lilah decided. 'You look desperate, and anyway –' shaking the string bag at me – 'I haven't got money to burn, y'know.'

'I know. Sorry. But couldn't it wait till tomorrow at least?'

'Yes,' Lauren put in. 'There might be guard dogs in there, or alarms. We could be arrested as vandals.'

'Too bad. Tomorrow's no good anyway. The moon will be waning tomorrow. She only has three days of power, and this is the third. We can't work magic when the moon is dark. That's when Hecate rules.'

Lauren began to panic. 'Not that I want to be a wet blanket or anything, but I don't want to be put on the young offenders list at my age. There's my future to think of – my career, I mean . . .'

But she was wittering on to Delilah's backside. Somehow or other, Lilah had wiggled her not in-considerable bulk through the railings, and was already hissing at us from the other side.

'Get a move on then. Am I supposed to be doing this by myself, or what?'

'You first,' I told Lauren. 'You're skinnier than me.'

Lauren groaned as she struggled through the gap, like a woman in the final stages of labour. 'This is madness, you realize. My entire reputation at stake, all for the sake of your rotten sex life.'

I squeezed in after her. 'Oh, gross! I think I've trodden in something.'

It was no use expecting sympathy from Delilah. She was off again, skirting the edge of the playing field, keeping to the shadows beneath the trees. Funny how different the park looked after hours. Here and there, security lights trailed silver arcs like giant snail tracks across the grass, picking out the bandstand and the adventure playground, with its bizarre towering structures jabbing the sky. In the houses overlooking the park, windows were strung like yellow lanterns. A dog was barking from one of the gardens.

Lauren was going on about our imminent arrest. 'This is illegal entry. We're probably being watched by security cameras. Any minute now and we'll be bathed in floodlights.'

'Oh yeah, and we'll have our faces plastered on WANTED posters all over Northgate. I can just see the headlines now – BROMFIELD GIRLS PLANT ILLEGAL GLADIOLUS BULB IN MILLENNIUM GARDENS. Oh, wow. We could get life for that.'

For this was where Delilah awaited us – the Millennium Gardens: a circular enclave with benches and water features. It was where the old ladies came to sniff the roses in summer. Now I could just make out the geometric-shaped beds, lapped by shadowy pathways.

'They might have left some tools lying around,' Delilah said. 'A trowel would have come in handy. Never mind, we'll just have to scrabble with our hands.'

Lauren, not about to soil her lily-white hands on my account, stuck them deep in her pockets.

Delilah looked like some demonic gnome in the

moonlight, standing hands on hips, the fuzzy outline of her hair like an over-planted hanging basket. 'Remember we're moon-sisters. We're here for each other, right? To help each other. Anyway, this is what we do. We plant the bulb, and lurve will surely blossom.' She shoved the bag at me.

I squinted through the gathering film of mist as Lilah kicked a patch of soil with the toe of her boot. 'Just make a hole there. And while you're doing it, concentrate.'

'Concentrate on what?'

She groaned, exasperated. 'What do you think? This bloke you fancy, the object of your desire. What you do is picture his face in your mind; repeat his name to yourself over and over.'

'I would, if I knew his name,' I muttered, my fingers searching the packet for a likely bulb. None of them were inspiring to the touch, but dry and rustly like the withered onions at the bottom of my mum's vegetable basket. I couldn't help wondering what would happen if I planted the lot. Would I have every eligible male in Northgate camped on my doorstep?

'Anyway,' I said, remembering suddenly, 'you haven't got your knife-thing.'

But Delilah said she didn't always need her *athame*. It was possible to improvise. Already she was drawing the pentagram in the air with her forefinger and calling on the elements, just like the day before. Once the circle was cast, I had no choice. There was nothing else for it but to dig. Or rather, scrabble, breaking my carefully tended fingernails in the mat of bark chippings that covered the soil. As I scooped and poked and prodded, worming my forefinger into the claggy soil, a strong humusy scent flooded my nostrils.

'Hail to thee, Levannah!' Delilah rasped, just like she had last night. 'Hail to thee, Lady of the Moon. Witness that the seed of love be planted. We ask that this seed should grow, blossom and bloom . . .'

By now I'd managed to make some sort of indentation, just big enough to settle the bulb in place. This was the moment. I began to panic. Name! I was supposed to be thinking of a name, but who the—? Then, just as I was covering the bulb with the loose bark chippings, a face suddenly swam before me. I could see it clearly, the light grey eyes, the quirky smile, that brown hair trailing over one eye: Delilah's brother Joel! My God, don't say I'd fallen for Delilah's totally uninterested and unobtainable and bound-for-Australia brother! Yet my inner voice was sighing over the name – JoelJoelJoelJoel . . .

'Let Abigail's love take root and flourish!' Delilah was nudging Lauren into a feeble echo of her own voice.

'*Let Abigail's love take root and flourish!*' they chorused together, a little out of time.

Still patting the bulb into its hiding place, I went on repeating the marvellous name – Joel, Joel, Joel – until it seemed that the name really belonged to me. By the time I'd finished it felt like the bulb had been planted not in the earth at all, but in me. Inside of me, in the deepest most unknowable part of my self, something was stirring, already putting out feelers towards the light.

Alas, this euphoria lasted only a few seconds. No sooner had I brushed the soil from my hands than Joel's face vanished entirely from my mind. The spell was broken. Not by security guards or fierce dogs foaming at the mouth – nothing like that. It was something far worse. It was that *feeling* again; the sensation that had turned me to stone in Delilah's garden the other night.

My heart sank. Could the others feel it too? A quick glance told me they could. Lauren had the trapped look of someone standing on a railway track when a train's approaching. As for Delilah, you could almost see her bristle, like a cat with its fur standing on end. She stood, head on one side, as if alert to something we couldn't hear. Not yet anyway. I strained my ears. There was only the background rumble of traffic from the main road. Then I heard it, approaching as if from a long way off: the faint but unmistakable clip of hooves on tarmac.

Lauren said in a puzzled tone, 'That sounds like a horse. You don't think the security guards are on horseback, do you?'

Delilah was mouthing something at us. I stared in dismay as her lips framed the two words, 'The Creep.'

Suddenly I was cold all over. I turned up the collar of my denim jacket, wanting to shrug myself into it and hide. Not again. Not here. Somehow, if I'd allowed myself to think of the Creep at all, I'd connected him with Delilah's place. The grim atmosphere bequeathed by Verne, the rituals, the bizarre array of gods and goddesses were virtually an advertisement to any available spook to do its worst.

But even as she mouthed the words, the hoofbeats were upon us. How did they get that close so fast? Close and soft, scuffing wavy patterns into the neatly raked gravel paths.

'Oh come on,' I murmured quietly to myself. 'Tell me this isn't happening, please.' My throat had gone dry.

There was an ache at the back of my neck as I forced myself to look up, beyond the phantom blur of hooves and tail and grey mane. The rider was sitting astride the horse, back stiff and soldierly, one hand relaxed on the reins.

Perhaps he'd been there all the time? All I had to do was open my eyes and there he was, swimming into focus until he blotted out the shadowy gardens and Northgate beyond, and London beyond that, and the everyday world as I knew it.

The face staring down at us was in shadow. Only the tall brimmed hat was unmistakable, outlined clearly against the yellowish sky. The Creep. The Creep had found us!

Delilah was yelling something to Lauren and me. What? All I could hear was: '*Don't!* Don't break the circle.'

At the same time I could feel Lauren tugging on my jacket sleeve, swaying dangerously as if she were ready to faint. 'Lilah, I'm going. Lilah, I can't take this. I'm . . .' She began to whimper as the Creep slowly raised his hat to us.

I squinted through tear-blurred eyes. My God, he was actually greeting us as 'gentlemen' did in those days, raising a hat to a lady. Yet I could feel his scorn, his contempt for us, as the hat was jammed smartly back on his draggled locks.

'Children —' the voice was plaintive, almost regretful — 'what brings you to this place, hmmm? What diabolical tricks are these?'

Lauren and I would have bolted that minute if Delilah hadn't somehow held us back. 'Wait, we must cut a doorway first!' She began striking the air with her finger as if it were an *athame*. She looked as if she were un-zipping a tent-flap. Only once she was satisfied that the door had been properly 'unzipped' did she shout, 'OK, *run*!'

These were Delilah's orders, just as the moon vanished behind a cloud, and we were plunged into darkness.

Chapter Six

A Discoverie of Witchcraft

'The Creep,' Lilah panted, when we'd hauled ourselves back through the railings. 'That miserable sod just never lets up.'

What seemed to worry her most, though, was leaving the 'circle' without a formal 'see ya later' to the Ancient Ones. 'I can't believe you freaked like that, Lauren,' she kept saying as we tottered wobbly-kneed up the street. 'I would never have broken the circle normally. Anything could happen. Thank God I managed to cut the doorway first.'

Lauren was clearly traumatized by the vision we'd just seen.

'Who *is* he anyway?' I asked Delilah, my voice sounding strange and husky to my ears. 'What the hell does he want? He spoke, Lilah. Did you hear him? Something about "diabolical tricks" . . . Eugh!' I shuddered. 'His voice made my skin crawl.'

Delilah frowned. 'I didn't hear that. I didn't hear him speak. But then it's no wonder, the way Lauren was wittering on. All I could hear was, "Ooh, Lilah, please, Lilah, I'm scared, Lilah!"'

It seemed she had no more idea than we did what the Creep wanted. At least she *said* she didn't. I wasn't sure I believed her. I'd begun to realize that this spectre that wafted such hatred was part of the darkness that wrapped itself about Delilah like a cloak. The darkness that was now drawing Lauren and me in, deeper and deeper.

I suppose we could have cut Delilah out of our lives at that point, and never set eyes on the Creep again. But that seemed cowardly. Delilah couldn't help her ghostly sidekick any more than she could help her awful stepfather. Could she?

As for that gladiolus bulb, I thought it must have just rotted in the ground or been eaten by a mouse or something because, in the days that followed our little planting ceremony, nothing much happened in the lurve department. I had to face it: moon magic or not, my chances of bumping into Joel again were practically zilch, what with Delilah's place being off limits. The Loathsome Verne was in residence, and more loathsome than ever, according to Lilah.

'I'm planning on flying a flag when he's at home,' she said grimly. 'Like the skull and crossbones. Just to warn everybody.'

But at least hanging around with Delilah made life more interesting. What else was going on? There was school, there was study, there was my Saturday morning job, and that was it.

Did I say job? It wasn't a real job exactly, working for my mother. Every Saturday morning I would do a couple of hours' cleaning at her newly opened surgery, Feet First. We had an arrangement: once Mum's fame as chiropodist *par excellence* had spread throughout the land and she was tending the tootsies of the rich and beautiful, then I would get a rise. Until that marvellous day arrived, I earned myself a tenner by scuttling around the surgery with a damp J-cloth, trying not to look at the posters of humungous foot diseases.

Actually, on the Saturday after our bulb-planting ceremony, the posters were a welcome distraction. It was one of those murky November mornings that made even my mother's sparkling windows look grimy. When I turned on the strip lights, they buzzed and flickered so much I began to feel spooked. It was hard not to think of the Creep. Imagine if I saw his shadow now; if it should rear demonically on the wall next to the Scholl sandal poster? I was just thinking this, when a sudden rap on the window zapped through me like a thousand volts, catapulting the Mr Sheen from my grasp.

'You frightened the life out of me,' I told Lauren and Delilah with relief, as I opened the door to them. 'What are you two doing here? You don't need your corns removing or anything, I hope. Perhaps I could oblige for a small fee. I have here zee leetle hack saw.' I flourished one of my mother's grisly torture instruments at them.

'Eugh! Gross!' Lauren shuddered.

Delilah said she'd pass, thanks, because her feet were in perfect shape. 'If you want to know, we came to take you away from all this, didn't we, Lauren?' She waved a hand to indicate the surgery. 'Cinderella, you *shall* go to the ball!'

Delilah made a strange fairy godmother, I have to say, in her long, dusty black coat and what looked like a dead weasel slung around her neck. Beneath the coat she was wearing a skimpy mini that revealed acres of pudgy, henna-decorated belly button and mad polka-dot tights.

'The ball?' I laid down my J-cloth. 'Great. We're going somewhere exciting at last.'

'Oh, dead exciting,' Delilah said. 'Are you ready for the thrills and spills of St Ethelreda's jumble sale?'

I groaned. 'Tell me you're joking.'

'No joke. I'm deadly serious, in fact.' Delilah flopped into one of the waiting-room chairs and began flicking through a copy of *Chiropody Monthly*.

'I'm not really into jumbles myself.' Lauren perched uneasily on the edge of her chair. 'Other people's cast-offs turn my stomach actually. You might catch some disease from wearing them. You might catch fleas.'

Delilah took great offence at this comment. She snorted that it was all right for girls like Lauren whose parents gave them allowances. 'I get a fiver a week if I'm lucky, which barely keeps me in Tampax.'

As one who regularly went shopping in bargain basements, I sympathized. Even so, I found it hard to understand why Delilah, who lived in an enormous house overlooking the park, should be so hard up. Perhaps reading my mind, she explained that Verne kept a tight rein on household expenses.

'He reckons any more dosh would turn me into a wanton shopaholic. Who needs fashion anyway? Verne says. Any Brethren female worth her salt wears some nice little sackcloth number with a headscarf to cover up her woman's glory.'

I looked down at myself. 'Funny place for a headscarf.'

'Not *there*, you moron. Your hair, I mean. He and my mum had a row because she wanted to have hers cut. Anyway, are you up for it? The jumble, I mean. Because we should leave if you are – it starts at one-thirty.'

I considered the Wrangler baggies and old rugby shirt that were my cleaning uniform. 'Why not? You never know, Geri Halliwell might be chucking out some of her Versace.'

Outside St Ethelreda's church hall the murk had thickened. A fat drop of rain trickled down my neck. As we jostled with old ladies and young mothers steering their double buggies like chariots, I began to wonder if this was worthwhile after all.

'Right.' Delilah prodded me as the doors opened. 'We have lift-off. Go for it.'

Inside the hall the old dears were certainly going for it. All I could see was a wall of raincoated backs, as they hurled anything they didn't like over their shoulders. Struggling free of a string vest the size of a North Sea trawler's fishing net, I cast about for a gap in the wall-to-wall macs. When I finally managed to slot myself in, it was a case of snatching dementedly at anything that wasn't made of pink brushed nylon.

A woman with orange pencilled eyebrows seized on a black sweater at the same time as me, and for a second or two we each tugged on an arm, until someone elbowed me out of the way. I fell back, clutching my pitiful spoils: a pair of day-glo green harem pants hung over one arm; a feather boa that looked like one of my mother's draught-excluders dangled from my neck.

'Hey!' I yelled out to Lauren, who hovered at the fringes. 'New Romantics, whaddya think?' I gave her a whirl of the feather boa. 'Is it me, or is it me?'

'There's a terrible niff in here,' was Lauren's pained response. 'It smells of old nylons and sweaty trainers.' She turned up her nose, but as it was already turned up, this looked more piggy than cute. 'Can't we wait for Lilah outside? She'll know where we are, won't she?'

Sometimes Lauren was no fun at all. I was about to tell her this in no uncertain terms, when the words died on my tongue. Suddenly, I wanted out of there as much as she did. It wasn't just the pong of old cast-offs. It was more of a feeling – that feeling of shame and horror that I was beginning to recognize, like the onset of some horrible pain.

Instinctively my eyes searched the crush of bargain hunters. It was weird, this searching for something – someone – I didn't want to find. Yet somehow I knew I *would* find it. And yes, there he was. My heart seemed to shrink inside me. The tall, dark figure was prowling among the women, babies wailing like synchronized cuckoo clocks as he passed.

'See him?' I clutched Lauren's arm so hard she winced.

'Ow! D'you mind? You know I bruise easily.' Then, as her eyes followed my pointing finger, 'What? The vicar, you mean?' She must have mistaken the swirling cape for a cassock, for his back was turned towards us.

'Wake up, Lauren. Since when did the vicar dress like that? Where's Delilah? We've got to warn her.'

'No, *you* warn her – although I don't know what you're on about. I'll be outside, OK?'

Peering through the crowd, I could just make out Delilah's crazy hair among the silvery perms and head-scarves. She hadn't noticed him yet. He was stooped over the bookstall, picking over books the way a crow picks over the entrails of a rabbit squashed by a car.

'Delilah!' I shouted. It was hopeless. She was drifting towards the bookstall. Another second and she would run smack into him.

As I pushed my way across the hall, feet tangling in pushchair wheels and carrier bags, I could see them both apparently browsing, shoulder to shoulder. Delilah hadn't noticed yet. She thought the tall bloke at her side was just another bargain hunter. She hadn't noticed that she was actually rubbing shoulders with the Creep!

'Lilah, come away, please, quick!' I managed to tug on the tail of the weasel fur that hung forlornly down her back.

She just carried on trailing a ringed finger along the tatty spines of old paperbacks. 'OK, OK, I'm just looking.' She made a puking sound. 'It's all rubbish romance stuff anyway. Who reads that crap?'

'Lilah, I—'

But the Creep had no intention of letting me drag Delilah off. His back seemed huge suddenly, barring my way, blocking my view as he bent towards her. And then he spoke. Not the whispery half-mumble we'd heard in the Millennium Gardens. This time he spoke as a real living human being might speak, his voice sly and gentle, like some farmer crooning to his cows.

'Perhaps I may be of service, my child. I do have a volume here that I think you may find interesting.' And he reached for something beneath his cloak.

The book he passed to Delilah might have been one of those old-fashioned family Bibles. A huge doorstop of a thing. Black. Dusty. 'Take it, daughter.' He pressed it on her, his face shielded from me by a greasy straggle of hair falling beneath his hat.

And Delilah *did* take it. That was what astonished me – the way she just stood there, receiving the book in her outstretched arms. The expression on her face was weird.

Kind of blank, like the real Delilah wasn't at home; as though even if you jumped up and down in front of her, crying, 'Halloo-oo! Delilah?' she wouldn't see you. She only had eyes for the book, which she accepted like some terrible honour, some burden meant only for her. Her whole body, I noticed, braced itself, as if the book were impossibly heavy, even heavier than it looked.

As the Creep continued in his sly country burble, saying that Delilah should 'ponder well every word therein, for the good of her mortal soul', I began to feel dizzy. It was so warm in here, the smell of dirty nappies and perm lotion and dust all humming together. Suddenly, I just had to get out into the fresh air.

'Lilah . . . Lilah, I'm going . . .' My voice was hoarse and whispery – how could she hear that? Especially with the Creep leaning over her, uttering the words almost in her ear: 'Hear my counsel, daughter, for it is I, who am the author of this *Discoverie*. Take heed.'

But that was all I heard, because the next minute I was standing outside the hall taking deep gulps of dank, fume-ridden air. Lauren seemed unimpressed by my gasping for breath. Brushing the tawny sleeve of her Afghan coat, she said, 'It's not fair. Some rotten bird just pooped on me. I've only had this three weeks, and now I'll have to send it to the cleaner's.'

'Lauren,' I gasped, 'we have more to worry about than your coat. Or Delilah does . . .'

For Delilah had just come bursting through the church hall doors, and was hurtling along the path that edged the heath, her long coat flaring behind, her weasel fur flapping at her neck as if the devil were after her. For a second or two I continued to watch the double doors, in case the Creep was following her. To my relief, there were only two fat women trailing a tribe of kids.

'Lilah, wait!'

Lauren and I fell into a jog behind her, Lauren groaning, 'What are we running for? What's the hurry suddenly?'

But Delilah wasn't stopping for anyone. At least, not until the book slid from her grasp. It landed, spine-up, spread-eagled in a shallow puddle.

'Arse!' Delilah stared at it in horror. From the look on her face, you'd think she'd just dropped a newborn baby on its head.

'It's all right, I've got it. I don't think it's damaged . . . Phew! Heavy, isn't it?' I gasped aloud as I grappled the book out of the slimy water.

Almost at once I regretted touching it. Something foul emanated from the book, as if all the horror and misery in the world were contained between its covers. 'The Creep gave you this . . . What is it? What's it about?'

'Read the title,' Delilah said dully.

The gold lettering was dulled and flaky. Yet I managed to read aloud: '*A Discoverie of Witchcraft* by Master Matthew Hopkins.'

We stood silent for a moment, as if we'd been caught red-handed in some terrible act. Like there was nowhere to run. We'd been found out. Caught. Discovered. But . . . by who? By a ghost? By the Creep?

Delilah's eyes on mine were bright, feverish. She held out her arms to me. 'Better hand it over, Abb. It's better if I hold onto it.'

When I passed the book back to Lilah it was like handing a baby back to its mother. An evil-hearted baby,

68

like a changeling in a fairy tale. Delilah didn't want the thing. Yet somehow it belonged to her.

'So what now?' Lauren said, bewildered. 'What do we do with it?'

'We go to my place. We look at it properly there.'

Delilah struggled on, still clutching the book, heading for the house on the avenue, where surely the Loathsome Verne was in residence. Waiting for us.

Chapter Seven

The Loathsome Verne

'Do we really want to see inside that book? I think we should just dump it.' I whispered my doubts to Lauren, as Delilah kicked open the kitchen door. Did we even want to see inside Lilah's house, come to that? Supposing Verne was lurking in the kitchen?

'This book could give him a claim on us,' I murmured.

'Give *who* a claim? It's only an old book that someone dumped,' Lauren said sulkily.

This was one of Lauren's infuriating quirks. When it came to the normal, everyday senses like sight and smell, she was needle-sharp. But when it came to the sixth sense, forget it! For someone with such a keenly honed sense of survival, Lauren was about as tuned in to psychic phenomena as a plank of wood.

Thankfully, though, all seemed normal in the kitchen, where Delilah's mother was scrubbing out glass jars – the enormous kind they used to have in sweet shops. Except these were grainy with dirt and green mould.

'What in the name of the goddess are you doing now, Mother?' Lilah demanded.

'Just cleaning out some jars, dear, and try not to shout. He's working.' She nodded nervously towards the ceiling and smiled 'hello' at Lauren and me.

'So? He's working, so what?' Delilah seemed to have recovered from her dazed spell in the church hall. She was quite her old bolshie self again, as she slammed the book on the table and glared at it. 'We don't have to observe a three-minute silence, do we? Anyway, what's with all the jars?'

Verne had found them on a tip, her mother explained patiently. 'And please don't take that tone with me, dear, it's quite unnecessary.'

She bent to one of four large hessian sacks and began scooping brown rice into one of the jars. Her hair fell forward onto her face and her sandals squeaked – those cloddy sandals that look made to last twenty lifetimes. The grains of rice rattled into the jar. 'It was such a lucky find. Now I can store all our grains and flour properly.'

Delilah groaned. She began explaining how Verne liked to have stocks of food in. 'For when the world ends, you know. According to him we've got – what is it, Mum? – one year? Two? Only the lucky few will survive, anyone who belongs to the Brethren, that is. Imagine it –' Delilah threw up her hands theatrically to indicate the heavens – 'the end of the world as we know it. We're about to be swallowed up by a black hole, or pulverized by a giant comet, or some maniac's about to nuke us into non-existence – and hey, there's Verne, he's one of the famed Puritan Brethren, so we'll give him a miss. Verne can live on in his bunker and nosh brown rice for the rest of his naturals. That's before he's beamed up into paradise, of course.'

Delilah grabbed the book again and clutched it defensively to her. 'Personally I'd rather just snuff it on the spot, like the rest of the no-good heathens.'

It gave me quite a turn to hear her say that. One year?

71

Two? End of the world or not, that was more years than Lilah had left to live by my reckoning.

'Does your, er, stepfather ever come in here?' I said five minutes later, as she slammed her bedroom door behind us.

'He'd better not try.' Delilah flung both the book and herself onto the bed. 'There's no way he can enter, in fact, because I've sealed the place tight.'

'Sealed?' Lauren glanced around, puzzled.

'I don't mean insulation tape.' Delilah tapped her nose mysteriously. '*I have my ways.*'

So far she'd made no attempt to open the book. I couldn't blame her. It lay on the bed, dark, ominous. Still, our eyes couldn't help but be drawn to it, as if it were an unexploded bomb. Who dared to look between its covers? Supposing one glance were to trigger something? Bring the Creep winging his way to us, like a curse.

Maybe the others were thinking the same thing. There was a moment or two of silence before Delilah walked her stubby, ringed fingers spider-like across the wrinkled leather cover. 'So, let's see what Master Matthew Hopkins has to say, shall we?'

Dust flew into our noses as she fanned pages that had the rubbery, mouldy look of those processed cheese slices. She finally stopped at an illustration. 'Looks like we've got the Creep.' Her finger hissed against the rough vellum. 'Abbie, look. The figure we saw at the jumble – this is him, right?'

She was showing me one of those ancient woodcuts, dark and grainy and sinister. This much I could see from where I stood at the foot of the bed. An upside-down view. It was enough.

Delilah looked up at me. 'Have you got zoom-lens eyes or what?' Reluctantly, I moved to her side. It was hard to explain, but everything in me flinched from looking at this book. It was like the locked room in the fairy tale, the one you're forbidden to explore. The one you can never resist.

'Would you say that's the Creep?' Delilah demanded again.

I stared. Yes. This was him all right. Just as I'd seen him this afternoon. A man of importance in his time, obviously. You could tell him, not just from the broad-brimmed hat or the cloak, but from the way he stood holding his staff, like he reckoned he was *someone*. I glimpsed hollow cheeks and a beard like the root of giant leek before I closed my eyes. Clearly the figure in the illustrations was the person we had seen in the Millennium Gardens and just now at the jumble sale. That is a dead person. A very dead person. A person who must have been dead for over three hundred years, judging by the costume he wore.

'Yes, that's him. Oh, turn the page, please, Lilah. Just turn the page!'

But Delilah seemed transfixed. She tapped her tongue-ring across her teeth. 'Bit of an ego-tripper, isn't he? He writes the book, then fills it with pictures of himself.'

'Let's see.' Lauren peered over my shoulder from a safe distance. 'That was the way the Puritans dressed, wasn't it, when Cromwell fought Charles the First during the Civil War? Maybe the vicar dresses like one of the Pilgrim Fathers.'

'Yeah, yeah, maybe the vicar wears a wig and kitten heels in his spare time.' I sighed. 'Lauren, why not admit the truth? What we've just seen is an apparition, a ghost, a very dead person, right? It's the same ghoul we saw at the moon ritual, and again in the park. And now it's spirited this horrible book to us somehow, from the other side.'

'Listen!' Delilah jerked her head at the door. 'Did you hear something just then?'

We listened. There was only the faint chink of glass from the kitchen far below us, the occasional car passing in the street. Somewhere beneath these everyday sounds, so faint that it hardly even registered on your conscious-ness, was the intermittent creak of a floorboard.

Delilah leapt up from the bed. 'If that's Verne snoop-ing, let's give him something to listen to.'

Rattling furiously through a heap of discs, she slotted one into her CD player. At once a hypnotic chanting, backed by an African-style drumbeat, pulsed through the room. What with the light fading outside the window and the book laid out like a tombstone upon the bed, I couldn't help thinking that anything more sinister than the *Simpsons* theme tune was a bad choice.

'That's fixed him.' Delilah returned to the book. She held up another woodcut for Lauren and me to see. 'Hopkins again,' she said, 'if I'm not mistaken.'

In this picture the cloaked figure towered forbiddingly over a couple of old crones. Both women were surrounded by a bizarre assortment of animals: a sausage dog with a cow's head, dogs and cats with lizard tails, wings, beaks and claws. Their pet names were printed alongside them. The cow-faced dog was called Vinegar

Tom; one, which looked like a spaniel with lizard's feet, was Grizzelldiguts. The pet names might have come from a children's fairy tale, yet there was a horror about them that made me shudder.

' "Witches and their familiars . . ." ' Delilah read aloud, with a kind of grim triumph. As if she knew something. As if she'd been proved right about something we hadn't even guessed at yet.

'What's all this about, Lilah?' I asked faintly. 'Who is Matthew Hopkins? And why is he . . . haunt— I mean, following you?'

'Who *was* Matthew Hopkins, you mean?' Her fingers fidgeted with one of her dreadlocks. 'Matthew Hopkins was a witchfinder. Surely you've worked it out by now? The clue is in the title –' she emphasized the words as if to a couple of dimwits – '*A Discoverie of Witchcraft*. That's what Hopkins did for a living. *Discovered* witches.'

'A witchfinder!' I held my hand flat against my ribcage where my heart was flapping away like a demented bat. 'That's why he keeps appearing to you – to *us*, I mean. He's come back from the dead to find himself some more witches . . . but that's gruesome!'

'Yeah, and Hopkins wasn't just any old witchfinder, he was the Witchfinder General. That made him practically as powerful as the King.' Delilah tapped the cover of the book. 'This was probably a bestseller in its day – nice grisly pictures of torture and that go down a treat with the Puritan lot. Come to think of it, Verne would probably love it.'

Lauren, twisting a plait nervously around one finger, began prattling about some film she'd seen called *The Crucible*. 'Practically every female in this village was hanged as a witch. I thought it was just a story, you know? Just fantasy.'

Delilah laughed grimly. 'Some fantasy! The witch-finders were real people all right. Great career if you happened to be a pervert.'

'Yeah,' I said, still trying to avoid looking at the picture of Hopkins. 'I remember reading about this town somewhere in Norfolk, where three hundred people were rounded up. If they suspected you, they'd search you all over for warts and stuff, then they'd stick you with pins to see if you bled and after that they'd probably chuck you in the nearest lake to see if you drowned.'

'Actually,' Delilah said, 'their very favourite torture was sleep deprivation. The witchfinders used to walk these women up and down all night, right, until they were fainting from exhaustion and their feet were all blistered. The idea was to get them totally ga-ga, so they'd tell the names of their familiars and that.'

' "Familiars" sounds so creepy,' Lauren said, peering at the hideous woodcut of Vinegar Tom and his mates. 'What are they anyway?'

'Imps of Satan, of course,' Delilah said. 'Witches were supposed to suckle them like babies. That's why women were searched all over for hidden teats. To a witchfinder, anything was suspect, even a pet canary. They thought if they kept the women up all night, the familiars would get hungry and show up for a quick slurp. If Vinegar Tom didn't put in an appearance, they'd drown you anyway.'

'A no-win situation, in other words,' I mumbled. I was doing my best to contain the panic that was beginning to rise in me. It was happening again! The ghostly stalker thing. Lauren and I had been there, done that. I was beginning to think we were like some kind of spiritual fly-paper, with unclean spirits swarming about us like blowflies.

'So, being a witchfinder, was it like some kind of religious quest?' Lauren asked.

'Partly.' Delilah scratched so maniacally in her dreadlocks, you'd think she had nits or something. 'Don't forget there was money in it too. Twenty shillings a town to rid it of witches. That's about a thousand quid in today's money. It wasn't a bad career option. Especially for a psycho like Hopkins.'

'And now he's a dead psycho,' I blurted, unnerved by the sudden flutter of curtain, the darkness falling outside. 'What are we going to do, Lilah? I mean, why is he here? Why the book?'

'I don't know,' Delilah admitted. 'It's like he wants us to know he's on our case.'

'*Our* case?' Lauren clutched nervously at her throat as if she could feel the noose there already. 'But that's not fair. I mean, *I'm* not a witch. I only rubbed in a bit of moon-dew after all.'

But Delilah didn't seem to hear this cowardly cop-out. She was gazing almost dreamily into space. 'He wants us to know he's come back to keep an eye on us. But if he's trying to scare me off, tough, because I don't scare that easy.'

'You're not saying he's actively hunting down witches again? And we—' I was about to say that we three must be prime suspects, but my voice seemed to pack up on me. Like the music. A sudden click, and it stopped mid-drumbeat. At the same time the light bulb flickered out. Darkness fell like a blanket thrown over our heads.

'Oh my God, it's him! It's him, isn't it?' As I backed over to the window, my hip knocked into the altar. The elephant god Ganesh tipped sideways onto his trunk. I held my breath. Any minute now and we'd hear it, the *tap-tap* of the witchfinder's staff on the bedroom door.

But, like Delilah said, she didn't scare easy. She was stomping over to the door, wrenching it open. 'I don't bloody believe it, the lecky's run out again. Mum! Verne! The lights are out. Mum!'

When no one responded to her yelling, she slammed the door so hard the house shook. Her currant eyes blazed. 'No need to climb up the curtains, you two. It's only Verne and his smegging economy drive.'

She began tipping assorted candles out of a shoe box – some tall and spindly, encrusted with stalactites of seeping wax, some just stubs stuck anyhow onto saucers. Only the two candles on the altar for the god and goddess remained unlit, I noticed.

'Sorry about this,' Delilah mumbled. For once her eyes flitted away from ours, embarrassed. 'He's such a tight-arsed git, we've got this slot meter for the lecky, and it's not even a coin thing. Verne gets these cards from the post office.'

'Cards?' I sat on the bed again, relieved that this was only Verne's doing. Loathsome he might be, but at least he was alive. Human. Or almost.

'Yeah, I know it sounds bizarre, but there are such things, believe me. They give you, say, ten quid's worth of lecky at a time. We don't just use what we need and pay our bills like normal people, are you kidding?'

'So,' I suggested, embarrassed for her having to explain all this to Lauren and me, 'when the card runs out, why don't you just slot another one in?'

'Because it's never that simple with Verne. He makes sure we run out deliberately, for the good of our souls. Sometimes we go to bed at eight, just to keep warm, and read by candlelight like in Victorian times.' She gazed around at the six flickering candles. 'Look, don't run away, you two. I'm going to sort this out. Won't be a minute.'

Lauren and I looked at each other.

'D'you think we should go?' Lauren said sheepishly. 'There might be a – you know, a scene.'

'Perhaps we should. I'm not sure I want to read that thing by the light of a guttering candle.' I nodded at the horrible book, collapsed face downwards on the bed. 'Poor Lilah though.'

Lauren and I snuck out onto the landing. Two floors below us, Delilah's furious yelling was punctuated by a measured, rumbling tone that must belong to Verne. I hesitated. I wanted to escape as much as Lauren did, but I didn't much fancy bumping into the Loathsome Verne in full flow.

'He can't really be such a monster,' Lauren said, tripping ahead of me down the first flight of stairs. 'Don't forget, I'm used to stepfathers. I have to put up with Harv-wit. We'll just say hello politely and make out we have to get home urgently.'

But on the second landing she stopped. From here we found ourselves peering down upon the thinning scalp of no less than the Loathsome Verne himself. There was just enough light sifting through the stained-glass panels in the front door to make out a slight figure in a huge sweater and cords. He looked much the same as anyone's dad. That is, boring. I'd almost expected horns and a forked tail the way Delilah described him.

'But you must have some more cards stashed away somewhere,' Delilah was pleading. 'It's Saturday night, and the post office won't be open till Monday morning. You can't expect us to go all bloody weekend without electricity.'

'Delilah, what have I told you before about swearing?' Verne spoke with the kind of weary, dogged patience a social worker might use on some young offender. 'I will *not* have foul language in this house. The electricity has run out. It is not, contrary to your belief, the end of the world. An entire third of the population of the globe manages very well without such luxuries, as I've told you on many occasions.'

Delilah was hurling herself about the hallway in a fury. 'Don't give me that third world crap, please. We don't live in the third world.'

'And what will you do when all the lights go out, heh, eh, Delilah? How will you manage without your mobiles and computers when the world is in chaos, all because some folk had to get greedy and take more than their fair share of world resources?' Verne sounded almost excited, as if he could hardly wait for this day to arrive.

'And I've got friends here, if you don't mind,' Lilah screeched, interrupting the lecture that I guessed she'd heard a million times. 'You can't expect my friends to sit in the dark all night!'

Verne's voice was so soft, so saintly, I barely caught the reply – something about not recalling Delilah asking if she might invite any friends. At which point her mother came out, anxiously wiping her hands on a teatowel and asking what was the row about?

Lauren and I grabbed our chance. We almost skidded

down the last few stairs, both of us chirruping our excuses to leave.

'See!' Lilah yelled. 'Happy now? Now that you've driven my friends away?'

I'd seen Delilah mad before but never this mad. With the power out, the downstairs hall was almost in darkness, but Delilah was radiating such a fizz of energy you could almost see it. The more she fizzed, the calmer Verne seemed to become. On and on he lectured in his quietly stubborn, reasonable way, not bothering even to acknowledge Lauren and me.

But Delilah, it seemed, had had enough. She grabbed her coat from the banisters, muttering like someone deranged. 'If you two want to sit in the dark all night like the bloody undead, that's fine with me. But count me out. I'm going! I'm bloody well going. And I'm not coming back!'

She must have been in a bad way, because she didn't even wait for Lauren and me. It was like she'd forgotten all about us. As the front door slammed behind her, we were left shuffling awkwardly at the foot of the stairs, wondering what on earth we could say to her parents.

Chapter Eight

Love Spell

Our first instinct was to chase after Delilah, of course, but it was a bit awkward, what with her mum bursting into tears like she'd never stop.

'Histrionics.' Verne just shrugged his mean shoulders. 'She only does it for attention. She'll be back as soon as she gets hungry.'

This wasn't a great comfort to Delilah's mother. It only made her realize she'd have to cook their dinner over the camping gas tonight. She began wittering on about lentil hotpots and parsnip soup, while Lauren and I edged towards the door.

I grabbed my jacket from the hall stand. 'Don't worry, we'll find her, won't we, Lauren? She won't have gone far.'

Delilah's mother peered at us with bleary gratitude. 'She gets herself into such a state. Sometimes I worry about what she might do. Delilah's very lucky to have friends like you girls. I hope she realizes that.'

'Too right she's lucky to have us,' Lauren said as we stood outside the house, searching the far horizon for a glimpse of dusty black coat and mad, dreadlocky hair. 'Now what do we do?'

'I thought she'd just be lurking about down the street somewhere, waiting for us,' I admitted.

'Where is she then?' Lauren looked pointedly right and left, all down the long, leafy length of Bromfield Avenue.

I sighed. 'She must've legged it. I don't blame her, do you?' I jerked my head in the direction of the house. 'What with that lot in there. I don't know which is worse, that creepy stepfather or the . . .'

'Or the what?'

I'd been going to say 'the Creep', but then I remembered we knew his name now. Hopkins. Matthew Hopkins. I wasn't going to say it aloud though. As we stood under a drift of rusty leaves from the great shadowy plane tree outside the house, I preferred not to think of Hopkins. Or of that hideous book abandoned in Delilah's room.

'Anyway,' I continued, 'if I was Delilah, I'd run all right. And I'd keep on running.'

This was all very well, Lauren pointed out, but where did it leave us? 'You just made that promise to her mother, which, if you want my opinion, was somewhat rash.' She flapped her arms hopelessly against her sides. 'I mean, she could be anywhere.'

I ignored her and started off down the street. 'Well, I suggest we just check out the obvious places. Are you coming or what?'

Two hours later the only obvious thing was that finding Delilah would not be easy. We'd tried her mobile, but either she'd switched it off or hadn't had time to take it with her. She wasn't in any of the usual places, like Gav's Café, or the chippy, or the park. We'd even asked the park keeper if he'd seen a girl with dreadlocks and a long black coat. The keeper said no, he hadn't, and he hoped she wasn't one of that gang who'd upturned all the litter bins earlier on, and anyway he was just closing the gates.

After that we trudged about The Triangle, which was just a pedestrianized shopping space with benches, and a favourite hang-out with kids from our school. After being propositioned by at least a dozen blokes, every one of them gross, Lauren announced that she was fainting with hunger and was going home. Apparently her mother was hosting one of her Moroccan evenings for the belly-dancing gang, and there might just be some tagine left in the pot.

'Tagine?'

'It's kind of a stew with couscous. It's quite tasty actually.'

'Well great, Lauren. You just run on home and enjoy your couscous, and I'll trog off back to Delilah's and tell her mother she's possibly been abducted by the Witchfinder General – how's that?'

Immediately I regretted these words. A wind seemed to blow up suddenly, knocking over a traffic cone in a disabled parking bay. As it rolled on its side, it reminded me of that sinister steeple hat. If I'd had any sense I would have followed Lauren's example and caught the next bus home. Instead, as she hurtled off on the 192 to Highgate in hot pursuit of her tagine, I turned off the main street and headed back towards the park.

It had come to me suddenly. OK, Delilah hadn't been there earlier, but there was nothing to stop her sneaking back after closing, was there? This seemed such a Delilah-ish thing to do – to skulk about in the chill of the Millennium Gardens planning revenge on Verne – that

I was soon struggling through the gap in the railings.

This time there was no full moon. I crossed the playing field like before, keeping close to the railings, avoiding the silver beam of the security lights. My heart was pounding so hard I was sure it would rouse the neighbourhood. Delilah must be here. She must! I knew, even before I caught sight of her slumped forwards on the bench. Even before she glanced up and murmured, 'Sod off and leave me alone.'

'That's charming, when we've been hunting for you everywhere.' As I drew nearer, I could see the litter of empty Special Brew cans at her feet. At least three. Now she was working her way steadily through a fourth.

'Lilah, why did you run off and leave us? Your mum's really upset. She's . . . she's . . .' I stopped short.

Clearly I wasn't getting through to her. The fourth can joined the others, clinking onto the gravel path. Slowly, luxuriously, Lilah produced an enormous belch.

'Lilah, you're disgusting.'

She laughed. A kind of snorting guffaw, cut short by another prize-winning belch.

'You're drunk, Lilah.'

'You donssay. Sowha?'

She was leaning, head down, staring at the empty cans as if you could read a message in the pattern they made, like the *I Ching*. She lifted her head slowly to stare at me. 'Whyshoo come anyway?' She waved her arm at me. 'Bugger off. Go home.'

'I wish I could, but I can't leave you like this, can I? You can't spend the night on a park bench like some old dosser. You'll get into trouble when they find you. And you'll freeze to death.'

'Oooh –' she was mocking me now – 'I'm so scared.' Then the ultimate insult: 'You sound like Lauren.'

The mention of Lauren seemed to amuse her so much, she laughed herself sick. Literally. She retched, right in the middle of a flowerbed, dangerously close to my gladiolus bulb.

'Sorry, Abb,' she mumbled, ashamed. As she shook the hair out of her eyes and gazed at me, her face had a sickly yellowish sheen. 'What'm I gonna do, Abb? Can't go home like this.'

'No. You can't.' I had to agree with her for once. The prospect of delivering a sloshed Delilah to the Loathsome Verne's Dark Domain filled me with as much dread as it did her. 'What do we do then? I'd take you back to my place, but my mum would probably force-feed you with Marmite toast, and call Childline or something. And that would be too . . . too— What are you doing?'

'Can't geddit. Arse!' Failing to punch out a number on her mobile, she thrust it at me, waggling her fingers. 'Call my brother. Call Joel.'

'Joel? Are you sure? I thought Joel would have nothing to do with your stepfather?'

She shook her head despairingly, just managing to get the words out – 'Not *home*, stupid. Joel's place –' before throwing up again; over the back of the bench this time.

I considered the mobile for a minute, before running through SEARCH, and pressing J.

'Yes?' Joel answered straight away. The 'yes' had a wary, suspicious sound, like he was expecting trouble.

Funny, I'd imagined he'd be out at this time on a Saturday night. I imagined a girlfriend for him, some beautiful brainy type with glossy dark hair and fantastic legs.

'Er, is that Joel? Joel, you probably don't remember me, but I'm Delilah's friend Abbie. I'm just ringing to ask you a favour.'

'What's that?' Even more suspicious.

'Well, er, Delilah, see . . . she's had a bit too much to drink. There was kind of an argument with Verne, and now we're in the park—'

'The park?'

'Bromfield Park – well, the Millennium Gardens actually, and Delilah's . . . well, there's been this row, and now she's scared to go home, and she wondered if you could sort of, like, come and get her or something . . .'

Silence.

'Could you? She's been a bit sick,' I added as the silence continued. 'Well, very sick actually. She's been sick twice, and I think she might be—'

'OK, OK. Suppose I don't have much choice, do I?'

'Thanks. I'll try and drag her to the entrance – I mean, the gap in the railings. Trouble is, she's a bit heavy, and—'

'Look, just stay where you are,' Joel cut in irritably. 'The place with the fountain, right, near the bowling green?'

'That's it. Will you be long or . . . ?'

'As long as it takes,' Joel said, before hanging up on me.

'He's coming for you,' I told Delilah as she retched once more into an innocent row of winter pansies. 'Your brother's coming.' Then, muttering under my breath, 'Which is just great, as it happens, what with me looking like a dog's breakfast.'

'Wha you say?' Delilah roused herself at last.

87

'I said . . . oh, nothing.'

It meant nothing to Delilah, of course, that by some twist of the divine plot her brother was about to turn up at the very spot where I'd whispered his name in a demented mantra of hope just a few days ago. What did she care? She had no idea that Joel was The One, the object of my lust, the sexy, super-cool victim of my gladiolus bulb ritual. How could she? I just had to sit there, patting her back while she puked, still wearing the disgusting old rugby shirt and wrinkle-crotch baggies I'd worn to clean a chiropodist surgery and flee through muddy puddles from the Witchfinder General.

Not that it mattered. Any hopes that the bulb would physically signal to Joel and transform me into a winsome babe were dashed when he finally showed up.

'Christ, Lilah, will you never grow up?'

He stood in the entrance to the gardens, lean and moody, hands thrust in pockets. He was so busy cursing Delilah, I could have been wearing winceyette jim-jams for all he cared.

'Do me a favour, Lil,' he began, brushing the sleeve of his leather jacket. 'Next time you get yourself legless and want rescuing, choose somewhere more accessible, will you? I nearly wrecked myself just now vaulting those railings. I just hope no one saw me.'

At last he turned to me, looking me up and down, obviously assessing my load-carrying abilities. 'Look, er . . . Annie . . .'

'Abbie.'

'Abbie, can you take one side, and I'll take the other. We'll have to drag her between us.'

It wasn't easy, manoeuvring Delilah out through the

gap in the railings. It was even worse trying to bundle her into the back seat of the clapped-out Fiesta parked at the end of the alleyway. It was like wrestling with a sack of potatoes, except that potatoes don't groan and tell you to 'get your sodding hands off' them.

'Jesus,' Joel muttered. 'Where did she get such a foul mouth?' He seemed a bit puffed and bewildered as he slammed the car door on her. Jerking back the flick of brown hair, he asked me, 'Can I give you a lift somewhere then? I live in Finsbury. If you're on the way, I can drop you off.' He stood, hands in pockets, shoulders braced, as if against the cold.

'Thanks. I live near Bounds Green tube – just round the corner that is.'

Sliding elegantly into the passenger seat was impossible, what with all the old newspapers, maps, chocolate wrappers and other junk. Joel reached over and swept them to the floor. 'Sorry about the mess.'

As he executed a jerky three-point turn, I said, 'You're taking her back to your place then?'

He glanced over his shoulder at his sister, now snoring on the back seat. 'Looks like it. Verne sees her like that, he'll go ballistic.'

'Oh dear. I wouldn't like to be around when that happens. He's scary enough when he's all quiet and whispering.'

When he didn't reply, I began to explain about Delilah's row earlier after the electricity went out. 'He said there were no cards for the meter, and they'd just have to manage without for the weekend. Lilah just went wild and stormed out. Lauren and I were looking for her for hours.'

Joel's silence made me chatter on like a demented squirrel. As he concentrated on the Saturday night traffic, I knew he was angry just thinking of Verne.

'Sorry,' I said. 'That we had to spoil your evening, I mean.'

He actually laughed. 'Yeah, yeah. You interrupted Indiana Jones. And my coffee's probably cold by now, but no problem.'

What about the raven-haired brain on legs? I wondered. Had he left her curled up in front of the TV, kettle on the boil for his return?

'I hope you didn't miss the bit in the snake-pit?' I said sympathetically.

The corner of his mouth twitched slightly. Was that a smile? Difficult to tell because his hair had flicked forward again. I resisted the urge to reach over and push the sexy brown tendril behind his ear. What was happening to me? I sat on my hands just in case the temptation got too strong.

'Lilah overreacts – that's her trouble.' Joel pushed back his hair, and I saw his mouth was set. As we stopped at the lights, a bloke outside Kytzu's Kebabs was waving a traffic cone and swearing at passing cars. 'I keep telling her, that's what Verne wants. She plays right into his hands every time.'

I said uneasily, 'He must be pretty hard to take.'

'Yeah, well, I'm going to have to take her back to-morrow when she's sobered up. Then the shit will really fly.'

Delilah gave a sudden pig-like snore in the back, as if she'd heard. I glanced out of the window. For once I was glad of the heavy traffic. It had turned a ten-minute journey into twenty at least, which gave me that bit longer to imagine that Joel and I were actually going somewhere, like on a proper date. Just the two of us. Without a drunken witch-sister snoring in the back seat.

'I suppose you're into weird stuff like my sister?' he said unexpectedly.

'Me? Oh no. I'm into completely normal kind of stuff. Anyway . . .' I hesitated. 'What do you mean by "weird stuff" exactly?'

'Prancing about half dressed in someone's garden in mid-November – it's not exactly what you'd call normal.'

'I wasn't *prancing*,' I said, annoyed, wishing my swimwear had been a bit more stylish.

'Whatever.' His eyes fixed on the lights of oncoming cars again.

'Anyway, that was Delilah's idea. It was kind of a healing ceremony. She's got real gifts, you know. She cured my friend Lauren of eczema.'

'Yeah? I'm impressed.' There was that twitch of a smile again.

'You're laughing at me.'

'I'm not laughing. What's Delilah done for *you* then?' He glanced sideways at me.

'Nothing. I don't have any medical problems.' Not yet anyway. Although, from the pulsating crimson my skin was turning, my blood pressure must be going through the roof. If only he knew what Delilah had done for me! Or tried to.

'You don't really believe in that stuff?' he said. 'Lilah only does it to get up Verne's nose. That Daughter of the Devil thing – that really gets him going.'

'Does it?'

'It's against his religion, isn't it? He even stopped Mum going to see an aromatherapist last year.'

'Why would he do that?'

'Aromatherapy is just the beginning, according to Verne. You start with a few oils and herbs and end up a Satanist.' He laughed bitterly. 'Not that I believe any of that crap. But in Verne's book all therapies are a form of occultism, and occultism is the slippery slope to hell-fire and damnation. My sister only does her witchy thing to piss him off.'

'Oh.' There was no point in arguing, although I knew Joel was wrong about Lilah. She really *believed* in her craft. It was more than an annoying hobby to wig Verne off. The Witchfinder General knew. As far as he was concerned, Delilah was the real thing all right. Remembering the book still lying open on her bed, I shuddered suddenly.

Joel must have noticed. He began apologizing for the heater: 'It packed up last month. There's no point getting it fixed. The wheels are about to drop off any day now.'

'Sounds serious.'

'Yeah, well, it gets me to work and back. As long as it lasts out the next couple of months, I'll be happy.'

A couple of months! He was leaving the country in a couple of months? How could he be so heartless when we'd only just met?

'Smedhurst Road – is that the next one on the left?'

'Oh, yes. You turn left at the off-licence.'

Journey's end. Damn. Home already, and we'd hardly had time to get to know one another. I glanced over my shoulder at Delilah, dead to the world, oblivious to the budding romance going on in front of her. Except that nothing *was* budding.

'I hope Lilah's OK tomorrow,' I said. 'I suppose you'll ring your mother and let her know she's with you?'

'Yeah, don't worry. I'll call her.' Joel was staring intently at the lamppost he'd just pulled in by, as I got out of the car.

'Thanks for the lift then. Tell Lilah when she wakes up, I'll see her on Monday.'

He nodded, or was it just that gesture of his that made me weak at the knees, shaking the hair out of his eyes?

So that was that then. Another huge non-event, another missed opportunity in the sad life of Abigail Carter. I crossed the road towards number 62 and the porch we shared with Mrs Croop, and I was just fumbling for my door key, when the car drew up along-side me.

'Just thought of something.' Joel was leaning across to wind down the passenger window. He was patting his jacket pocket. 'I don't have your number, do I?'

My number? He wanted my phone number! A bit of fumbling went on while one of us provided a scrap of paper, the other a biro, and I scribbled my mobile number down. Which was a bit daft, because he could easily have got it from Delilah next morning, when she'd sobered up.

'Thanks.' He waved it at me. 'In case I need to get hold of Lilah some time. She's always switching hers off and forgetting.'

'Ah. Right then.'

Our eyes met just long enough for me to know this was rubbish. An excuse. Joel wasn't the kind of bloke to push himself at a girl. He needed to think things out first. To be sure. But he did like me. I was sure of that. *He really did like me.*

Later on, in bed with a mug of hot chocolate and my dad's book, *The Gardener's Guru*, propped open on my knees, I turned to the section on bulbs. More specifically, gladiolus bulbs. What I needed to know was, how long did they take to flower? Because, incredible as it seemed, I was sure that tonight had something to do with that shrivelled, unpromising onion thing buried in the Millennium Gardens. Already it was stirring into life, thrusting out feelers in the darkness. You had to hand it to Delilah: she had the gift all right. It looked like she had pulled off an impossible trick. Slowly but surely, love was beginning to sprout.

Chapter Nine

Odd Customers

I longed to tell Delilah – to tell her that her spell might just be starting to work – but there was no chance. Come Monday, Delilah was definitely not her normal self. Her normal *weird* self, that is.

'Probably a hangover,' I whispered to Lauren as we plonked our school bags under the café table. 'She's in a right mood. I mean, you'd think she'd be a bit grateful at least, me rescuing her from a night on a park bench.'

'I thought you said her brother rescued her. Anyway, some hangover! It hasn't put her off her food any,' Lauren remarked.

It was midday and we were in Gav's, one of the cheapest lunchtime joints Northgate had to offer. Now Delilah was at the counter, ordering a sausage baguette, big as a torpedo and stuffed with enough relish to strip the enamel from your teeth.

Lauren took a pained sip of her mineral water. 'I wish I had *her* appetite. Actually, I doubt I'll ever eat again. I think it was that tagine my mum made. It tasted off. But then her hygiene is not the best.'

'Whoops, too bad if the Muzbelles got belly-ache,' I tittered.

Lilah joined us, mouth already stuffed with sausage. She shook out a newspaper and grease drizzled onto the headline STARGAZE WITH STELLA. Obviously she wasn't in the mood for talking.

This was frustrating, to say the least. I was dying to pump her for some insider info on Joel. Not just the obvious things, like, Was he in a relationship right now? I wanted every detail: his favourite colour, music, breakfast cereal; the name of his pet rabbit when he was a kid. All that cheesy stuff only a sister could know.

'So, er . . .' I began craftily, 'you still haven't told us what happened, Lilah. When Joel took you home yesterday. How did your stepfather take it?'

'Oh yeah, thanks,' Delilah said grudgingly. 'For fixing it with Joel, I mean; taking care of me.'

'No problem. You know, you're lucky to have a brother like him. I mean, giving up his Saturday night and everything.'

'Oh yeah, I'm dead lucky,' Delilah grunted. She was pretending to read her stars in the newspaper.

'So, what does it say for Scorpio?' Lauren asked chirpily.

'It says it's going to be a shitty week – no, make that a shitty year. A shitty rest of my life, why not?'

Lauren simpered, 'It can't be that bad surely?'

'Yeah, it can. It can be that bad.' Delilah carried on reading. Today she was sporting more metal accessories than an armoured tank. Blobs of sausage-grease oozed through her ringed fingers and onto the page.

'Just promise me one thing,' I said lightly. 'No more boozing on park benches, eh? You really had me worried that night.'

Delilah just grunted.

'It was so lucky your brother came by,' I pressed on

slyly. Somehow I just had to get the conversation onto Joel.

But Delilah was mumbling something through mouthfuls of baguette. Something about how I'd never have to worry about her again. ''Cos I won't be here.' She almost spat the words, porky bits splattering everywhere.

'Won't be here?' My heart jolted. For a minute – and I knew this was stupid – I thought she meant this as in, won't be here on earth. At all. *Alive*. It was just something about the way she said it. 'You mean, you won't be here in—?'

'Sunny Northgate, where else? I told you, Verne never sticks long in one place. We're moving again, to the country.'

'But you can't just leave us,' Lauren burst out, alarmed. 'You only just moved here.'

Selfish or what! I knew what she was worried about. Having Delilah on her doorstep was like having her own personal witch doctor, should any more rashes or other infirmities dare to arise.

Delilah glanced up from her stars at last. 'Good to know *someone*'ll miss me. I'm touched, really. But you needn't worry. I'm working on something. A plan.'

She began to tell us how the Puritan Brethren were moving their headquarters to Shropshire. 'Verne has to be there 'cos he's a leading light –' she rolled her eyes – 'head preacher or something. Wow.'

'Where *is* Shropshire?' Lauren wanted to know.

'Exactly. Where *is* Shropshire? Out in the smegging wilds of nowhere is where it is probably.' Delilah was concentrating on the sachets of ketchup and salad cream that came with every baguette, squeezing them onto her plate like it was an artist's palette.

'So what's the plan? You're not thinking of running away?' I suggested.

'I can't. Not yet. I can't run out on my mum.' Having run out of sachets to squeeze, she turned to the salt pot, drizzling a white trail across the plate.

'But doesn't your mum have a say in the matter?' Lauren said.

Delilah scoffed. 'My mother is brainwashed, in case you never noticed. Wherever Verne goes, Mum toddles along behind. Anyway, what Mum does has nothing to do with this. I can deal with Verne.'

The way she said this, we couldn't fail to understand what she meant. Delilah had her own ways of dealing with people. Even here, in the steamy warmth of Gav's, with its stink of chips and hissing espresso machine, I felt nervous suddenly. As if Hopkins had sidled through the door when we weren't looking. Maybe he was here, leaning at the counter, hidden by the brawny backs of builders at their all-day breakfast. Listening, spying, gathering evidence.

'Lilah, you're not . . . ?' I leaned closer, my sleeve brushing the debris of sachets and sugar wrappers. 'I mean, you told us already, if you do bad stuff it comes back on you. Three times over. And anyway, what about *him*, the Creep, Hopkins? What about that book?'

'What about it? It's in a safe place, if that's what you mean.'

'Maybe you should burn it. Supposing he comes back, looking for it?'

'Huh! Let him try,' Delilah grunted. 'Anyway, it'll just

be like a warning. Something to scare Verne off. What I want to know is –' she concentrated on the salt pot, propelling it around the table clockwise, as if casting the circle – 'I want to know, are you two up for it? Are you going to help me teach Verne a lesson he won't forget?'

Lauren and I fidgeted uneasily. What was she proposing exactly?

'This isn't going to involve anything gruesome, is it?' Lauren asked. 'Like, you know, blood . . . or sacrifices, or anything?'

'Or toenail clippings,' I put in hastily. 'Because I draw the line at them.'

Delilah actually grinned for the first time that day. 'You two! What are you like? We're not talking about a Satanic mass, for God's sake.'

I sighed. 'Yeah, OK then. We'll help you, won't we, Lauren?'

'Oh yes . . . I suppose . . . I mean, *absolument*,' Lauren agreed finally, a sickly smile on her face, as if the tagine had chosen this moment to come back up.

'Yeah!' Delilah seemed to relax at last. She stuck both thumbs up in triumph. 'You know, for a moment I doubted you two. But you're not such a pair of wusses as I first took you for.'

'Thanks.'

If only she knew how wussy I actually felt when she began explaining about how we must perform the ritual during the phase of the Dark Moon.

'That's when *she* rules.' She looked sly as she swivelled her empty plate round for Lauren and me to see. The name of the goddess Hecate was scrawled in a wavery salt-trail, encircled by blobs of ketchup that might have been blood. We watched in silence as she dabbed a finger in the letter H and licked it slowly. 'Hecate, is, for your information, supreme goddess of the Dark Moon.'

The goddess, Delilah said, was on her side. Which was just as well, because Hecate (alias Queen of the Underworld) wasn't the kind of deity you'd want as an enemy. For a start, a hairdo of writhing serpents does not exactly inspire confidence. Also she never went anywhere without her trusty pack of bloodhounds. Anyway, Delilah reckoned the goddess was rooting for her because, as luck would have it, the dark moon conveniently coincided with Verne's house-hunting trip in Shropshire.

It was the Saturday after the drunk-in-the-park episode, and Delilah didn't waste any time. No sooner had Verne's car chuntered round the corner of Bromfield Avenue than she whipped out her shopping list and hauled Lauren and me off to Imelda's Web. The list read as follows:

3 small pieces of onyx
patchouli leaves
malt vinegar
1 grey candle

'Malt vinegar?' I queried. 'Are you pickling onions or something?'

'It's all part of the recipe, child,' Delilah said. 'You'll see.'

Whenever Delilah called you 'child', you knew she was in her goddess mode, which was worrying. I did not have a good feeling as we trailed round the shop, sidestepping a gang of giggly twelve-year-olds who were greedily pawing the polished stones.

'I wish these kids would get out of my road,' Lilah complained. She stalked among them like a bird of ill omen, black coat dragging like tail feathers. 'They are seriously wigging me off. Excuse me.' Virtually pushing one girl aside, she plunged a ringed paw into a basket and brought out the three pieces of onyx. 'Cheers.'

Lauren was browsing in the aromatherapy section. She nudged me. 'That woman gives me the creeps. Why is she watching us like that?'

I turned. The web-woman, whose bottle-blonde hair billowed beneath a leather cap, stood arms folded, watching our every move. Her expression wasn't exactly friendly. She looked like she suspected us of shoplifting.

'Yeah, what *is* she staring at?' I felt guilty, even though I hadn't done anything wrong. Well, not yet.

Delilah glanced over to the till. 'One thing I do know, her aura's even worse than Verne's. It's the colour of old blood. Like dried-up scab.'

'Eugh!' Lauren crowed, pleased to know there was a worse colour than pigeon-grey.

'Have you got everything?' I urged Lilah. ' 'Cos if you have, let's get out of here.'

'Wait a minute, I need a grey candle.' Delilah refused to be put off her quest. 'Why should we run off because of that old cow? I'm a paying customer, aren't I?'

It was then that I noticed that the younger girls had vanished. Without their chatter, the shop felt empty, hostile.

'Does it have to be grey?' My eyes scoured the shelves. Candles came in every shape and colour, it seemed: fat and creamy, gold and glitzy, scented, floating, slender spills of rainbow colours; everything, that is, but plain ordinary grey.

Delilah had grown impatient. Slamming her basket down next to the till, she jerked her head at the shelves. 'Are they all the candles you've got?'

'Everything I've got is on display,' the woman said shortly, piercing us with her ice-blue gaze. There was something strange about her pupils — tiny, far-off, like black pin-pricks. She folded her arms, and a leathery cleavage spilled from a tight black top decorated with zips. 'Are you all together?'

What was she on about? She wasn't even looking at us. She stared beyond us to the back of the shop, where an exotic bead curtain divided the sales area from a back room.

'Yeah, we're together,' Delilah said in her 'what's it to you?' voice.

The woman continued to stare past us fixedly. Her cherry-glossed lips formed the words slowly, as if we were hard of hearing. 'Would you ask your friend if he's going to actually buy any of those goods he's been pawing?'

He? Pawing?

We swivelled round, all three of us, to look at the shelves behind us. There was no one. Nothing but the display of candles, jars, twirling dream-catchers, wind chimes, books, crystals. We were the only customers in the shop. Then I saw Delilah's face. I knew that she'd seen something. Hopkins. Who else would follow us here?

'We're together, me and my two friends.' Delilah stuck

her chin out. Only the slight huskiness in her voice gave her away. Whatever she'd seen, she was scared.

'I know he's with you lot,' Web-woman insisted, her eyes flashing hatred. 'You brought him with you the last time.'

'We did?'

'Yes, you did. Autumn sales, remember? Your friend came too. Well, you can tell him from me, he's not welcome. Scaring the customers off.' She waved her arm at the door. 'Saturday afternoon, and it's dead as a dodo. And it's not only that. I don't like people who maul the goods – items they've no intention of buying.' She frowned. 'What's he scribbling down? Bloody cheek. Pawing the goods, scribbling away like he's doing the stock-taking. Look, you'd better all go. Now. OK?'

Beside me, Delilah bristled. 'Look, I don't know what you're on about, I just want to buy a candle, right? An ordinary grey candle. Do you have such a thing in stock or don't you?'

'No.' Web-woman spoke without hesitation. 'No. I don't.'

'Well then, I'll just take these.'

The woman rang up the items, red nails whizzing across the keys, drawer pinging open. She took the money, tight-lipped, and counted the change into Lilah's hand. As she did so, there was no mistaking the chink of glass from the aromatherapy shelves. One of the dream-catchers launched into life suddenly, whirling turquoise feathers.

'I don't like him,' the web-woman hissed at Delilah. 'I won't have him in here – understand? He's *your* problem, not mine. Just keep him away from me.'

Delilah must have known what she meant, but she pretended not to. 'Don't worry. I won't be shopping in here again. You're a nutter. And by the way, your dream-catchers are crap.'

'Just get out of here!' Fire dashed from the ice-blue eyes. Red nails hovered over the counter. 'If I press that buzzer, it goes straight through to security. Do you lot want throwing out?'

'No, no. We're leaving – now . . . Sorry . . .' I pushed Lilah in the small of the back. Hard. She moved towards the door, yet I could feel the weight of her stubborn resistance leaning on me.

'Oh yeah, and have a nice day!' Delilah yelled back over her shoulder.

The woman didn't reply. She was too busy seeing us out. The three of us, I mean – me, Lauren and Delilah. Then she stood aside, waiting for the fourth customer, our invisible friend, to follow us.

In any case, we were up the escalator and onto the next level before you could say 'hocus pocus'. Delilah didn't stop until she reached Dixons, flumping down on a bench beneath a plastic palm tree. Lauren and I flopped down beside her.

Lauren, never having been turned out of a shop before, was grossly offended. 'In my opinion, someone should tell that woman, the customer is always right. I still don't understand what she was accusing us of. Why did she keep going on about our friend? There was no one there but us three.'

'How come . . . ?' I said to Delilah. 'How come she could see him and we didn't? How come he didn't show himself to us this time?'

104

Delilah just plugged her mouth with more gum. 'I told you she's one of the Dark Ones. She could be a seventh generation witch for all I know.' As if to herself she said, 'I bet she knows him of old. That's why she got her knickers in such a twist – us, bringing an old enemy into the shop. There were such bad vibes in that place. I thought it was just her – she's got this, like, spiritual body odour which isn't nice. Did you notice the wind chimes? How they gave out that kind of dull tone when they rang?'

I shook my head. I was trying to concentrate on the families piling into Dixons, where already the microwaves and washing machines were glitzed up with Christmas tinsel, the windows splashed with CHRISTMAS BARGAIN stickers. The sheer ordinariness of this was a kind of comfort. I confided my worst fear to Delilah: 'Supposing he's here now? Sitting on this bench, right next to Lauren?'

Lauren shifted up slightly, a disgusted look on her face, as if some smelly old tramp had plonked himself beside her. 'I wish someone would tell me what's going on. We're not talking about that character at the jumble sale again, are we?'

Delilah suddenly looked pleased with herself. A gleam came into her eye. 'You know what I think? I think we've left him down there in the shop. Why d'you think that old crone in there nearly wet herself? Because . . . because . . . ?' Delilah urged me to answer.

'Because she's one of the . . . Dark Ones?'

'Yeah, exactly. I mean, if you were the Witchfinder General returned from the grave, looking for a witch to haunt, who would *you* choose? Listen, compared to the

Daughter of Darkness down there, we're just small fry. A few feathers, a few candles? Bet you that's nothing to the skulls and sacrificial cockerels and stuff *she's* got back at home.'

I could only hope she was right. At the corner of my eye, the escalator slithered out of sight. I imagined the woman closing Imelda's Web early, cursing us. Somehow the thought that her malevolence might be directed at us was even more creepy than the idea of Hopkins on our trail.

'You're trying to tell me that the Witchfinder General was in the shop with us?' Lauren said. 'That you've passed on a ghost to someone else? Off-loaded him like . . . like some kind of disease?'

I held up my hands as if to some heavenly presence. 'Praise be. The light has dawned! Lauren finally gets her head around the ghostly stalker concept.'

'It's not something I want to get my head around, thanks very much,' Lauren snapped.

'Anyway!' Delilah said, slapping her knees as if everything were decided. 'Shift your arses, you two. We've got work to do.'

Work? Spells, she meant. Rituals. Ceremonies. Curses. I wasn't so sure I wanted to go through with this now.

'What about Hopkins though?' I panted after her, as she swept through the glass doors that led to the street, where the bloke in the bobble hat sold the *Big Issue*. 'And we haven't got your grey candle. We can't do it without a grey candle.'

'Who says?'

'You did. Didn't you?'

'Never heard of improvisation?' Lilah snorted, adding

that the house was a Verne-free zone, so there was no need to be scared of bumping into him. 'In fact, you two can stay the night,' she said, turning to Lauren and me. 'Then you won't have to rush off after the ritual.'

As we passed the brightly lit shops, where girls like us (yet *not* like us) were trying on their Saturday night outfits, Delilah glanced up at the washed-out violet sky.

'We'll do it as soon as it gets dark. The dark moon is the time for banishing, and I intend to banish Verne.' She turned to Lauren and me, eyes bright, challenging. 'And just let anyone try to stop me.'

Chapter Ten

The Casting Out

It was almost dark when we reached Delilah's.

'I suppose your brother might call by,' I casually suggested to Delilah, 'now that Verne's out of the way.'

This was my one hope, the only thing that persuaded me to spend a Saturday night messing about with candles and crystals. But it seemed the only person likely to 'drop by' was Hecate, Queen of the Underworld. If we were invoking the goddess, Delilah said, rattling her key in the lock, it was better to have no men about.

'She just doesn't like them. And anyway, Joel's still pissed off with me about last week. Wrecking his evening and that.'

Wrecking his evening? Alone on the sofa with an Indiana Jones video? Did she know something I didn't?

Talking of wrecked evenings, you'd think that with Verne out of the way Delilah's mum would have been uncorking the champagne and boogying around the room to old Abba songs. In fact she was knitting in front of the gas fire. With a shawl spread about her shoulders, green Alice shoes peeking out beneath her skirts, she looked like a peasant woman in a fairy tale. Stripy garments flew like rainbows from her needles.

'What beautiful colours!' Lauren immediately launched the charm offensive she reserved for other people's mothers. (This was probably because she considered her own mother to be sadly negligent.) 'What are you making?'

Delilah's mother pushed her glasses up her nose and told her they were legwarmers. 'They're so easy to make.'

'Are they? I've been absolutely begging my mother to knit me a pair of legwarmers, but she hasn't got the time.'

'Oh, Mum'll make you a pair, won't you, Mum?' Delilah offered with a hint of pride. 'She's the fastest knitter in the west.' She seemed pleased to have her mother to herself for once. She flopped down beside her, smoothing the knitted rainbow over her own lap.

Her mother looked vaguely alarmed. 'Lilah, love, this isn't a fashion enterprise. It's forward planning, that's all.'

'Forward planning?'

'I hear that Shropshire can be one of the coldest spots in the country, especially up in the hills . . .'

'Shropshire!' The very word sent Delilah springing from the sofa in outrage. 'Mum, let's get this straight, please. I am not, repeat *not*, going to live in the hills with you and Verne. With or without bloody legwarmers. I mean it. I'm not!'

Then she was thundering up the stairs, leaving Lauren and me feebly discussing the merits of plain and purl, while her mother wiped a tear from her eye.

Delilah hadn't gone straight to her room. As Lauren and I reached the first-floor landing, the door of Verne's study creaked open. Delilah beckoned irritably to us. 'Well come in then. He's not hiding in the cupboard or anything.'

We shuffled into the Loathsome Verne's den, feeling as if the very walls could see, would tell on us. I glanced around. A black lamp was poised cobra-like over a vast polished desk, and bookshelves were stuffed with the kind of books you only read if you're forced to. My eyes wandered over the titles: *Denying the Self, Survive the Apocalypse, The Organic Growers' Guide* . . .

Delilah sat in Verne's spoke-backed chair, picking up pens and testing them out on the blotter. 'You have now reached the inner sanctum of the Puritan Brethren. I hope you're suitably impressed.'

'Thrilled,' I said. 'Well, more chilled actually. Does this house have a damp problem or something? It's, like, sub-zero in here.'

But Delilah was peering at the map pinned on the wall above the desk – one of those old county maps with spidery brown roads and green blobs of hills and blue veins of rivers that made you think of an England before motorways and Welcome Breaks. In the bottom right-hand corner the map was marred by a crimson ink-splodge.

'Ludlow!' Delilah stabbed the spot with an accusing black fingernail. 'It's practically in Wales. Why do they have to have their stupid headquarters there anyway?'

Lauren mumbled that she'd seen Ludlow on some countryside programme on TV. 'It's really pretty, you know, with these black and white houses and a castle and—'

'Please, Lauren.' I nudged her. 'Now is not the time for the tourist board ad. Lilah doesn't want to go and live in the hills with a lot of blathering old sheep, does she? I mean, Northgate is bad enough, but at least it's civilized.'

'He wants to bury us out there.' Delilah's voice was

quiet, almost a whisper. 'Me and Mum.' She closed her eyes. 'I could send him something really bad. I could. I could have his car crash into a tree, or he could choke on a herring at breakfast, or he could fall down the twisty stairs at the B&B he's staying at and break his neck.'

'How do you know the stairs are twisty?' Lauren said.

'I just do, OK.' Delilah's eyes flashed open again. To my great relief she said, 'But I don't do dark stuff, not even on him. I won't be led into that.'

She began rummaging among the papers on the desk 'Here it is, the very document we require.'

It looked like a menu from a posh restaurant: slanting copper-plate writing framed in a fancy border. I read the heading aloud: ' "The Puritan Brethren – Simple Rules for Righteous Living".'

'In other words,' Delilah said, 'the grim guide for miserable gits.'

Unable to resist, I scanned the next few paragraphs, phrases jumping out at me: *Gluttony and idle gossip are an abomination to the Lord . . . Fasting is the way to righteousness . . . A still tongue is the surest route to grace.*

'Do they have many followers?' I wondered aloud.

'You'd be amazed.' Delilah took up a pair of scissors. 'You'd be surprised how many people go for that stuff.' She snipped a perfect square from Verne's text, leaving a meaningless jumble of 'ation to the Lord', 'ill tongue is the' etc.

'Won't he, like, kill you when he sees what you've done?' I murmured.

But Delilah said no. Murder was against Brethren rules. 'And anyway, he'd better not try, or he'll have the goddess to deal with, won't he?'

I don't do dark stuff, Delilah had said. Upstairs in her room, with the curtains drawn and the candles lit, I kept reminding myself of her promise. Not that I really cared what happened to her nutty stepfather either way. All the same, I wouldn't want to have anyone's death on my conscience, not even Verne's.

'Lilah, this isn't going to be, like, a curse sort of thing, is it?' I began to panic as she set out the tools on her altar like a surgeon preparing for an operation: *athame*, salt, dragon's blood incense. When she looked up at me, it was like someone else was staring out from her bright eyes. Someone fierce, ancient; someone not to be messed with.

She frowned. 'It's not a curse. It's a warning. I told you.'

'Oh. Good. Sorry to go on, but –' I heard myself giggle idiotically – 'I just don't want to hurt anybody. I'm just thinking, you know, about . . .'

'About?' Delilah sighed impatiently as she lit the incense, her thick brows knitting together.

'Well, this thing about bad stuff coming back on you three times over. If you put a curse on someone, and they, like, *died*, how would that work? I mean, you can't die three times over, can you?'

'Yes you can, actually,' Lauren put in. 'Technically speaking, your heart could stop, but that doesn't make you officially, like, brain-dead. This man in our street, he died three times, and they kept bringing him back to—'

'Technically speaking, are you two up for this or not?' Delilah snapped. 'Make up your minds, 'cos I don't want you blathering on once I've summoned the Ancient Ones.'

Lauren and I all but stood to attention. Up for it? Of course we were. 'Just tell us what you want us to do.' I tried to sound enthusiastic, ready for anything. But Delilah growled that she only wanted us to stand there and repeat a few words after her, if we could manage it. First, though, she had some preparation to do.

As usual the circle was cast and the Ancient Ones summoned. Something about the casting of the circle changed the atmosphere in the room. I'd noticed this before. The circle calmed you, steadied you. It was almost a churchy feeling, as if the most insignificant act, like scratching your nose or yawning, were being scrutinized by the Ancient Ones.

Lauren and I fell silent as Delilah approached the old cracked washbasin in the corner of her room. Water trickled from the tap and I imagined that she was about to give herself a kind of pre-ritual cleansing. However, when the basin was full, she produced a packet from her pocket and added a pinch of white powder and three black peppercorns to the water.

'Now we insert the words of wisdom,' Delilah said, as the water turned into a kind of blue soup. The scrap of paper was duly submerged. We watched as the words ABOMINATION and FORNICATION dissolved into the blue, leaving only a faint stain behind them. So this was the casting-out. Not black magic certainly, but not white either. Grey maybe? Was this why she'd wanted a grey candle?

The scrap of paper was left to dry out on the altar. I stood, tense, as Delilah lit a green candle, half expecting that shameful horror to take hold of me again. But it didn't. The fat globe of wax burned steadily. Its flame was reflected in the black square of window like a golden tulip.

'The light is low on earth.' Delilah began talking in her husky 'ritual' voice. It made me feel oddly dreamy. You could hear the usual sounds from outside – a dog barking, cars, aeroplanes droning overhead – but they all seemed remote, as if they came from another world that had nothing to do with us. 'This is the time of Hecate,' Delilah went on. 'O Hecate, Great Mother of the Dark Moon, we ask that you witness our casting-out.'

Lit from underneath, Delilah's striking eyebrows, sharp nose and chin were somehow handsome and witchy all at once. Her hair, which in the real world appeared grungy and dated, now looked fantastic, a riot of black mambas wiggling into her eyes. A single dreadlock tickled the tip of the flame as she held the square of paper close to it.

Now she said slowly, 'The person we think of goes by the name of Vernon Barry, known to most people as Verne.' Staring deep into the flame, she recited her warning in such ominous tones, you almost expected an accompanying crack of thunder. '*I tell thee, Vernon Barry, bedevil me no more. All done to me rebounds on you – so mote it be.*'

This was where Lauren and I came in. We chorused obediently at her signal, '*So mote it be.*'

And *bang!* We stared at each other. For one silly moment I thought it was part of the ritual – Verne going off *bang*, like a human firecracker. When four more bangs followed, I realized it was just the front door.

'Arse!' was Delilah's response, as she blew out the candle. Only when she'd undone the circle and thanked

114

the Ancient Ones did she say, 'I'm bloody sick of these interruptions. Just as well we'd finished. Who the hell is it, anyway? No one ever pays us a visit.'

I went to the window and peered down at the street below. 'Whoa! Flash car, whoever it is.' A gold-sprayed limo was a rare sight, at least in Northgate.

Delilah joined me at the window. 'Well, it's not one of Verne's cronies, that's for sure. Their favoured mode of transport is a bicycle. Or, if they're feeling really daring, a Robin Reliant.'

I giggled, relieved that the ceremony was finished. And no sign of the witchfinder sticking his long nose in. Phew!

There were voices in the hall, then Delilah's mother calling up the stairs in her melancholy drawl, 'Lilah? There's someone here to see you, dear.'

Delilah looked somewhat taken aback. 'For me? Blimey.'

'Perhaps you've got a secret admirer, Lilah?' Lauren suggested.

'Yeah,' I said. 'You haven't been casting any "send me a billionaire lover" spells, have you, Lilah?'

Naturally, Lauren and I couldn't help being curious. We followed Delilah downstairs at a discreet distance. However, at the last landing she stopped dead in her tracks. 'It's *her*! It's bloody *her*. From the shop.'

Lauren and I froze. It seemed absurd. Why would Web-woman follow us here, to Delilah's house? But then we peered over the banister and found ourselves looking down on the peaked leather cap, the brassy puff of hair. The voice twanged like broken guitar strings as she attempted small talk with Delilah's mother.

'They do say it's going to be a hard winter, don't they? Not that you can believe the weather forecasters, can you? I expect we've got the worst to come.'

As conversations went, nothing could be more mundane. Yet the way my heart was behaving, she might have been calling on Hecate to damn us all to the dark beyond.

'What's she doing here?' I said.

'And how does she know where you live?' Lauren whispered. 'Maybe she's come to complain to your mother about us.'

'I think I know what she wants.' Delilah's voice was like armoured steel.

'Nice house you've got here, I must say,' Web-woman twanged. 'How many bedrooms, did you say?' With that her eyes wandered upstairs and caught sight of us three pressed against the banisters, like flies in a web. 'Oh, there's your daughter . . .'

Delilah's mother peered up at us. 'Lilah, dear, this lady has very kindly brought you something from her shop.'

Web-woman stretched her scarlet lips over her teeth. She waggled her ringed fingers at us. 'Hi there, girls!'

Delilah didn't have much choice. She descended a few more stairs, then said coldly, 'What d'you want? Where did you get my address?'

'Lilah!' her mother exclaimed, embarrassed. 'There's no need to be so rude. This lady has gone out of her way on your account.'

'Oh, no, no.' Web-woman denied this: she was just passing through – it was no bother. 'Wouldn't you know it, I told you we had no grey candles in stock, didn't I? Well, silly old me. I'm afraid I told a lie. You'd only just

116

left when I remembered a whole box of them out in the stock room.' She turned to Delilah's mother and explained chattily, 'We don't get much call for grey usually.'

'It seems a lot of bother to go to for one candle,' Delilah's mother said. 'Would you like a cup of tea or anything?'

Lauren and I had joined Delilah at the foot of the stairs. We held our breath, waiting for Web-woman to answer. When she actually said, Yes, what a kind thought, she was in fact gasping for a nice cup of tea, we almost choked. The next thing we knew, Delilah's mother was telling us to take our visitor into the sitting room.

'Do make yourself comfortable, won't you? I won't be long.' With that, she went shuffling off to the kitchen.

Delilah nudged me. 'If only we had an electric kettle like normal people. It takes bloody ages to boil water on the stove. She'll be here all bloody night!'

Web-woman, it seemed, didn't care how long she was here for. She was already arranging herself on the sofa, crossing her legs, the black fishnet tights making a rasping sound. As she sat rotating her ankle in front of the gas fire, my eyes fixed on her shoes. They had a vicious look, impossibly pointy and narrow, like giant hornets poised to sting.

'Well then, girls. Isn't this nice!'

Delilah stood squarely in the middle of the room. 'Look, don't make yourself too comfortable. In fact, why don't you forget the tea? My mother's got enough to do without waiting on you.'

My heart missed a beat. A hornet was one thing. But an angry hornet had only one option, didn't it? Better to just open the window and let it out. No harm done.

'Let's not mess about, eh?' Web-woman said. 'You girls know why I'm here. Something you left in the shop, right? Some little thing you left behind you.' She tutted. 'So careless! Thought you could foist him off on me, did you?'

Delilah said roughly, 'You're paranoid. If I were you, I'd go and see a doctor.'

Web-woman snarled back, 'And if I were *you*, young lady, I'd be careful who I kept company with. You can't just dump him on me, you know. Think I was born yesterday? I've been around a long time, miss. Longer than you imagine.'

Lauren, who had been hovering by the door, twisting one of her plaits around a finger, cleared her throat. 'Ahem . . . perhaps I could help your mum with the tea, Lilah?'

'What a little treasure you are!' Web-woman snapped. 'But I'm sure your friend's mumsy can manage a pot of tea by herself. You just stay put, dear, because what I've got to say is for all three of you.'

Delilah yawned. 'Look, can't you just say it and get it over with?'

'With pleasure. You don't really think I want to stick around in this dump and yatter about the weather with your dippy ma, do you? I've just come to give you a friendly warning. Don't worry – it won't take long.'

'Good.'

Web-woman didn't answer. Her attention seemed caught by something in the corner of the room. Just for a second, in place of the tall wrought-iron candle sconce, which stood incongruously by the gas fire, I thought I saw *him* there, Hopkins, folding himself into the dust and shadows like a furled-up umbrella. *She* must have seen him too. The flicker of fear which crossed her face was unmistakable.

'I just want you girls to know, he's *your* problem, not mine. Maybe he was my problem once, a long time ago. But that's in the past.' She hesitated. 'I hope you're paying attention to what I say, because if you don't, there'll be trouble. For all of you.'

Delilah laughed. 'Oh yeah? What kind of trouble?'

Web-woman studied her scarlet talons. 'Well, that would depend. Lauren, for instance . . .' She paused, smirking. 'No need to jump like that, poppet. Wondering how I know your name, are you? You'd be surprised what I know about you, dear – your skin problem, for instance . . .'

The way she said it – *skin problem* – was so horrible, Lauren's hand flew automatically to her cheek, to check its smoothness. 'How do you know about that?' she whispered.

'Oh, come!' Web-woman sniggered. 'Girls of your age get spots, don't they? All those disgusting hormones surging away, oozing pus – eugh!' She gave an exaggerated shudder. 'Acne, eczema – it all looks disgusting at the end of the day. It all looks like *zits*. Have you ever seen a really serious case of acne, angel child?'

Lauren shook her head numbly.

'Well, let me tell you, it's not pretty. Show your silly face in my shop again, and all the skin creams and potions in the world won't help you. Your skin will slough off, like a snake's.' She held a hand to her head as if the image was just too revolting. 'Oh look, you get the picture. I'll change the subject, because frankly it's making me feel sick. Let's just move on to Abigail, shall we?

'By the way, poppet, how's the love life? No boyfriend yet?' She shook her head slowly from side to side, as if in despair. 'And how old are you – fifteen, sixteen? You know, it's weird how there are some girls who are just destined to be alone. Doesn't matter how pretty they are. The boys just don't fancy them.' She shrugged. 'It's one of life's little mysteries. Some of them even resort to spells – hah! Well, you'd have to be desperate, wouldn't you? I heard of some girl who planted a bulb in the park and imagined the face of this boy she fancied – yes, really! Oh, you're going all red, poppet. Was it something I said?'

I swallowed. I was thinking of Joel. Joel's face. My eyes stung with tears. What was she saying? What was she threatening me with?

'You wouldn't want to be one of those girls, would you? Repellent to men. A complete turn-off. It could happen, you know, if you don't keep *him* away from me and my business.'

Web-woman suddenly got up, brushing her skirt in disgust, as if the sofa were some filthy park bench. She turned to Delilah and sighed. 'And now,' she said with relish, as if leaving the best till last, 'now for the junior priestess here. Little Miss Magic. Delilah the Dabbler.' She considered for a moment. 'Yes, that's a fitting title, don't you think, for a girl of your –' she coughed sarcastically – 'powers.'

There was to be nothing so trivial as spots or un-popularity with the opposite sex for Delilah. Oh no.

Web-woman was threatening to take her powers away.

'Not that they're anything special.' Sliding the grey candle from her bag, she tapped it in her palm. 'I mean, candles, crystals . . . Kid's stuff. And by the goddess!' She turned to cast a withering gaze on the room. 'You need your powers, don't you, poppet, to deal with this shambles.' Moving closer to Delilah, she hissed, 'Come to my shop again and all your so-called rituals will have no more effect than Ring-a-Ring-a-Roses, got it? Your loopy ma and that twisted stepfather of yours will rule your little life and make it one hell on earth. Do I make myself clear?'

'Here we are, then.' Of course, Delilah's mother would choose this very moment to enter the room with a tea tray. 'Sorry it took so long, but the fire was getting a bit low, and the kettle— Oh, you're . . . Is something wrong?'

She stood, perplexed, as Web-woman pushed past her, though not before thrusting the grey candle into Delilah's hand.

'Wrong? Heavens, no. Your charming daughter and her friends have been entertaining me, haven't you, girls?' Consulting her watch, she flashed a diamond the size of a small planet. 'But time rushes on, you know, and I've got an appointment. Delightful to meet you, Mrs, er . . . So sorry I couldn't stay.' Turning her spiteful gaze on us for the last time, she added, 'Remember my little words of advice, won't you, girls? And no burning the candle at both ends, eh.'

We stood for a moment, speechless, as the front door slammed behind her. Only Delilah moved to the window, twitching the dingy lace curtain. There was a sound like ripped velvet, as Web-woman's limo accelerated smoothly into the night. With a sigh, Delilah let the curtain fall. 'She's gone. And she'd better not show her ugly face here ever again.'

Chapter Eleven
Blind Date

There are certain things you don't do, even for your best friends. I liked Delilah. I liked her a lot. She was different, fun, interesting, despite her sod-awful home life.

There were things I would have done for Delilah, certainly. I'd stick up for her at school, help with her history homework, lend her my best outfit (not that she'd want it); I'd go along with her spells and rituals even when they seemed totally daft. But one thing I wouldn't do. I wouldn't get caught up in this haunting of hers. No way. It was enough that the ghost of Hopkins was on our trail, without the psycho blonde from Imelda's Web joining in. Things were getting complicated. Clearly it was time to bail out.

So, to my shame, I have to admit that while Delilah stood in the sitting room, clutching the candle like a poisoned chalice, I was desperately thinking up escape routes. It must have been providence that, at this very moment, my mobile bleeped, flashing its message sign. I pressed the NAVI key, and read the miraculous words:

HI ABBIE. FANCY A CURRY 2NITE? CALL ME. CHEERS, JOEL

I read it twice to make sure. Just a plain old text message, yet it might have been a Shakespearian sonnet the way my heart was pounding. It wasn't *just* the thought of being with Joel again. The curry was tempting too – there were as yet no enticing smells wafting from Delilah's kitchen. Her mother was muttering something about Delilah's manners, and how she hoped she hadn't been rude to that kind woman. Frankly, she looked too vacant to put any kind of a meal together, and my stomach was making 'feed me now!' noises.

Now, under normal circumstances, Lauren would have wanted to know who was texting me, but she was too distracted. She whipped a mirror from her bag and scrutinized her skin for the faintest hint of a dreaded red patch. 'That woman is a total monster! You don't think she could really do those things, do you? Abbie, look.' She stuck her face inches from mine. 'Can you see anything? Is it coming back? Is my skin OK?'

I sighed. 'Lauren, it's peachy, OK? It's like flawless silk. It's like . . . I can't think what it's like – is that enough for you?'

Delilah gave her a disgusted look. 'We've got more important things to worry about than your face. She's brought him back with her, hasn't she?' She glanced about her at the pools of shadow, those odd corners neglected by Verne's economy low-wattage lighting. 'He's here, now. It's like Pass the bloody Parcel.'

I tried not to look at the candle sconce over by the gas fire. If the others hadn't seen the Creep lurking there, why worry them now?

'Maybe she's just trying to scare us,' I jabbered unconvincingly. 'Spirits go their own way, don't they? They have their own means of transport. I mean, she could hardly bundle Hopkins in the back of the car and deliver him like a sack of potatoes.' My fingers closed over my mobile and the precious text. I was itching to call Joel back.

Delilah grunted, 'That's exactly what she *could* do, a woman of her powers. You heard what she said – she's been around a long time. A long time . . . You bet she has. Like a few centuries. I told you she was one of the Old Ones.'

'I thought you said, Dark Ones.'

'Dark Ones, Old Ones, they're the same thing.'

'Really? Well, she knocking on a bit, I'll grant you. Someone should tell her that cap doesn't do anything for her.'

Lauren gave me an odd look. 'I don't know what you've got to be so glib about. Remember what she threatened you with.'

'Yeah, I know, don't remind me. I don't exactly want to spend the rest of my life loveless and utterly repellent to the male sex, thank you very much. I don't even want to think about it. We just stay away from her tacky old shop in future, like she wants, and we'll be all right. Won't we, Lilah?'

But Delilah was prowling around the furniture, sniffing the air in this really creepy way. 'Can you smell it?' she asked us.

To show willing, I sniffed and got a full blast of essence of lily mixed with paint stripper. 'Phaw! That perfume of Web-woman's is toxic.'

'Not the perfume, stupid. *Him.*' Delilah stood glaring at the battered furniture, the gas fire, the remnants of her mum's knitting, as if daring Hopkins to show himself. 'It's kind of a farm smell – horse muck and leather and old straw . . . and . . .' She paused. 'What the smeg is wrong with Lauren now?'

Lauren was clutching at her stomach like she'd been poisoned. 'I feel sick. It came on so suddenly. It must be the smell. Or it could be that leftover couscous my mother served up last night, with those pukey bits of meat in it . . . Oh my God. She's poisoned me. Sorry, Lilah, I really don't think I should stay the night.'

'Actually, Lilah –' I seized my chance – 'I can't stay either. I just got a message: an old friend just turned up at my house, sort of out of the blue. I mean, they really should have warned me first but— Oh God, Lauren. It's not that bad, is it?'

Lauren was doubled up as if in agony. Her groans were so convincing I was almost fooled myself. I put my arm round her. 'Listen, Lilah, I really think I should walk home with her, and then . . .'

Delilah nodded. She didn't seem to be taking in what I was saying.

'You'll be OK?' I checked, praying she wouldn't plead with us to stay. 'I mean, now that Web-woman's had her fun, we'll probably never see her again. And we've done the ritual and everything. Verne should be a pussycat when he gets back, shouldn't he?'

Delilah muttered, 'He doesn't scare me anyway. I can handle him.'

Was she talking about Verne, or the Witchfinder General? I didn't wait to find out. Another 'I'm about to puke any minute' type groan from Lauren, and I was helping her on with her coat.

'Tell you what, I'll give you a ring tomorrow, make sure you're OK.'

'Sorry to break things up, Lilah,' Lauren called out in bravely pathetic tones.

But Delilah was making it easy for us. She held the front door open, scanning the street as if to check that Web-woman's limo hadn't slunk back round the corner.

'We'll see you at school on Monday then?' I said. 'That's if Lauren lives that long.' Even as I said this, I remembered Delilah's miserably short life line and a wave of shame rushed through me.

'Yeah. See you,' Delilah said shortly. She seemed pre-occupied as she closed the door on us. Perhaps she didn't feel abandoned at all. Still, I felt bad about leaving her to the spooks. She deserved better. And I should have been honest with her. I should have told her about Joel.

The moment we were out of sight of the house Lauren made a miraculous recovery. 'You can let go of my arm, thanks. I'm not that sick. Only mildly nauseous.'

I let go at once. We exchanged brief, sheepish glances. Then Lauren said miserably, 'We've deserted her, haven't we? We've deserted Lilah in her hour of need.'

'Deserted is a bit over the top, isn't it? Anyway, don't rub it in. You said yourself, even before the moon-dew episode, that you didn't want to get involved in this kind of stuff.'

'Yes, but that was before we *were* involved. When that woman turned up I nearly had kittens. She must have followed us from The Gates.'

'Maybe. Anyway, listen, something I gotta do. Wait a minute, will you?' By now we'd reached my bus stop. Lauren didn't go on to her own stop, but stood watching suspiciously as I whipped out my mobile and punched out Joel's number. He answered after only one ring, as if he'd been waiting.

'Hi. Joel? I, er, got your message just now, and as it happens I do quite fancy a curry. What time shall we—? The Angel? Eight o'clock? Fine, that's OK, I'll meet you there. Byeee.'

I turned to Lauren. 'So, what are you gawping at?'

She wrinkled her nose at me. 'Joel? Not Joel as in Delilah's brother Joel?'

'Yep, I confess, they are one and the same Joel.' I told her about the text message back at the house, only to be greeted with a look of contempt.

'So that's why you couldn't wait to get out of there. Nothing to do with concern for my health. First chance of a date and you're off like a rocket.' She nodded slowly, like I was some arch traitor. 'That's not very loyal, is it, Abbie?'

'It's not very loyal to put on your dying swan act either.' My eyes strained for the approach of the bus that would take me away from this place and into the arms of Joel. I glanced sideways at Lauren, wondering how far I should go. 'You know, Joel's really sweet. I mean *really*. He was so, like, kind and concerned and brotherly and all that when we rescued Lilah from the park.' I folded my arms, doing that impatient 'waiting for a bus in the cold' jiggle, like I was dancing to some invisible tune inside my head. 'Besides, I'm bloody starving. Oh, come on, Lauren, don't look at me like that, OK? You know that thing your mother always says?'

'Not the old "life is short" line, please.' Lauren looked truly agonized.

'Life is short. Exactly. Listen, Lauren, if I don't start

128

living mine soon, I'll be an old crone of thirty with . . . with . . . cellulite on my bum, trundling round Asda with a trolley full of brats, OK?'

'Whatever.' Lauren gazed at me sadly as my bus came into view. She shouldered her bag and tramped on to her own stop. 'Far be it from me to spoil your fun.'

In the dark of the bus window, my own face reflected back at me like Hecate's moon. Lauren didn't need to spoil my fun. By the time we pulled up at The Angel, I was already shouldering a guilt trip the size of a nuclear mushroom cloud.

Lauren was right. What she implied was right: that I was a traitor who dumped her mates at the merest whiff of testosterone. But she was just as guilty. It was as if we'd betrayed Delilah, betrayed her to a real live witchfinder, and left him to do his worst. Like it or not, we had a debt of gratitude to her. I only had to look across the road and see Joel to know this for a fact. Would he be here at all, furtively scanning the high street like a bank robber's look-out, were it not for that gladiolus bulb?

I don't think so.

'You all right?' I won't say his face lit up when he saw me, but it seemed to relax, as if he'd been really worried I wouldn't come. He gave me that same crooked grin his sister had. 'Sorry about the short notice. It was, you know, an impulse.'

'It was a good impulse,' I said. 'I was, um, at a friend's house. I don't think she has her dinner till really late. I was starving actually.'

'I wasn't sure if you'd like curry,' Joel said. The hair trailing over one eye gave him that hunted look I'd

129

noticed before. The effect was so sexy, my heart leapt into my throat. I hurried to assure him that curry was fine – 'As long as it isn't my mother's version. She never gets the spices right. Last time it took our tongues a week to recover. She's better on the bland English stuff, if you know what I mean.'

Damn. I almost swallowed my own tongue in disgust. This was what happened when I got nervous. My tongue went into overdrive. It gabbled away with absolutely no prior instruction from my brain. There was also this sickening little giggle that I fixed at the end of each sentence, as if everything I said was hilarious.

Surely it was enough to put Joel right off me, and make him regret the curry immediately. But the way he looked at me, I might have been spouting gems of wisdom on the origins of the universe.

He took my arm. 'Let's go in then, shall we?' When he looked deep into my eyes, he almost took my breath away. It was like he could see the *real* me – the super-intelligent, sensitive, mystic-type person that lay hidden beneath the gibbering idiot.

I'd only been into The Angel once before. It wasn't exactly a hang-out for the *it* crowd of Northgate. There was a red, swirly carpet and the bar was wreathed in plastic hops. The clientele was on the dodgy side. Tonight it consisted of a girl with a partially shaved scalp and an enormous cagoule serenading two drunks with a chorus of 'Irish Rover'. Otherwise it was mainly bleak-eyed middle-aged people puffing on fags and telling naff jokes. And me and Joel of course.

We took our drinks down the couple of stairs to the dining-bar and sat opposite each other in one of the booths. I was just instructing my tongue to keep still while I strove to maintain a coolly seductive exterior, when Joel came straight out with it. 'I got to tell you this, Abbie: I've been thinking of you all week.' He scratched his head helplessly, like he couldn't figure this out.

Thinking of the gladiolus bulb, I couldn't help flushing. 'Really?' I chortled idiotically.

'Yeah. Really. It's just like . . . like . . .' He held his palm to the side of his head, as if it hurt. 'It's like you're taking up all my head space. I just had to see you again. Listen, I don't usually come out with this kind of shit on a first date. It's just . . . just . . .' He looked at me helplessly. 'You're so beautiful.'

Beautiful! This was so over the top, I decided to laugh it off. 'Ha-ha! Joel, do you think you should, like, push that hair out of your eyes or something?' I knew for a fact that tonight was not one of my beautiful or even tolerably attractive nights. Coming straight from Delilah's, I hadn't even had time to wash my hair. Then I'd had to renew my eyeliner on the bus – never a good idea when you're sitting over the wheel.

But Joel just pushed his hair behind his ear and leaned closer. 'OK, it's out of my eyes, and you're still beautiful.'

'Joel,' I sighed, 'it's nice of you to say so, but I know I'm not beautiful, OK? Catherine Zeta Jones is beautiful, Julia Roberts is beautiful. You don't have to flatter me, really.'

He suddenly looked desperate. 'I'm not feeding you a line – it's the truth.'

This was getting silly. Confronted by his adoring gaze, I began to doubt my own feelings. What had happened to the cool dude who drove me home the other night?

Obviously Joel was unable to tell a beauty queen from an old boot. Either that, or the gladiolus bulb was doing its work underground, and the poor bloke was totally blinded by love! Strangely enough, this didn't reassure me. It felt like a cheat.

'Two chicken curries?' Luckily we were interrupted at this point by a girl bringing our food. I tucked in immediately. The sight of my hamster cheeks would surely wipe the rose-tinted specs from Joel's eyes. Then we could really talk, get to know each other.

'This looks great,' I said. 'I've never been in here before. It's kind of an old man's place, isn't it?'

Uh-oh, wrong thing to say. Joel flushed the colour of the chilli on his plate. 'Yeah, I'm sorry about the venue, really – it's crap, isn't it? Thing is, my car is off the road. You know I said the other night about the wheel dropping off any minute? Well, the exhaust dropped off instead. It dropped off the next day, after I'd taken Lilah back home. Otherwise we could have gone somewhere—'

'Oh, it doesn't matter. I mean, I don't care . . .' I rushed in, flustered. This was mad, the way we kept apologizing to each other. 'Joel, d'you mind telling me how you got that?' Desperate to change the subject, I pointed to the thin white scar which ran diagonally above his upper lip.

'This?' He fingered it, as if he'd forgotten it was there. 'That was years ago. When I was a kid.'

'Really? Well, it suits you. It kind of goes with your face.'

'Verne did me a favour then.'

'Verne did that? Your stepfather? You mean deliberately?'

He shrugged.

'Oh, but that's . . . that's abuse. That's awful, Joel. I didn't realize he was, like, *violent*.'

'Yeah, well, I should have ducked faster.' He stabbed half-heartedly at a piece of chicken, as if he'd lost his appetite. 'He used to set us this little character-building exercise. I was about fourteen, I think. Verne would hide the food, bury tins of beans in the garden, then hide the tin opener. If we found it, we ate that day. If not, we didn't. Well, only the stuff Mum smuggled us. It was supposed to make us appreciate what it's like to live in the third world. This happened a couple of times. Then one day I just rang Dial-a-Pizza, and when Verne got home he went ape-shit and threw the tin opener at me.' Joel drained his glass. 'End of story.'

'That's terrible.' I seemed to have lost my appetite suddenly. I felt spoiled, fortunate. How could I understand the kind of thing Joel and Delilah had had to go through – were still going through?

'Joel, did you know about Shropshire?' I blurted out.

It seemed he did. Delilah had told him a couple of days ago.

'Lilah won't go. She won't stand for it. It was bad enough when we lived in Wales.'

'Wales? Was that where you got the—?'

'Scar?' He nodded.

'I didn't know they had Dial-a-Pizza in Wales.'

For the first time Joel seemed to relax. He actually laughed. 'Neither did Verne. When he found out he thought it was the end of civilization as we know it. A few years later he tried to buy an island, this godforsaken pimple out in the Atlantic. It didn't work out, though, luckily for Mum and Lilah.'

'And you.'

'I'd left for St Andrews by then. I was doing an archaeology degree, but –' he shrugged – 'I couldn't keep going on the grant. So now I'm digging in flowerbeds instead of digging for bones. Great, eh?'

'That's tough,' I admitted. Joel wasn't playing for sympathy, I knew. Yet his story was so sad I had to resist the urge to clutch his head to my bosom and soothe his fevered brow.

'Yeah, well, it's not so bad.' As if sensing he'd revealed too much, he tried to make light of it. 'Anyway, listen, I'm sorry. This isn't much of a date, is it? I don't know what part of the chicken this is supposed to be.' He prodded a shred of meat. 'Must've been the parson's nose or something.'

Poor Joel. He looked so confused, I couldn't resist reaching out and tracing his scar with my finger.

'He's a bastard,' I said, 'to do that to you. But don't worry. I think he's about to get what's coming to him.'

It was a pity Joel's exhaust had fallen off, because even the back seat of an old banger would have come in useful on a rainy November night. A pity, too, that I didn't have the kind of parents who go out on a Saturday night and leave the house conveniently free. We had to make do, Joel and I, with smooching in the entrance to some old garages just off the high street.

Close up, he was good enough to eat. His hair, which tickled my nose as we kissed, smelt of rain. And the hand that cupped my face was like you'd expect a gardener's hand to be, a bit chunky and battered, but sensitive too.

His body beneath the flying jacket was lean and wiry, and kind of insistent.

OK, it wasn't the most romantic of settings, but the way Joel kissed me, it hardly mattered. I'd had a few snogs in my time, of course: wet kisses, French kisses and shy, pecky kisses. But Joel's kiss was out there on its own. Joel's was that kind of loving, hungry kiss you reserve for someone special. Someone beautiful. For the love of your life.

When, finally, we pulled apart, we both seemed lost for words. We strolled the few blocks towards Smedhurst Road and Joel's bus stop, arms locked around each other's waists beneath our jackets as if we were one person.

'Next time,' Joel muttered, 'let's not talk about Verne, OK?'

'Fine by me.'

'I've got to study after work next week – some research for this dig I might be going on. But I'll call you next weekend, and maybe we'll do an exhibition or something?'

'Yeah, great. Oh, by the way, I forgot to ask, what star sign are you?'

Joel did that crinkly thing with his eyes that made my throat go dry. 'I'm Capricorn. Is that OK with you? I mean, if we're not astrologically compatible, maybe we should forget it right now?'

'No, no, Capricorn's fine,' I said, although I knew he was teasing me. 'Well actually, it's my opposite sign because I'm a Cancer, but opposites . . . well, opposites . . .'

'Attract?'

'Yeah, sort of.'

He scratched his head, mock serious. 'That must explain it then, why I'm so attracted to you.'

I laughed. If only he knew what the real cause was!

We parted at the end of Smedhurst Road and I floated the rest of the way home, with the ghost of Joel's kiss and a silly smile on my face.

Chapter Twelve

Visitations and Vanishings

Never had crummy old Smedhurst Road looked so lovely as on that night, after saying goodbye to Joel. The bumper-to-bumper cars, the ragged privet hedges, even the rubbish bags slumped on front steps all looked heavenly to my eyes. That is, until I stepped into the porch of Number 62.

OK, the porch was hardly a thing of beauty. Usually it smelt of Mrs Croop's fish dinners. But tonight I sensed something else, as if something dark and old had passed this way. Something that wasn't Mrs Croop.

I opened my front door to the sound of raised voices. Incredible! My mother and father were having a row. This might be a normal event in most households, but not mine. My parents were the kind who claim on their sixtieth wedding anniversary that they've never had a cross word.

The reason soon became clear. The TV was on the blink.

'Your father's trying to fix it himself.' My mother looked flustered. 'I told him to call out the repair man, someone who knows what he's doing.'

Dad grunted that he knew what he was doing. 'Thank you for the vote of confidence, Maureen.' He was on his hands and knees, twiddling wires, the whole back of the TV off. 'It's probably just a missing connection.'

'It's a missing connection all right. Please, Jim, you'll electrocute yourself in a minute.'

'What was on anyway?' I asked my father.

'Snooker. It's the final tonight.'

'So what happened? Did it just fizzle out or something?'

I was trying to sound concerned. Actually, now that I was in love, I felt sorry for old folks like my parents who only had the telly to entertain them.

'It was just when that religious maniac knocked at the door. He knocks, and the telly goes *bang*. Just like that.'

'Religious maniac?' I laughed. 'Are you kidding? At this time of night?' It was eleven o'clock. 'I didn't know the Jehovahs kept such late hours.'

Mum said she had no idea what religion he was. 'All I know is, I couldn't get rid of the man. He had his foot in the door. Harassment, you might call it. I had to call your dad, and then I go back upstairs and he's got the telly dismantled—'

'This, er, religious nut,' I said slowly. 'What did he look like exactly?'

My mother was too distracted by the TV and the possibility of Dad blowing himself up to worry about doorstep nutters. I had to keep on and on: 'He was wearing one of those suits, I suppose? Mum, I said, was he wearing a suit?'

She hovered over my father with a screwdriver. 'What? Oh, I don't know, looked like fancy dress to me. I can't abide a man who wears a hat like that. So affected. And sinister, frankly.' She looked at me suddenly. 'Abigail? Are you all right? Where have you been anyway? Did you eat at Delilah's house?'

'Yeah – I mean, yeah, I'm all right, and yeah, I've eaten. What did he say, this nutter?'

My mother answered irritably that there was a pamphlet on the kitchen table, if I was so interested. Personally she had more important things to worry about, and she could hardly understand the language he spoke in any case. 'It wasn't English exactly, as we know it. It was sort of old-fashioned, with a country burr to it. I mean, calling me "my good woman" – blooming cheek—' She broke off and gave me one of her searching looks. 'You'd better throw that rubbish he left behind in the bin. We don't want you getting involved in any peculiar cults, Abigail, not after all that other nonsense last summer.'

The paper on the worktop reminded me of the wood-cuts in Delilah's book. The same kind of heavy, old-fashioned print, set out like a public proclamation. I read silently, the hairs standing up on the back of my neck as I did so.

TO THE PEOPLE OF THIS TOWN
Cast out all witches and devils which hath lately annoyed these parts with several grevious molestations and curiosities.
Some councils directing a due improvement of the terrible things lately occurred in this neighbourhood hath been alarmed by the unusual and amazing range of Evil Spirits. Prevent the wrongs which these Evil Angels may intend against us.
In the Year of Our Lord 1645

★ ★ ★

Did I sleep at all that night? I should have been dreaming sweetly of Joel, but all I could think of was Hopkins. Hopkins, here on my doorstep; he had opened his foul ghoul's mouth and communicated with my mother. My mother, the most down-to-earth, un-psychic of women, had been trying to push a spook off her doorstep!

The question was, Why? Why bother with me, when Delilah was the one with the hot-line to Hecate, Queen of the Dark Moon. Yes, I'd dabbled a bit in palms and astrology and that, and once I thought I might get myself a crystal ball and become a fortune-teller, but I was hardly a witch! Or was I?

Sometime in the early hours the realization came to me: Delilah might be chief witch and spell-caster, but the moon-dew and bulb rituals had been performed for the benefit of Lauren and me. Hadn't I planted that stupid bulb with my own hands? Hadn't I wished and prayed to the moon for a lover? And now the super-cool Joel, who'd always been more interested in archaeology than girls (or so Lilah once said), was crazy with love for me. Proof enough for any witchfinder that I was into the magic arts up to my neck.

What scared me most was that if Web-woman really *had* delivered Hopkins back to Delilah, then he hadn't stuck around long. He must have somehow intercepted my message from Joel and tracked me to the pub. He might even have been spying on us when we snogged by the garages. Going straight to my mother was a crafty move, though. Was he trying to tell on me? Inform her that her daughter was a no-good whore and a witch, and deserved to die? God knows.

I turned over in bed, sighed and stuck the pillow over

my head. One thing I knew: the spells had got to stop if we were ever to get Hopkins off our backs. And they had to stop *now*.

Next morning Lauren answered the door wearing pyjamas and yawning. She groaned suspiciously. 'Oh, don't tell me you've come to bore me with every tedious detail of your romantic evening, because if you have I'm—'

'No, just let me in, Lauren. Please. It's important.'

As we wandered through to the kitchen, Lauren made a face. 'You look terrible.'

'Thanks. So would you if you'd had a night like I've just had.' Before she could plug her ears, I told her the story. Everything that happened post romantic moments, that is, beginning with the TV breakdown and ending with the visiting religious maniac.

Lauren stopped crunching her gluten-free soya flakes and stared at me, spoon halfway to her mouth. 'He came to your house? But how can you be sure it was him?'

I gazed steadily at her. 'Lauren, since when have the born-again Christians worn funny hats, talked in olde English and gone on about "not suffering witches to live"? Hmm? Answer me that.'

Lauren couldn't answer. She seemed lost for words.

'Well then,' I said, 'I rest my case. What we do is, we go to Lilah's place right now and we tell her the magic has got to stop. No more dabbling in stuff we can't control or understand, OK?'

Lauren shrugged. '*Absolument*. Whatever you say. But Delilah's not going to like it.'

* * *

141

However, the moment we approached Delilah's house something told me, Uh-oh, bad, bad plan. It looked the same as always, the jungly front garden, the tall windows screened by thick curtains, the witchy turret that was Lilah's room, yet something had changed. I knew, even before I grabbed the brass knocker shaped like a clenched fist, that the house was empty.

Lauren was hovering by the front gate. 'I'll wait here.'

'Yeah, don't worry about a thing, Lauren. You just cringe by the hedge like a big wuss.'

'Well, it was your idea. Personally I haven't had any visits from this so-called witchfinder.'

'Not yet,' I muttered.

At that moment the door of the neighbouring house flew open. A woman in a headscarf with anchors all over it, and a fierce-looking Alsatian on a lead, gave us a suspicious look.

'You want the Barrys? They've gone.' She spoke as if she were glad of this.

'They've gone?' I repeated.

'In the middle of the night. Here one minute, gone the next. Are you a . . . ?'

'We're friends actually,' Lauren said, in her snootiest 'mind your own business' voice.

'Oh yes? Well, I can't give you a forwarding address, I'm afraid.' She added darkly, 'This is the sort of thing that happens with rental properties. You get all sorts. Brings down the tone of the whole neighbourhood.'

As the Alsatian dragged her to the gate, I called after her, 'But surely they might come back? I mean, how do you know they've gone for good?'

She half turned, struggling to maintain her balance as

the dog tugged on the lead. 'People don't usually take all their furniture with them when they go out for the day, do they? Banging and thumping all night. The removal lorry didn't get here till midnight. Midnight! I might tell you, my husband and I haven't had a wink of sleep.' With that, she stomped off in the direction of the park, as if her sleepless night was all our fault.

The park was almost empty when we crossed it once more. Black-bellied clouds billowed in from the west like the sails of some deathly flotilla. The fitful sun had given up the ghost, and a wind moaned low over the football pitch.

Lauren and I sauntered in a kind of daze, almost sleep-walking along the tarmac path. 'But her mother was knitting those legwarmers only yesterday afternoon,' Lauren said. 'No one moves house that quickly, surely?'

'I know, it's odd. Verne must have found a house and packed them off before Lilah could even protest. Wait a minute. Let's try her mobile.' I fished mine out and keyed in Lilah's number. Nothing. Only the pre-recorded voice, telling me the person I'd called was not available. As if I didn't know.

'What about school? Her education and everything?' Lauren said.

'Yeah. Poor Delilah.'

'Poor Delilah? Poor *me*. Supposing my eczema comes back again?' Lauren rolled up her sleeve to check. 'I haven't the faintest idea how to get hold of that moon-dew stuff.'

I gazed at her in disgust. 'I have to say that's about the most selfish thing I ever heard. Here's poor Lilah, spirited off to the back of beyond by her mad stepfather, the ghost of the Witchfinder General in hot pursuit, and you expect her to leave you instructions for the making of moon-dew. That's just— What's up?'

Instead of defending herself, Lauren was staring past me, across the lake, towards the Millennium Gardens. 'Abbie . . . Abbie . . . that man over there . . .'

I followed her gaze. The gardens were separated from the rest of the park by low conifer hedges. Somewhere behind that hedge was my precious gladiolus bulb. And standing in front of it, still as a statue among the skeletal stalks of the roses, was a tall, dark figure.

'Is that –' Lauren nodded, her face pale – 'is that who I think it is?'

The figure didn't move. Not an inch. That was the scariest thing – the utter stillness of the man in the cloak. You couldn't see his eyes from this distance, yet you knew he was watching. You could *feel* his stare, the same way a grazing bush animal must sense the eyes of a predator. The statue-like pose had an uncanny effect upon us. For a minute it seemed *we* were the statues, Lauren and me, turned to stone by that intense gaze.

Then a sudden gust of wind lifted the cloak like a dark cloud, and the spell was broken. The figure raised a hand to steady the steeple hat. And we were off, running towards the gate where the passing bus would take us back to Lauren's house.

'Whassup, you two?' Lauren's mother Izzie said cheerfully, as we flattened ourselves against the front door, panting like old war horses. 'In training for the London Marathon or something?'

She was drifting about in a flimsy kaftan – the kind of

thing women in films change into to make themselves 'more comfortable'. 'No offence, but I reckon you two need to work out. Young people these days! Can't even run for a bus without going into total collapse.'

Recovering slightly, Lauren pushed past her mother to the kitchen. 'We're really not in the mood for your witticisms, Mother, hilarious as they are.'

Izzie rolled her eyes at me in mock terror. 'Come and have some coffee, eh, love? I've just made a really strong pot. I need it for the shock.'

'Shock?' I followed Izzie and Lauren into the kitchen, in the wake of musky Muzbelle perfume.

'Yeah, some nutter at the door just now.' Izzie poured coffee into tall, jazzy mugs and tipped double-chocolate-chip bickies out of a packet.

My hand shook as I took the mug from her. 'Nutter?' I repeated.

'Nutter, as in historical-looking nutter?' Lauren echoed me fearfully. 'All dressed in black?'

Izzie looked taken aback. 'That's the fella. Oh my God. Not one of your pals, is he?'

'No, no,' I said quickly. 'We saw him. Just now. In the park.'

Izzie looked suspicious. 'Is that why you were running like the devil was after you? Did he approach you? Say something?'

'No,' said Lauren. 'We just noticed him, that's all.'

'Who wouldn't?' I said. 'A weirdo like that?'

Izzie sighed and sipped her coffee, cradling the mug with both hands. 'Yeah, well, to tell the truth, I nearly got Harvey to call the police, the way he was going on about "wanton women" and staring at my boobs.' She shuddered. 'Although actually, I blame the government. People like that should be properly cared for in a hospital, where they can't do any harm to anyone.'

In the old, pre-Henry days Lauren's clean, varnished, Ikea-inspired room had been a hostile environment for the house-dust mite. Now it was also a no-go zone for spooks. The bright-blue pentagram she'd painted across the varnished floorboards a few months back was still there, hiding beneath the jute herringbone rug. Now she positioned her crystals to maximum effect on the window ledge and flicked her wind chimes into a frenzied pealing.

'D'you mind taking your trainers off, by the way, Abbie? You've just walked something yucky into my floorboards.'

'Oh, beg your pardon, I'm sure.' I hoicked them off and found that my toe had waggled a hole in my socks again. 'It's only a few old dead leaves, for God's sake.'

'It may be a few old dead leaves to you,' Lauren said, flicking them with a duster. 'It could mean a week's itching for me. There are micro-organisms in that mud. I've got to be extra careful now that I've run out of moon-dew.'

The bottle of moon-dew on the shelf still contained a few trickles. Lauren knelt on the rug, rolled up her sleeves and gave her forearms a quick, light coating.

I watched her with a heavy heart. Here was the evidence. Proof. The reason Hopkins was still hanging around, watching us. I explained my theory to Lauren.

'Those spells are on-going, aren't they? As long as we are still benefiting from them, then we're guilty in his eyes. I've been thinking about it half the night, and I

146

reckon you're probably in the clear, provided you don't try to gather more moon-dew. It's *me* who's in trouble.'

'You?'

'Yeah, the gladiolus bulb, remember? I mean, it's done the trick, hasn't it? It's actually worked.'

Lauren stopped rubbing in invisible moon-dew and gawped at me. 'Not . . . You mean it was *his* name you thought of – Delilah's brother?'

'Well who else?'

'I don't know. I thought it was that ape-guy at school – you know, the one with the black hairs on the back of his hands? Jake . . . something or other . . .'

'I don't know any ape-men, thanks. And hairy hands are not exactly a turn-on. Joel's hands are so nice . . .' I murmured, suddenly aware of the immensity of the sacrifice I was contemplating. 'In fact he's nice, you know, all over.'

'A bit too nice for you, I'd have thought,' Lauren said, a detectable sniff of jealousy in her voice.

'Thanks, Lauren. All I know is he really, like, *cares* for me. Smirk all you want, but I really think this is *it*, you know? Love. That rotten old bag of worm-eaten bones is spoiling everything for me, Lauren. He's going to totally ruin my life. Oh, what am I going to say to Joel? Am I really going to have to give him up? *Can* I? What am I going to do?'

Lauren stood looking blank. She was like that. Totally hopeless in the comfort department. If you wanted a sympathetic ear, then you didn't go to Lauren. Might as well pour your heart out to the wall.

'You could dig it up, I suppose,' was Lauren's cool suggestion.

'Dig up the bulb? Oh yeah, I can just see me scrabbling around in the Millennium Gardens with my trusty spade in the dead of night. How am I supposed to find that exact one again, for God's sake? Bulbs all look the same in the dark, don't they? And anyway, if I did manage to find it, what then? Rose-tinted specs peel away from Joel's eyes, he sees me as I really am. Next thing you know, I'm dumped.' I put my head in my hands. 'You have to admit it's a no-win situation.'

'Well then,' Lauren said, unable to hide the tiny stream of satisfaction in her voice, 'you'll just have to tell him, Abbie. Do it now. Before you get in any deeper. Send him a text or something.'

'A text?' I peered out at her through my fingers. 'Just like that? What d'you suggest: U R DUMPED? For Christ's sake, Lauren, have you actually *got* a heart, or are you stuffed with some kind of allergy-free, man-made fibres or something?'

Lauren smacked the empty bottle down on the shelf and said there was no need to take out my frustration on her. 'I've got my own problems, don't forget. What about my future, eh? It'll be back to the allergy clinic for me, and I can tell you, Chinese herbs are not exactly pleasant! Anyway, it's no skin off my nose if you make mad, passionate love with your wonder-boy. But don't be surprised if . . .' She glanced up at the rain hammering on the skylight.

'*If?*'

'Just . . . if . . .' she said. Then, to emphasize the seriousness of the situation, she flipped back the jute rug and slowly traced the outline of the pentagram with her bare toe.

Chapter Thirteen

The Letter

Thus began one of the sorriest chapters of my life. You know when people say stuff like, the magic has gone out of their relationship? Well, that's how it was for Lauren and me after Delilah left. The magic had gone out of our lives. Quite literally.

The first thing that happened was that Lauren's eczema and allergies returned with a vengeance. Once again she was a snivelling wreck, sleeves bulging with tissues, skin eruptions all over the place, and the only dates she had were with the Chinese medicine clinic.

As for me, well, my life was an empty shell, a wasteland, a desert . . . let's just say it was total crap.

Poor Joel. He had taken some convincing that our relationship was over even before it started. I'd decided to write him a letter in the end. After wasting practically an entire rainforest's worth of paper, I came up with the feeble excuse that my heart had been broken once before, and now I'd decided to concentrate on my A levels.

I could hardly expect him to fall for this guff. The third time he rang, my mother was out and I picked up the phone.

'It's because of my car, isn't it?' Joel said. 'It's because my car's off the road.'

'Your car? You think I'm the kind of girl who cares what kind of car you drive? Please, Joel—'

'Only if it's the car—'

'It's not the car. Listen, Joel, you're trying to save money. You're going to Australia. What's the point of us getting it together, if you're off to the other side of the world in a few weeks?'

'Is it because I'm a Capricorn?'

'No it's . . . OK, some people think Capricorns are a bit on the dull side, but you could have Leo rising or something. And anyway—'

'I'm coming round,' was all he said. 'Abbie, to hell with Australia, I've got to see you.' Then he put the phone down on me.

When he turned up at the front door, it was all I could do not to fly down and hug him so tight I'd squeeze the breath out of him. Only the thought of the steeple hat and the dark swirling cloak gave me the strength to send my mother out to make excuses. This was unwise, as it happened, because Joel was the kind of guy who brings out the mumsy instinct in older women.

'That poor lad,' my mother said, having sent him packing as gently as she could. 'He's got it bad for you, Abigail. You should be flattered. Such a nice boy. Intelligent, by the look of him – you can tell.' She gave me that wise-owly look through her bifocals. 'I suppose that's his trouble – he's too nice for you.'

'Oh yes, Mother,' I said sarcastically. 'I'm the original "treat 'em mean keep 'em keen" floosie after all.'

Then I went off to cry my eyeballs out in private. I cried all that night, and the night after that. I didn't even care that my eyes turned into red slits and my nose swelled up to twice its normal (that is, not inconsiderable) size. How could I explain to anyone? How could I

150

say to Joel, 'See, you're only here because of a bulb'? Finally, I convinced myself that I was doing both him and me a favour. Come next November, when the gladiolus was just a few shrivelled brown petals clinging to a dried-up stem, Joel would look at me and see the blobby nose, the slight gap between my front teeth, and wonder what the hell he'd let himself in for. And that would be it. End of beautiful romance.

Even so, the last time Joel came, I had to hide in my room, hands jammed fast over my ears so I couldn't hear his voice, when my mother told him, 'I'm sorry, dear, she's not in.'

I couldn't bear even to peek at him from the window. Just the sight of him, loping forlornly down Smedhurst Road, would have broken my resolve. And then I'd have been galloping after him, arms outstretched like you see in movies, and the next thing you knew, the Witchfinder General would be on my doorstep, wanting to examine my witch's mark.

Life might be boring, Lauren reminded me in case I cracked; it might be a pain, but we had no choice.

'We don't want any more visits from the man in black, do we? After all, we're both paying the price. You're not the only one to suffer,' she finished with an accusing sneeze.

There were no more visits from the man in black, as it happened. At least, not for a while. Life had returned to normal. At school we copied out notes till our wrists ached, and debated Blake with Uncle Phil: was he a genius or a madman, and who cared really? I swept up toenail clippings on Saturday mornings, and Lauren smothered herself in marigold ointment. Saturday afternoons we'd wander around The Gates, trying out new lipsticks in Boots and taking care to avoid the web-woman. The evenings would find us at Cine-world, snivelling into our giant popcorns and wishing we looked like Gwyneth Paltrow.

Sometimes one of the Fionas would drawl, 'Wonder what became of that skanky witch-girl? Must have taken off on her broomstick!'

Apart from that, no one mentioned Delilah. Lauren and I had tried her mobile several times, but all we got was, 'The number you are dialling has not been recognized.' Joel must have known where Delilah was, but I couldn't ask him. It had been a week and three and a half days since I'd last heard from him, and for all I knew he might already be mending his broken heart on the far side of the world, with the help of some Aussie girl.

I did worry about Delilah, though. Suppose the Loathsome Verne had finally flipped and had her locked up somewhere, like Rapunzel in her tower? Suppose we opened the newspaper some day to read of a girl fitting Delilah's description found buried in a Shropshire wood, or floating Ophelia-like down the river Severn? How would we ever forgive ourselves?

Still, as Lauren pointed out, Delilah was hardly a natural victim. She was tough, wasn't she? 'If you want my opinion,' Lauren said, 'she's probably run away and is back here in London somewhere.'

I agreed she might have a point. Somehow I couldn't see Lilah in the country, toddling off to some yokel school wearing her mum's legwarmers and woolly helmet. Obviously it was time to put this whole episode of my life behind me along with all the other duff episodes, and look forward to a future of, well . . . more successful episodes. Although just thinking of my future made me feel weary. For a start, how was I ever going to find a bloke as perfect as Joel without the aid of a gladiolus bulb?

Then, three weeks before Christmas, the letter arrived: one of those handmade envelopes that look like there's bits of bird's nest embedded in the paper. I recognized the bold spidery scrawl at once. Delilah! It couldn't be anyone else.

Heart pounding for some unknown reason, I took it to my room, well away from my mother's prying eyes. The envelope was so firmly stuck down, I had to rip it off in shreds, my hands trembling. This was ridiculous. I hadn't been so worked up over a letter since opening my exam results. God knows what I was expecting. Some kind of bad news, I suppose. A warning. Some horror story about the Loathsome Verne or Delilah's own ghostly side-kick. I read fast, skimming over individual words in a fearful gulp.

Dear Abbie,
This is Flopshire calling Earth: Are you receiving me? Listen, if you think Northgate is dead, let me tell you, from up here it seems like Sin City.

Sorry I didn't get the chance to say goodbye. Not long after you left, Verne turned up with a whole flock of his pervy religious nut cronies and an estate agent's blurb on Crud Cottage. Before we knew it the removal men from hell had us packed up and shipped out like it was some kind of life-or-death emergency. I couldn't even ring you because the battery on my mobile gave out, can you believe it? Just when I needed it most.

I could have kicked myself. Remember we used that green candle in the protection ritual when it specifically said 'grey'? If we'd used grey in the first place, well, I might still be living in the Wicked City, like some halfway normal person.

Anyway, what happens next is my mother gets ill. We reach this hovel (I kid you not) in the hills, and Mum just goes to bed and doesn't get up. The doctor says it's nothing physical, just some kind of nervous breakdown.

So my life is total shit right now. The college in Ludlow is a three-mile walk then a bus ride away, but mostly I stay home with Mum. I'd bugger off to-morrow, get some job in London – anywhere – but how can I leave my mum alone with that creep? He's always sitting over her and muttering prayers and stuff. He'd probably start casting out devils or something if I wasn't around to keep an eye on things.

Anyway, what I was thinking was, could you and Lauren get up here for Christmas? You don't need to panic about Verne because he's either out preaching all day or hanging around HQ, and Mum says she'd like to see you both.

Perlease, Abbie, please come! I've been to loads of schools, but you and Lauren are the best mates I ever had. We don't have to hang out at Crud Cottage all the time. We could check out Flopshire's hot spots. I mean, there must be some, if you know where to look.

Let me know soon. Of course, if you'd rather spend
Christmas in Northgate . . .
    Please come and save my life,
    Love, Lilah xxxx

After the gulp-read, I digested it slowly. Every word.
Between the lines. The thing that struck me most was
that there was absolutely no mention of Hopkins. What
had happened to him then? Maybe he hadn't followed
them to Shropshire after all. Maybe he just came with
that house like any ordinary old spook. Or maybe he was
just confused, still wandering in that murky space
between this world and the next, sniffing out dark deeds
where he could find them. Or, more likely, Delilah
hadn't mentioned him because she'd given up magic.
Had she lost interest? Grown out of spells? Or was
she just too busy looking after her mum and Crud
Cottage?

'Well?' I could hardly stand it.
    Lauren was reading Lilah's letter as she leant against
the cloakroom radiator.
    'Well,' she replied. It struck me suddenly what was
wrong. She'd gone into a huff because Delilah had
addressed the letter to me instead of her.
    'Well,' I urged impatiently, 'are we going or aren't we?'
    Lauren was sitting on the radiator now, like she'd climb
inside it if she could. 'What d'you mean "we", anyway?
She wrote to you, didn't she?'
    I snatched up the letter with a sigh and read aloud,
'You and Lauren were the best mates I ever had. Lauren.
That's your name, isn't it? For God's sake, Lauren, she

probably forgot your address or something. Does it matter who she wrote to?'

'I'm allergic to the country,' Lauren said stubbornly. 'Whenever we went to Devon on holidays, I never stopped sneezing.'

'That was in the summer. There's not going to be any pollen about in the dead of winter, is there?'

'Maybe not, but I don't like the sound of this cottage. She says it's a hovel, doesn't she? That means no central heating, no mod cons, no comforts of any kind. If damp air gets onto my chest, I've had it. I can get seriously—'

'Yeah, and you can get piles sitting on radiators, did you know that?' I said, thinking this would be just deserts for such a pain in the arse. 'Poor Delilah. We were supposed to be her friends. Must admit I feel a bit bad about leaving my parents and that, but she *needs* us, Lauren. Her life is just so shitty – think how she'll feel if we don't go. She'll have to pull crackers with the Loathsome Verne.'

'I suppose . . .' Lauren was biting her lower lip, a good sign that I was wearing down her defences.

'And it sounds like she's given up her witch-thing. If she hadn't, well, she'd just magic her sick mum out of bed, wouldn't she? Well, what do you say then?' I was beside myself with impatience by now. 'Christmas in the country? Oh go on, say yes, Lauren, pleasepleaseplease . . . I don't want to go on my own.'

'I'm not sure.' Enjoying her moment of power, Lauren deliberated. 'I've never spent Christmas away from home before.'

'Lauren!' I all but screeched.

'Oh, all right then,' Lauren said, with the air of one

making a great sacrifice. 'I suppose I'll have to say yes or I'll never get any peace. Although since I'm not allowed to use any more moon-dew, I can't see there's much point. And I warn you –' wagging her finger at me – 'if I get frost-bite or anything, I'll blame you, OK.'

'Blame me,' I said, trying not to look as happy as I felt. 'Blame me all you like.'

The next hurdle was persuading my mother. When I told her the story (leaving out the witchy bits, of course), she insisted it would be better if Delilah came to Smedhurst Road for Christmas. 'If her poor mother is ill, she's not going to want three great teenagers clumping about the place, is she?'

'I'm glad you mentioned "clumping", Mother,' I said, describing Delilah's attachment to her Doc Marts. 'Delilah is, like, the original clumper. Mrs Croop would have a permanent migraine if she stayed here.'

Still Mum wasn't convinced. She kept on about how I was sure to feel homesick without her and Dad at Christmas. It took a phone call from Delilah's mother to assure her that Lauren and I were truly welcome. Mum seemed a bit humbled when she got off the phone. 'Apparently she can't manage without Delilah. The poor woman is practically house-bound. It sounds like agoraphobia,' she added darkly. 'What a terrible burden for that poor girl.' She gave me one of her looks. 'Well, I suppose you'd better go then. Although with the mood you've been in lately, Abigail, I can't see you bringing much Christmas cheer to that unfortunate household.'

Chapter Fourteen

The Middle of Nowhere

Two weeks later and we were on the train to 'Flopshire', me trying to quell a sneaking feeling, as we chugged out of Paddington Station, that this was a bad idea, after all. Snow was forecast and the train kept grinding to a halt, as if it felt the same way I did.

'Leaves on the line,' the ticket collector explained at first, then, 'Kids throwing stones. Nothing to worry about. Happens all the time.'

Nothing to worry about, he said. I tried not to. Still, had it not been for the thought of Christmas at Smedhurst Road, *The Wizard of Oz* on telly and Mrs Croop cracking nuts with her gums, I might have got off at the next stop.

'I can't think why my parents always have to invite Mrs Croop,' I grumbled to Lauren. 'Just because she's on her own, they think it's their Christian duty.'

Lauren reckoned I should consider myself lucky. 'My mother's throwing a Muzbelle Christmas special. It'll be couscous and pelvic swivels all the way. That is just so *not* the way to spend Christmas.'

'Mmmm . . . I suppose.' Looking out at the landscape of field and sky, all blended together in shades of sludge, I was thinking that the only way to spend it would be in Joel's arms. And imagining I *was* – in Joel's arms, I mean – somehow kept me going as the train rolled onwards, eating up the land that lay between us and Crud Cottage, Delilah, her sick mother and the Loathsome Verne.

It was almost dark by the time the taxi dumped us at the end of a lane, in what must surely be the middle of nowhere. Lauren and I stood shivering by the sign for Crow Cottage. Someone had scratched out the last two letters of CROW and changed it to CRUD. This had caused some confusion with the taxi driver.

'Delilah can be so juvenile at times.' Lauren turned up the collar of her coat. 'God knows where we might have ended up.'

'Yeah, we might have ended up somewhere even cruddier.' I glanced around. 'I knew that Flopshire was, like, the country, but this is a bit more country than I'd imagined.'

For a start, there wasn't a house to be seen. Where was the village with the friendly twinkling lights? Where was the pub with the fit yokels waiting to be bowled over by our urban sophistication? On either side of us trees scrabbled along the edge of the track to Crud Cottage, branches creaking like loose floorboards. There was a piquant scent of cow-shit in the air. From deep within the wood, some unknown bird cackled like it had smoker's cough.

'You never said it would be this remote,' Lauren mumbled accusingly from the depths of her furry collar.

'Well, how was I to know? Anyway, at least you're dressed for the occasion. What about me?' I indicated my pride and joy, pink cowgirl boots purchased with early Christmas money, and cunningly combined with a knee-hobbling skirt and plunge-neck T-shirt. As an arctic wind took liberties with my cleavage, I shrugged my denim jacket closer around me.

'Are we still in England? Or have we, like, crossed into the frozen wastes by mistake? Oh, Lauren, how am I going to get up this track in these heels? It's full of potholes.'

Lauren just snapped that the whole idea of coming here at all was a big mistake, and if I wanted to dress up like I was off line dancing, that was my look-out.

'Line dancing!' I hobbled after her, as she marched off up the track. Wearing buckled wellies and snug ankle-length Afghan, Lauren obviously had a better idea of country style than I did.

'Listen!' She stopped just ahead of me. 'Somebody's chopping wood. And there's smoke, see. Well, I'm glad they've got the fire lit at least.'

We rounded the corner, and there was Crud Cottage in all its glory. More of an upmarket hut than a cottage, with a ramshackle porch. In front of the porch someone in a massive duffel coat and sheepskin balaclava was wielding an axe.

Delilah!

Delilah throwing down the axe and gallumphing towards us, arms outstretched and shrieking like a Sioux warrior.

'Hey, Lilah!' I cried, tolerating her smelly bear hug. 'You look like the mad axeman. And, you rotter, you never told us about all this mud and stuff!'

'Nice to see you, Lilah,' Lauren simpered, two-faced as ever. Except you could hardly see her face peering over her collar.

Delilah stared at us as if she hadn't really believed we'd

come. 'Hail, moon maidens!' Lilah said — a greeting which, frankly, I hoped was a joke. I really did not want to get into that moon-maiden stuff again. 'Come inside then.' She gave us both a hearty push towards the cabin. 'Come and see Crud Cottage.'

'Whaddya think then?' Lilah said when we'd defrosted a little. 'Shit, isn't it?'

We looked around at the splintery beams, the coconut matting over cracked tiles and a stove belching black smoke as Lilah stoked it with logs. I sniffed. Mice. Old newspapers. Cupboards under the stairs. Dereliction.

'OK,' I said. 'I've seen worse.'

'You have? Where?' Lilah wanted to know. 'My God, Abbie, you don't have to be polite. It stinks, face it. Would you live here? Anyway, come on up and see Mum.'

We followed her up a spindly winding stair that led straight from the kitchen. There were only two bedrooms upstairs, one of which we were to share with Delilah. In the other, her mother sat up in bed with a shawl over her nightie and one of those helmets she'd been knitting wedged over her straggly curls. She looked pale as the ice that laced the inside of the windows, but she smiled at us.

'Lauren, Abbie — I'm really glad to see you girls. Lilah's been looking after me so well, but she really needs company of her own age.'

I nodded gormlessly, wondering, what the hell do you say to someone who is suffering from some kind of nerve-thing?

'We're so sorry you've been ill, Mrs, er, Barry,' Lauren cooed. 'Really, I hope we won't be any bother to you.'

'Me too,' I rushed in. 'Are you still, er, doing your knitting at all?'

161

Back in the kitchen, Lauren rolled her eyes at me. 'What a stupid thing to say to a sick person.'

'I only wondered if she had, like, time to knit a spare pair of legwarmers,' I mumbled.

Delilah began hacking slices of bread for our cheese-on-toast supper. Her mother was improving, she said. 'Or she was, until she heard Joel wasn't coming home for Christmas.'

'Joel?' I said faintly. Of course. Joel. It hadn't occurred to me that he might turn up at Crud Cottage. I'd been too busy imagining him in Australia.

'Is that because of your stepfather?' Lauren said, rubbing her blue fingers together over the stove.

Delilah looked mischievous as she waved the bread knife in my direction. 'Joel can handle Verne all right. He's not so sure about girls, though.'

'Girls?' I repeated, flushing.

'Yeah, girls! Girls as in Abigail Carter in particular. Come on, Abbie, spit it out. Joel's taken a fancy to you and you've got the hots for someone else, right? The bloke whose name you thought of – remember, when we did our little spot of gardening that night?'

'Well, er, no, not exactly right,' I admitted, leaning over to stroke the cat, so that she wouldn't see my face.

'Oh, come off it, it's worked, hasn't it? That spell never fails. You had to send my poor bruv packing because of some hunk. Joel told me that—'

'Joel doesn't know,' I rushed in. 'It *is* him. I mean, it was Joel's name I thought of that night.'

Delilah left off whopping mustard on our toasties and gave me a hard stare. 'So all the time you fancied my big brother. You secretive little devil!'

'It was *meant* to be a secret, wasn't it?' I said. 'That was the whole point.'

'Excuse me for being dumb –' Delilah slapped her head – 'but I'm not getting this. If you like Joel and he likes you and the bulb is sprouting away and obviously doing its stuff, then what's the problem? Why did he go all uptight the minute I said you were coming?'

Lauren and I looked at each other. Lauren raised her eyebrows slightly, a gesture I interpreted as saying we'd got to tell her some time.

'OK,' I sighed. 'You tell her, Lauren.'

Outside the window darkness pressed, as if the flank of a great black animal were blotting out the light. I wished Delilah would draw the curtains.

Lauren twisted a plait around her forefinger and launched into the story of the three appearances: Hopkins haranguing my mother on the doorstep, then watching us from the Millennium Gardens. 'And when we got to my place we found he'd been harassing my mother too,' she finished.

'You're telling me.' Delilah propped herself against the edge of the table, as if for support. 'You're telling me that while I've been up here, you've both . . . *seen* him?'

I nodded. 'Remember when Web-woman paid us a surprise visit, and you reckoned that she'd off-loaded Hopkins on you again?'

'How could I forget?'

'Well, if she did, he must have followed me that same evening, because he knew I was meeting Joel.'

'You were meeting my brother that night?'

'Yeah, sorry. I should have told you. But now you see why I had to write this letter to Joel? It was like he was part of the spell. As long as we were seeing each other, then the magic was working. Which would make me a witch. Kind of.'

'That's Abbie's theory anyway.' Lauren rolled up her sleeve to show Lilah some scabby bits on the inside of her elbow where she'd scratched herself until she bled. 'The moon-dew has run out – but she says I can't use it any more anyway. So now I'm back to marigold ointment. Might as well smother myself in lard.'

'The point is,' I said, 'it worked. Since Lauren gave up the moon-dew and I gave up Joel, we haven't seen hide nor hair of him, have we?'

Delilah wore her far-away, frowning look. We waited for her to say something incredibly wise. Admire us for our great sacrifice. Promise never to touch the magic arts again. But all she did was to screech, 'Shit! The toast!'

The ancient-looking grill pan was on fire, flames licking the toast crusts, the kitchen filling with black smoke in seconds. The next few minutes were taken up with Delilah rushing around swearing and waving a tea towel, while I scraped black bits from our toasties and Lauren coughed herself hoarse. It wasn't until we finally settled down to munching our burnt offerings, helped down by large dollups of ketchup, that I realized Delilah hadn't made any comment about Matthew Hopkins. Not a word. The toast-burning had been a welcome interruption, and I suspected I knew why.

After supper Delilah lit candles and a fire in the sitting room, and flourished her pack of tarot cards. 'I've never given you a reading, have I? Who goes first?'

'Not me, thanks,' I said quickly. Tarot cards were creepy

164

at the best of times. And supposing the old man with the scythe came up, just when our ears were straining for the sound of Verne's old Citroën on the gravel outside? Or even the ghostly tap of hooves. 'I mean, sorry. Perhaps another time. I'm feeling a bit, you know, jumpy.'

'I'm not really in the mood either.' Lauren hunched over the damp, spitting logs, looking pained. 'I shouldn't have had that cheese. Cheese is like poison to my entire system.'

Delilah looked disappointed. 'Listen, we have to make our own entertainment here, you know. As you see, we have no telly. The devil's work, Verne reckons. Go on, Abbie, give them a shuffle. Go on!'

She slapped the pack of cards into my hand. They gave off a faint heat, I noticed. Was it my own palms sweating, or were the cards themselves exuding a kind of stickiness? With Delilah looking on, I cut them automatically, without even thinking. Then gasped. 'Oh no. Oh my God . . .' The figure on the card staring up at me had a goat face and bat wings. He held aloft a flaming trident. Two minions, cringing on either side of their master, were chained at the neck. The devil's eyes blazed right out of the card, as if they could actually see me.

'Eugh!' I flung them down. 'Take them away, please, Lilah. Those eyes. They're staring at me!'

'I know what it is,' Delilah reasoned. 'You're worried about Verne turning up and catching us in the act. Well, soon you won't have to worry about him any more.'

'Why not?' Lauren asked.

'What d'you think I invited you two down here for?' Delilah was prowling around the room, idly shuffling the horrible cards between her palms. 'I need my moon maidens, don't I?' As Lauren and I continued to look blank, she blasted at us, 'For the spell, you morons!'

'Spell?' Lauren whimpered. 'What spell?'

'*The* spell. The spell I'm going to cast on Verne, of course.'

'But Lilah, the first one didn't work,' I reminded her, alarm bells ringing. 'Maybe Verne is, like, immune or something.'

Delilah snorted. 'That was kid's stuff. Anyone can get that rubbish out of a book.' She bent to put another log on the fire: wood beetles scrabbled for their lives and the mossy bark threw out a greenish smoke. 'It's the *intent* that matters. If you're going to send out anything, good or bad, you have to mean it, get me?' She thumped her chest with her fist. 'In here. You have to *feel* it in your heart, in the tips of your fingers. You have to *mean* it, think it so hard you can see your thought take shape.'

Delilah's eyes stared so fixedly into mine, I could see her thought already. The monstrous shape of it.

'I know what you're thinking, but I have to do something, don't I, to save my mum? You've seen her. You know. Verne has broken her down bit by bit until she's a zombie. I have to save my mum, and destroying him is the only way to do it.'

What could I say? Delilah might sound fierce, but there were tears in her eyes.

'Delilah,' I whispered, 'you know what happens. You said yourself. You said you'd never do the dark stuff.'

'I know what I said. But if my mother stays like this, I'll go up there one day and she'll be . . . gone, like— Oh —' she cocked her head at the door — 'here he is. Speak of the devil.'

I almost jumped out of the window before I realized who she meant. The Loathsome Verne was home. Thanks to the wind snarling in the chimney, we hadn't even heard the car pull up. Lauren and I waited uneasily. There was a clink of cutlery, the hiss of water from a tap, the clatter of wooden soles on quarry tiles, and then the door opened, and there stood Verne.

'You've burnt something, Delilah,' he said, yanking the tie from his neck. 'The kitchen is full of smoke.'

He looked smaller than I remembered him. He was wearing a black suit which clashed bizarrely with his footwear. Instead of loafing in slippers when he got home from work, Verne favoured clogs. They clacked across the tiles like shiny green beetles. As for his face, maybe it was the firelight that gave him that fanatical stare, like someone who hadn't slept for a week. I noticed the gingery stubble on his chin, the cold blue eyes shining at Delilah. Suddenly I understood exactly how Delilah felt. Why she was prepared to risk everything to get rid of this creep?

'It was only a bit of toast,' she replied. 'By the way, these are my friends, Lauren and Abigail. They're staying for Christmas. Mum said it was OK. It's considered polite to say hello, you know.'

Lauren and I cringed. We didn't want Verne to be polite to us. We didn't want him even to notice us.

'How many logs have you burned on that fire?' was Verne's next question.

'How should I know? I haven't exactly counted them,' Delilah said, with unconvincing bravado. It scared me to see the flicker of fear in her eyes. Delilah, who feared no one, was terrified of her stepfather, of what he might do.

But all he did was consult his watch. 'It is now nine o'clock. If you're going to stay up for much longer, you manage without a fire. Understand me, Delilah? These logs have to last us the winter. I won't have you wantonly wasting fuel, while you gossip all night with your friends.' Turning towards the door, he added, 'And please don't disturb your mother when you come up. She needs her rest.'

The minute he'd gone, Delilah leaped up, sticking out her lower jaw like a deranged Neanderthal and stabbing the middle fingers of both hands towards the ceiling. 'And sweet smegging dreams to you too!'

For all that, I noticed that she didn't burn any more logs that night. When the last one had smouldered into a pile of black ash, she blew out the candles and placed the guard in front of the fireplace.

'Don't worry,' she said, seeing our faces, 'we don't have to stick around here every night. We'll go out, find some action, yeah? And we'll fix him too —' casting venomous glances up the stairs — 'no doubt about that. The moon is dark again in a few days, then we act.'

And, on this far from reassuring note, we followed her up to bed.

Chapter Fifteen
The Devil's List

The nightmare began in an ordinary sort of way. I mean, sharing a bed with Lauren, *that* was nightmare enough. The problem was, Crud Cottage came complete with cruddier furniture. There was one sagging double bed in Delilah's room, with the kind of rock-hard bolsters that put your neck permanently out of joint. Then there was the floor. As hostess, Delilah gamely agreed to take the floor.

'I can sleep anywhere,' she said, shaking out a bed-roll, which apparently Joel had once taken camping. I almost volunteered to sleep on it myself when I heard this, but Delilah, wearing just her pants and DEATH METAL T-shirt, was already slithering inside. 'Valerian root –' she rattled a bottle of pills at us – 'I've just taken some. Mum takes it as an alternative to the stuff the doctor gives her. It's meant to sedate the nervous system. Works a treat if you're a bit, you know, on edge. Want some?'

'No thanks,' Lauren and I chorused in unison. I was on edge all right – a bit too on edge to trust any of Delilah's medication – and Lauren wouldn't take anything that hadn't been OK'd by her allergy therapist. She pulled the dingy-looking sheet up to her chin and glared at me. 'Don't you dare breathe on me, Abbie.'

I glared back and told her not to worry. 'I'm not going anywhere near you. What d'you take me for? Just stick to your side of the bed, OK?'

Finally we decided to mark out our territory with a dividing bolster. This was like sleeping three in a bed, but no matter. Whether it was the journey, the country air, or sheer terror at sleeping under the same roof as Verne, I was knackered. When Delilah snapped out the light around eleven thirty, I expected to fall asleep in no time. I probably would have if the rest of the household hadn't got there before me: within ten minutes of me closing my eyes, a symphony of snoring was all but rocking the foundations of Crud Cottage.

I burrowed my head deeper into my bolster. Verne was the worst. Even asleep he managed to dominate the entire household with his monotonous rumbling. Not far behind him was Delilah. The valerian root must have given her bad dreams. Every now and then she'd fall silent, only to launch into a bout of rapid panting as if she were running from something, or someone, and getting nowhere fast.

Lauren wasn't asleep yet, but she had the fidgets.

I hissed into the darkness, 'What's wrong with you?'

She hissed back, 'Nylon sheets! We always have cotton at home. Man-made fibres upset the PH balance of my skin.'

I murmured into the darkness, 'If I don't get some bloody sleep, your PH balance will be totally up the spout.'

But then, what do you know? Lauren abruptly stopped twitching and went so still I thought she must be dead. That is, until her whimpering sighs joined the baritone Verne and the grunting Delilah in the melody from hell.

Well, that was it. It seemed impossible that anyone

who wasn't actually stone deaf could sleep through this racket. I lay for what seemed like hours, silently cursing the snorers and wishing I'd never got on the train that morning. I even longed for my little bed with the teddy bear duvet and the comforting streetlight outside my window in Smedhurst Road. There were no streetlights at Crud Cottage. Just starlight. And not much of that because of the clouds.

The night deepened. As if things weren't bad enough already, I became aware of other noises surfacing above the rumbles. The rustly, scratching sounds were easy enough to identify – the place was sure to be overrun with mice. And even a townie like me could recognize the screech of an owl when she heard one. It was the soft whinnying just below the window that really got to me.

A horse? In the middle of the night? Maybe it was a wild pony from the moors? Some kind of weird bird that sounded like an old nag? The local lunatic? My imagination?

God knows how long I lay there, listening, trying not to listen, every nerve and muscle tensed to stop myself from strangling Lauren. Soon I was exhausted. I was also thirsty. Suddenly I knew I had to move. I just had to go downstairs for a glass of water.

Gently I lifted the covers, gasping as the chill from the lino gripped my bare feet. I wriggled into my pink cow-girl boots, trying not to think of how they looked with my red jersey pyjamas.

If only I'd brought a torch. Negotiating the twisty stairs in the pitch darkness was quite an undertaking. How did I know where the creaky steps were? Actually they were all creaky. I winced with almost every step and waited, holding my breath. What if I woke the Loathsome Verne? Suppose he came down to the kitchen and discovered me in my jim-jams. The very thought made my mouth go dry with fear.

There is nothing so lonely as being the only person awake in a household. And worse, finding your way around a strange house in the middle of the night. Where the hell was the kitchen light switch? At last my fingers closed over the plastic knob, and the kitchen was illuminated by a shuddery yellow light. Something black and shiny disappeared under the skirting board. What? Did Crud Cottage also have cockroaches?

Suppressing a shudder, I quickly washed out a mug and turned on the tap. Ouch. The pipes began banging like a Caribbean steel band, loud enough to wake the dead. Also the water looked a funny greenish colour. Delilah had mentioned something about the water supply coming from a well. At least it tasted sweet on my tongue, and deliciously cold as it trickled down my parched throat. I guzzled back a whole mugful and sighed. There was nothing for it but to go back to bed. I was so tired, the snores would probably just drift past me and I'd sleep like a baby till morning.

I turned off the kitchen light, then, just as my foot touched the bottom stair, I noticed that the sitting-room door to my right was slightly open. Through the crack I saw a flickering light. I hesitated. Hadn't Delilah turned out all the lights before going to bed? It was more than her life was worth to waste energy. There was no way she'd leave a candle alight either: Crud Cottage was mainly built of timber and it was too much of a fire hazard. Also, I remembered that she'd closed the door. It couldn't be Verne in there – his snores were reverberating through the entire house.

Who then? I glanced up the stairs, calculating. It would take me a second or two to clear them. In a few more seconds I could be in a warm bed, pillow over my head. Safe. Yet somehow I couldn't ignore that flickering light. Someone was in the sitting room, and I just had to know who it was.

Or maybe I already knew. As I pushed at the door, my breath seemed to freeze in my throat.

'You cannot sleep, mistress?' It was as if he'd been expecting me. 'Something troubles your conscience perhaps, hmmm?'

Hopkins was sitting at a desk by the window, writing. The sound of his pen slowly scraping across the page was somehow terrible, as if it was carving its precise, copper-plate characters in my own skin.

'Be so kind, mistress, as to close the door, that we may conduct our meeting in privacy.'

Later I often asked myself why I didn't simply scream my head off for Lauren and Delilah? Why I didn't run? There was nothing to stop me, was there? Yet somehow the air was snuffed from my lungs. My legs felt heavy, the way they'd felt when I had flu a while back, as if I couldn't trust them to support me. As I moved to close the door, the certain knowledge hit me like a bolt of lightning. I knew I would not be able to leave until the witchfinder was satisfied; until he was ready to part with me.

'Come closer, girl.' I shuddered as he laid down his pen. I seemed to glide across the thin rug that covered the quarry tiles, until I was close enough to see the hollow-cheeked face, pitted with old smallpox scars. His eyes were slow and searching. They slid over me, like a couple of snails leaving a slimy track shivering on my skin. 'I have your name here somewhere, here on my Devil's List.' He consulted his ledger.

As I watched his finger travel down the page, I noticed the other book at his elbow – *A Discoverie of Witchcraft*. So it was here. When I'd mentioned it to Delilah, she'd mumbled something about how she'd dumped it just before the move from London.

'Ah, now I see it. Abigail, is it not? Abigail Carter?'

I nodded.

'Carter.' He seemed to savour my surname on his tongue like a choice sweet. 'Then, child, you must be the Carter's daughter.'

'No, sir. My father is an ambulance driver, sir.'

He seemed to pounce on this. 'Amulet, you say?'

'No, *ambulance*. It's like a van that you take sick people to hospital in.'

'You speak of magic, mistress. You speak of the dark arts. Come, come, you can speak freely. You can tell me.' Tapping the nib of his pen on a blotting pad, *peck peck*, like the beak of a bird, he added slyly, 'It has been my experience that girls like yourself feel much improved for making a clean breast of these matters.'

When I remained silent, he leaned across the desk, balancing the pen between his fingers. 'Or mayhap you fear your master is listening?'

'Master?' For some reason I thought he meant Verne.

Then, almost tenderly, like someone unwrapping a fragile present, he explained, 'The devil, my child. Satan.'

174

My fingers clenched. 'I think, sir . . . I think the devil is here already.'

At once the pen dipped into the inkpot, poised ready over the page. Hopkins's tongue darted out, licking a fleck of spit from his lower lip. 'Yes, yes, go on, child. The devil, you say . . . Tell me. Tell me all.'

He misunderstood. I only meant that he was the devil. But then I saw that whatever I said, he would take my words and twist them to suit his own purpose.

'The devil is inside you, is he not?' The pen hesitated over the page. 'Come, girl, you have lain with the devil, have you not? You have lain close enough to feel his fiery breath on your cheek—'

'No,' I burst out. 'No, I have not. I've been lying with Lauren actually.' Irritating she might be, but hardly the devil. And her breath smelled of cheese toasties.

Hopkins laid down his pen, laced his fingers together. 'Lauren? Ah yes, I have her name here also. Your friend, Lauren Alexander. I have seen this Lauren. The child has the mark, does she not? Enough to suckle a thousand familiars.'

'Oh, her eczema, you mean? That's not the mark. It's . . . it's, like, a medical condition.'

I watched, transfixed, as he began extracting some implement from a leather pouch. Something long and sharp. The candlelight dashed sparks from the needle as he turned it thoughtfully between his palms.

'Dost thou know what this is, mistress?'

I shook my head. Watching the needle turn and flash in the light made me feel dazed and dreamy.

''Tis a sticking pin, child. A pin to search out the mark. You witches are most cunning creatures. You hide these teats for your familiars in your most secret parts. I shall use this later, on your friend. We shall see if the child Lauren doth bleed.'

My eyelids drooped. I felt so tired suddenly. 'Please,' I heard myself plead faintly, 'let me go. I want to go to bed.'

'And so you shall, mistress,' he said easily, 'in good time. When you have told me the names of your familiars.'

'My—?'

'If you do not tell me their names, you shall not see your bedchamber this night, Perhaps you shall never see it. Come, come, child – names! I am a patient man, but my patience doth wear thin tonight. Enough of this game, and confess!'

'Let me go. I want to sleep.'

Sleep. It was odd how I could still hear the snores rumbling from the rooms upstairs. The snoring, which had driven me wild earlier, now seemed strangely comforting. Only a few steps away, the others lay sleeping. Yet trapped as I was, they might have been light years away.

Now I was aware of Hopkins's voice, a soft, steady burbling in the background. Perhaps he'd given up on getting me to confess. He seemed to be talking to someone else. Then at last I heard a phrase I understood: 'Walk her!'

The next thing I knew, something had me firmly gripped by both elbows. Something was propelling me round and round, until the room spun. If it hadn't been for my spiky heels catching in the rug, I might have doubted it was real. Lights flickered past me. Sometimes I thought they were candles, sometimes torches. In my confused state I even saw the tarot card devil sitting in

Hopkins's chair, waving his flaming trident and laughing at me.

How long this ordeal lasted I had no idea. Time had no meaning. Each time I drooped, my body swooning into unconsciousness, something dragged me to my feet again, something shrieked in my ear, 'Walk! Walk, witch! Or tell me their names!'

Had I given him names eventually? I must have done. Silly names I remembered reading in some book: Grizzlegump and Spinnikins and Horash. Creatures like freaks of nature: dogs with lizard tails, cats with wings. Griffins. Demons. Familiars.

All I know is, I opened my mouth and words spilled out of their own accord. Any old rubbish that came into my head – names, dreams, nightmares. On and on I babbled. How I'd met the devil only last night, in this very room, and how his eyes had blazed at me like live coals.

'And you made the pact with him, did you not?'

'Oh yeah, we did some deal. I promised him my eternal soul and he promised me all the riches of the kingdom – queendom, sorry – and said I'd be as rich as Posh Spice and twice as beautiful, but that depends on your point of view of course. And then he kissed me, and his breath smelt like he'd been eating *chilli con carne* washed down with Jack Daniels and . . . and . . . and . . .'

What more could you say about the devil?

The pen scratched frantically as it rushed to keep up with the torrent of total garbage spilling from my mouth. How, finally, he let me go, I couldn't afterwards remember. There must have been a point when I ran out of 'devil' stories, and said in a small, pathetic voice, 'Can I go now? My feet hurt.'

And then I was dragging my body upstairs, foraging in the snore-ridden darkness for the warm space in the bed, aware of the lump that was Lauren beside me, Delilah's sleeping bag like some great cocoon by the window. Then, nothing. Oblivion. Deep, dreamless, beautiful sleep.

Chapter Sixteen

The Witchfinder's Women

Next morning I woke to Delilah yelling down my ear, 'Abigail Carter! Wake up, you lazy cow, or we'll go without you.'

My eyes opened to bright splinters of stabbing light. I closed them again. Groaned. 'Oh God. How long? How long have I been asleep?'

'About a hundred years. Listen, *I* was the one who took the valerian root last night, not you. Jesus, are you a heavy sleeper!'

Opening my eyes a crack, I could see Delilah bending over to tie her bootlaces. Lauren sat at the foot of the bed, tugging on a pair of stripy legwarmers and looking accusingly at me. 'I hope you're not ill. I hope you haven't been breathing your buggy old germs over me all night.'

'I haven't got any germs.' Heaving myself into a sitting position, I rubbed the sleep from my eyes, trying to make sense of things. Surely it must be obvious to them, the ordeal I'd been through? No one could go through such an experience and look normal.

I tried to explain. 'Listen, I didn't get any sleep last night. I went downstairs for a drink . . . and . . . and . . . How do I look, by the way?'

'Oh, gorgeous as ever,' Lauren sighed without even looking.

'I don't look, like . . . traumatized?'

'No more than usual,' Lauren said.

'No, seriously – I don't look like I've seen a ghost?'

At last I'd got their attention. They both stopped what they were doing to stare at me. 'I'm trying to tell you.' I ran my fingers through my hair. '*He* was here. He was here, in this house. In the sitting room. He kept me prisoner all night.'

A look of fear, then annoyance, flashed across Delilah's face. This, I knew, was the last thing she wanted to hear. Hardly surprising that she chose to disbelieve me and scoffed, 'Yeah, yeah. We don't want to know about your little fantasies, do we, Lauren? Anyway, shift yourself. We've got a bus to catch. There's one along in an hour, and if we don't catch it, we have to walk into town.'

'Better move it, Abb,' Lauren added. 'You know it takes you a full hour to do your face.'

So they chose to ignore me. Let them. The words 'bus to catch' had the desired effect. Bus to catch. Train to catch. Throwing back the blankets, I was aware of an ache in my thigh, and my feet . . . God – my right foot had developed two throbbing red blisters. 'Lauren, ring the station,' I ordered. 'Find out the times of the trains to London, will you?'

Delilah folded her arms and stared at me. 'Hey, was it something I said?'

Already I was wriggling into my knee-hobbling skirt, ready for my journey back to civilization. 'I'm trying to tell you,' I told Delilah. 'I'm trying to tell you that the Witchfinder General was here last night. You've got to believe me.'

* * *

180

Downstairs, the sitting room looked much as we'd left it last night.

'He was over there at the desk.' I pointed. 'He was writing names in a book. He called it the Devil's List.'

Lauren stood chewing the tips of her fingers. 'Abbie, are you sure that cheese on toast didn't give you nightmares? We haven't seen him for ages. Why should he bother us now, when we haven't done anything to encourage him?'

'What's this?' Something in Delilah's voice made us turn at once. *A Discoverie of Witchcraft* lay open on the table. 'How did that get here?' The colour had drained from her face. 'I dumped it before we moved up here. I put it out for the dustman with next door's rubbish.'

'Well, the dustman obviously never received it,' I said. Then, noticing the leather marker, 'He's marked the page. What is it? What does he want us to see?'

We crowded round the desk. Another woodcut. Of course. Pictures spoke louder than words. An illustration of a woman, naked, wrists bound to her ankles, imps and devils cavorting around her as she was dragged to her ducking.

I shuddered. 'I think he's trying to tell us something.'

Delilah slammed the covers shut and, as she did so, a sharp, metallic object rolled out from the pages. 'What the hell . . . ?'

We stood, our eyes glued to the object as it rolled across the desk.

'Believe me now?' I said quietly. 'He showed me that last night. It's a sticking pin.'

Delilah needed no explanation of what a sticking pin was. 'How bloody dare he!' She hurled it into the empty grate, where it lay glinting in the ashes. 'How dare he come here, when I've got serious work to do? When I have to save my mum.'

Lauren looked puzzled. 'Is that one of your mum's needles, Lilah?'

I explained to her the true, sinister purpose of the pin. 'They searched out your warts, moles, zits, you name it, then pricked them to see if they bled. Actually, er, Lauren, I don't know if I should tell you this, but your name came up last night.'

'My name?'

'Yes, in connection with the sticking pin. He said . . . he said you had enough marks to suckle a thousand familiars.'

'Marks? What did he mean, marks?'

'Um, I think he meant your eczema,' I said, unable to look her in the eye. It was bad enough suffering a horrible skin disease, without being branded a witch because of it.

'He wants to prick me?' Lauren said in a voice faint with terror. She looked a bit green.

Delilah said grimly, 'The victims hardly ever bled in fact. Know why? Because when you're scared practically shitless, right, your blood whooshes into your legs so you can leg it to safety if they—'

'Stop! Please!' Lauren plugged both her ears. 'Don't tell me. I don't want to hear this.'

I took hold of her wrists, forcing her hands away from her ears. 'Lauren, that's why we've got to go back home.' I turned to Delilah. 'I'm sorry. I know it seems like we keep running out on you and—'

'He's got your names.' Delilah folded her arms and

went on coolly, 'You said he'd got all our names on his Devil's List. Running back to Northgate won't make any difference. He'll be there, waiting for you.'

'But what does he want from us?' Lauren howled.

Delilah took hold of the poker and gently nudged the sticking pin further into the ash. 'He wants our fear.' She said this with a kind of cold certainty that sent a chill down my spine.

'Yeah, well, he's got that all right,' I muttered.

Delilah looked me in the eye. 'That's why we've got to be strong. Show him we're not like his other victims. We know our own minds. We're not afraid, right? We're *free.*'

I wasn't convinced. Right now, I felt like those women must have felt three hundred-odd years ago, when even a pimple in the wrong place might see you dangling at the crossroads by moonlight.

'We've got to stick together, right?' Delilah said. 'Right, Lauren? Abbie?'

Before either of us could answer, her mobile bleeped. A text. I held my breath. Supposing it was him? *I know thee for what thou art, witch.*

Then, as Delilah scanned the text, I knew, with one of those rare telepathic flashes you sometimes get, who it was. Even before she said, 'Wouldn't you bloody know it, it's my brother! "Tell Mum I'll be there tomorrow," he says.' Delilah's pale, angry face relaxed into a grin. 'Joel's coming for Christmas, after all.'

Our original plan was to go into town to escape Crud Cottage, the plaintive, blathering sheep and the sodden fields; to be among people again. Suddenly we had a more definite purpose. *Two* definite purposes. One, we were supposed to be shopping ready for Joel's arrival; two, the tables had turned and now *we* were on the trail of Matthew Hopkins.

'It's called knowing your enemy,' Delilah said, prodding us through the heavy glass door of a building that said, MUSEUM AND INFORMATION CENTRE. 'He must have included Ludlow on his countrywide tour of terror, after all. Maybe it's time we found out more about him.'

'What *is* she up to now?' Lauren rolled her eyes, exasperated. Delilah was accosting the tourist woman, who was filling a carousel with postcards. 'I thought we were supposed to be checking out train times?'

'Well, we don't have to do it this afternoon, do we? It's a bit late now.'

'What happened to all that "leaving this very after-noon" stuff?'

I flicked through a booklet on forest walks. 'Yeah, well, there's no, like, urgency.'

Lauren nodded like someone who has just realized she's been betrayed by her most trusted friend. 'I get the picture now. I see it all.'

'You see what all?'

'Just *it*. Your sudden change of heart. Anyway, don't you worry your head about me. I mean, just because some sexist ghoul wants to stick pins in me, so what? Why should you care if I'm about to be got at by a known woman-torturer? Especially when the beloved one is on the way.'

'Come on, Lauren, that's not fair—' I began.

She held up one mittened hand. 'It's OK, really. Just sacrifice your best friend for the sake of your love life, why don't you?'

Delilah stood between us suddenly. 'This is not the time for girlie chats about your love lives, you two. Follow me.'

We followed her through the doorway at the back of the shop which led into the fossil gallery – lumps of rock in glass cases with unreadable labels. Through another door, and here was the town's history, cased and catalogued. Mainly tedious stuff about the glove-manufacturing industry.

However, one of the glass cases displayed some more interesting artefacts. Delilah stabbed her finger against the glass, leaving a dirty smudge. 'Notice,' she said, 'they didn't have any of these charming objects for men.'

The objects on display made me shudder. The scold's bridle, which looked like a primitive pony harness, was intended to shut up a woman when she got a bit gabby. Having been tortured for the past couple of years by a dental brace that made my front teeth look like a cheese grater, I had some idea how this must have felt. Then there was the ducking stool, which looked like a giant battering ram, its oak seat worn smooth by the bottoms of God knows how many poor women. The sticking pin was long enough for a giant kebab.

'Listen to this.' Delilah began reading from the explanatory text: ' "In the autumn of 1647 a dozen women of this town were condemned as witches. Their names were Annette Humphries, Jennet Cross, Eliza Dalton, Alice Nuttall . . ." ' She paused to take a breath, her voice dropping to a hoarse whisper. ' "Sarah Didlick, Sarah Tipton, Susannah Perkins, Hope Perkins, Mary Dodds, Miranda Warburton, Ellie Lurch and Corinna Thorpe." '

185

We were silent for a moment. The sheer numbers took your breath away.

'My God.' I read the names silently to myself. 'Twelve! Twelve women, and look, two of them must have been from the same family.' I pointed to the Perkins sisters.

'Yeah, he was thorough all right. Left no stone unturned. Maybe this town was, like, the wicked city of the west,' Delilah said in a bitter tone. 'Rich pickings.'

'All those women, just put to death like murderers.' This sinister roll-call of names brought Lauren to our side at last. 'It must have been like some kind of cull.'

Delilah went on reading aloud, but in a quieter, more subdued voice – out of respect for her forebears, I supposed. '"These unfortunate women were brought to 'justice' by Matthew Hopkins, the Witchfinder General, during his tour of the Welsh Marches. This being at the height of the witch-hunt mania sweeping across northern Europe. Hopkins is known to have resided at the magistrate's house, Gridford House, during his sojourn in the town of Ludlow."' She turned to us. 'So he *did* come here.'

'Yeah,' I said. 'And now he's back.'

Gridford House was actually marked on the town map, encircled in red ink. As soon as I saw that red ink circle, I knew that Delilah would insist on going there. That this was our fate. The circle had been drawn around us too.

Armed with the map, we set off down the steeply curving Broad Street towards the old town gate. It was already mid-afternoon, one of those grey, murky winter days that hardly seems distinguishable from night. There was no time for the tourist bit; I just had an impression of church spires and teashops, the kind of wobbly black and white buildings you find on a granny's calendar. Flapping woefully along behind Delilah and me in her Afghan coat, Lauren was still carping on about train timetables.

I made excuses for her. 'Lauren's got the heebie-jeebs. She doesn't much fancy becoming a pincushion.'

Not that Delilah cared. She never questioned our obedience as we edged our way in single file beneath the town gate. The pavements narrowed here. My heel caught in the cobbles where they dropped steeply towards the river, and my blisters throbbed. I couldn't help thinking of those twelve condemned women. Had they taken the very same route to the gallows? I imagined them, wrists bound behind their backs, dressed in the coarse linen shifts of lunatics and criminals, being loaded into carts like sacks of potatoes, iron wheels rattling their bones across these cobbles to their doom.

As I trotted along behind Delilah, my thoughts turned to Joel. Was his heart still broken? Did he lie awake thinking of me?

'What are you grinning about?' Lauren wanted to know as we crossed a humpy bridge, the cold grey river whooshing beneath.

'I'm not grinning,' I lied, trying to look at least half as miserable as she did. It was difficult though. The fact was that Hopkins's appearance last night, had done me a favour. What was the point of denying our love, if my name was already on the witchfinder's list? What did it matter about magical gladiolus bulbs and love spells if Hopkins would have me join the likes of Sarah Didlick and co. at some ghostly gallows?

'Yes you are, grinning all over your face like a grinning idiot,' Lauren said, pitching her voice into the famous whine. 'And if you want my opinion, there is nothing whatsoever to grin about. Lilah, how much further? I think my toes have got frostbite, I can't even feel them.'

But Delilah said we were here already, and of course she knew where Gridford House was because she'd passed it every day on the school bus. The bridge had taken us just outside the town, to what had probably been an earlier settlement. To our left was a church and a cluster of ancient cottages with as many chimneys as windows, built from pretty, honeycombed brick. Smoke wafted from these into the bleached stillness of the sky. Ahead of us, the formidable wall of Gridford House ran alongside the old Ludlow road, the dingy, buttressed stonework topped with iron spikes. Delilah stopped a few metres short of the gateway. 'Look at this.'

We looked. A narrow, iron-grilled window was set in the wall, so low it was almost level with the pavement. We took it in turns to peer through the rusted bars. There was nothing to see but an impenetrable darkness. The stink of something dank and dungy like rotted straw was so thick, I drew back hurriedly.

'This must have been a cell.' Delilah's eyes glinted with excitement. 'The lawyers lived in the house, so they probably held the criminals here before their trial.'

Lauren sniffed. 'You mean those women we read about in the museum? Could they have been held here?'

'Definitely, I'd say. Bastards!' Delilah flung a stone through the grille and a pigeon flew warbling into the rafters, in an explosion of feathers. I glanced back the way we'd just walked: the sky and the river seemed to merge in varying tones of grey. It was only three o'clock, yet already the lights of the town shimmered on the other side of the bridge.

'Shall we go back now?' I suggested, trying not to sound too desperate. 'Did you see that teashop place with the cream cakes in the window? We could have chocolate éclairs. Well, Lauren, you could have a toasted teacake or something, without the butter.'

It was no use. Delilah was still hurling stones through the grille and cursing under her breath like a total loony. I looped my scarf, one of Delilah's mother's knitting projects, higher about my face. The air was so cold, it seemed to freeze your blood.

Delilah had produced a marker pen from her pocket. She began scrawling something across the historic stonework beneath the window: GO TO HELL, HOPKINS.

Keen to disassociate ourselves from this wanton vandalism, Lauren and I wandered further along the street, to the gatehouse.

Lauren hissed at me, 'If she gets arrested for defacing the historic gems of Ludlow, we're not with her, OK?'

I tried to make light of it. 'It's only a bit of marker pen, it'll wipe off.'

Just ahead of us, a figure emerged from the stone archway; a weasel-faced youth, wearing a long black raincoat that didn't go with the rest of him. He was more your anorak kind of guy; the grubby kind that goes with zits and crafty eyes. Behind him, in the courtyard, a number of cars were parked in front of a long, low, Tudor-type building.

'What's your mate up to then?' he asked us.

Delilah was on the scene at once. 'What's it to you?'

'What's it to me?' the boy squeaked, proudly flourishing some kind of walkie-talkie radio thing at us. 'Quite a lot, if you want to know. We've got a meeting going on here. This is private property. And I'm the gatekeeper.'

'Oh, that's nice for you.' I grabbed Delilah's elbow. 'Well, come on, Lilah, we've got shopping to do, remember. Nice meeting you,' I called over my shoulder to the weasel.

Some hope. Delilah wasn't budging. 'If you're the gatekeeper, you must know the history of this place,' she figured.

'History? Oh I know all the history, love.'

That did it. Delilah wasn't the sort of girl who takes kindly to being called 'love', especially not by a dork like this, who was possibly only a couple of years older than us.

'Get this straight, I'm not your "love", OK?' Delilah said. 'I just want to know about that window back there with the iron grille. Was that a holding cell or something? This was where the big-wigs hung out, wasn't it? The lawyers and judges and that.'

'What's it to you?' Weasel-faced sneered. 'You don't look like you belong to that historical research society lot. We get a lot of them round here.'

'It's for school,' I said quickly. 'We're doing a project, but, er, thank you, I think we have all the information we need right now, don't we, Lilah? Lilah?'

But 'I'll show yer if you like,' came the unexpected offer. 'I'll show you the room if you're so interested.'

'Oh yeah?' Delilah was suspicious. 'What's in it for you? Why would you want to give us a private showing?'

Weasel-face sighed. ''Cos I'm bored, all right? No

funny business. Makes no difference to me anyway – 's only a room in the outer wall, innit? Take it or leave it.'

'We'll leave it,' I said decisively.

'Yeah, we'll leave it,' Lauren put in. 'We've got to get to the shops before they close, haven't we, Lilah?'

Naturally Delilah ignored us totally. 'Go on then,' she challenged Weasel-face, who was looking around and whistling tunelessly. 'Show us.'

At once the gatekeeper drew a large bunch of keys from his pocket. 'This way, girls.'

Behind his back Delilah stuck up her thumb at Lauren and me. 'Cracked it! Nothing like the personal guided tour, eh?'

We followed Weasel-face back along the inside of the wall. Across the courtyard, lights had come on in the main house. Whoever was living or working there wouldn't be too happy about this impromptu tour, I reckoned.

'Here we are then, the door!' Weasel-face, selecting the right key from the bunch, sounded pleased with himself, like he was about to show us some secret vault with the crown jewels or the lost Ark of the Covenant or something.

Well, you never knew. The door was of thick oak planks. There was a rusted ring handle and a tiny grille at the top, like a peephole. Obviously it hadn't been opened for a long time. Weasel-face had to lean his shoulder against it to make it budge. When it did finally give, he staggered. Dust and darkness rushed at us. A scurrying. Then emptiness. The kind of emptiness that hasn't been disturbed for centuries; that resents intrusion.

'Shit!' Weasel-face brushed cobwebs from the smart

raincoat like they were some kind of personal insult.

'Very interesting.' I lingered in the doorway. 'Can we go now, please, Lilah?' I had no intention of going in there myself.

But Delilah was stomping about like she was a prospective buyer being shown over a new house. 'So, who were the poor sods they kept in here then?'

Still brushing himself off, Weasel-face said piously that it was 'all-sorts probably: petty thieves, murderers, all the no-goods of the town; people that did wrong.'

I sighed. It looked like we'd have to go in there, if only to physically drag Delilah out.

'Watch out for the step,' Weasel-face warned, grinning as I tripped. Luckily Lauren was beside me to catch hold of my arm.

'The bus,' she cried. 'I just thought of the bus, Lilah. You said four o'clock. Your mum'll wonder where we are, won't she?'

'Oh dear.' Weasel-face consulted his watch. 'Reckon you've missed that. Last one, was it? Never mind, eh? You'll just have to spend the night here, won't yer.'

You had to admit he was a fast mover. Crafty too. One minute he was there in the room with us, jingling his keys and brushing his raincoat; the next he was out of the door. *Bang!* The door closed much more easily than it had opened. When it wanged shut, it was as if it had closed on us for ever, sealing us up in total, absolute darkness.

Chapter Seventeen

Prisoners

'Hey! Hey. Puke-face! Let us out of here!' Delilah launched herself at the door. 'What are you, some kind of perv? Come back here!' She turned to Lauren and me. 'Don't worry, he's just trying to scare us. Makes him feel big. He'll come back.'

'You think so?' I wanted to believe her. It was just that I knew he wouldn't come. No one would. This room might have been a padded cell. We might kick and scream ourselves hoarse, but no one would hear us. The thick stone walls muffled every sound.

'Course he will. Hey you!' Delilah pounded some more.

Suddenly I could have throttled her. What had she got us into now, with her big mouth, her bloody-mindedness? Hadn't we got enough problems without being locked up by the town loony?

'I told you,' I said, trying to keep the accusation out of my voice. 'We could have been in that café by now, in the warm. It had an open fire too, I saw it.' For some reason, all I could think of were the chocolate éclairs I'd seen in the teashop window, and how Delilah had deprived me of them.

Lauren began whimpering, 'Oh my God, we're his prisoners. He's locked us up and no one will ever know. He could, you know, keep us here for ever, as sex slaves or something, until we die of hypothermia or some sexually related disease, or . . . or . . . rat bite . . . or . . .'

'Lauren—' I began.

'Or starvation. We could starve to death in here and no one would ever know.'

'Lauren, please, you're not helping.'

'They won't know till they discover our emaciated corpses, and they'll have to identify us from our teeth and everything . . . and—'

'Lauren, shut up!' This was Delilah. 'Holy bloody Hecate, woman, you do go on, don't you? I told you, he'll come back. He's just some saddo with a warped sense of humour. He's not the sex-monster from Mars, for God's sake.'

'How do you know? How can you be sure?'

Lauren had a point. We stood, straining our ears for the sound of returning footsteps, a give-away giggle – anything. But there was only the rumble of passing cars; office workers, shoppers going home to their fires and their hot dinners, lucky sods. The headlights slid over the slimy walls, revealing a mound of sacking, an old cartwheel, a roll of wire-netting. Obviously this place had been used as a store room for some time.

Lauren was scrabbling in her crochet bag with the appliquéd daisies. 'Sex monster or not, I'm calling the police. Now.'

'Hey! Weirdo!' Delilah resumed her kicking. 'This is abduction, right. Fancy ten years in Brixton with all the other pervs? Open this poxy door, you zit-faced shit! Hear me, open—'

She paused, as Lauren's cold little voice announced,

'That's funny. My screen's not lighting up. The battery must be dead.'

Something about this announcement had Delilah and me drawing our own mobiles like guns from holsters. God bless the mobile! It wasn't just for gassing endlessly to your mates; it was a life line. Survival. Escape. Or was it? Even as I punched the ON button, I knew what to expect. No light. No signal. Nothing.

'Is yours the same?' I hardly dared meet Delilah's eye.

She nodded. 'Could be there's no signal down here.'

'Three mobiles,' Lauren said in a small voice, 'and they're all useless.'

'Wait a minute,' Delilah cried. 'Mine's come on. It just lit up. Blimey, I've got a text. Oh . . . oh no . . .' We watched in horror as her grip loosened, her arm drooping, defeated, as the mobile slipped from her hand. It crashed onto the hard stone floor.

'What's the matter? What's it say?' I scrabbled about in the dust and straw, my hands closing at last over the smooth plastic. I turned it over. There on the green illuminated panel was the message. Just one word, shimmering up at me:

WITCH

With a trembling hand, I held it up for Lauren to read. Then, in the next second, we were all three of us hurling ourselves at the door, pounding, kicking, screaming. For suddenly this was no longer a silly game. It was life or death. We just had to get out of there, even if we had to claw our way out.

'Help, please help us!' After two minutes of this, Lauren

195

resorted to shrieking through the roadside window we'd stared through moments ago. Trouble was, this was a road that hardly anyone walked along. There were no shops, no more houses after Gridford House. Only the cars streaming past, windows closed against the cold.

'Shhh! Listen!' Delilah cried out suddenly. 'Hear that?'

We waited. Footsteps. Feet crunching across the gravel forecourt towards us. Someone was coming from the direction of the house. The owner must have heard us and was coming to investigate.

'Thank God!' I leant against the door, my heart beating wildly. 'Thank God, they've heard us.'

Delilah made sure by thumping the door with her fist and yanking herself up so that her face was level with the barred peephole. 'We're in here! Over here!'

What happened next seemed to take place in slow motion. I watched, horrified, as the door ground open with a violent wrench and Delilah, losing her hold, staggered backwards, cursing. There was a tantalizing glimpse of sky, a draught of icy air.

The dark figure stood, framed for a second in the doorway, before the door slammed shut, enfolding us in darkness again.

Hopkins murmured softly, crossing himself. 'So here we have them. May the Lord have mercy on their souls.'

Someone was screaming. Lauren. I clamped my hands to my ears. 'Lauren, stop, for God's sake!' Then, when she did, I wished she hadn't. The silence was filled with whispers. Urgent. Despairing. Women, girls whispering, hissing to each other. What? Words of comfort? Schemes? Plans for escape? No . . . *prayers*, I realized. The ghosts of

Hopkins's victims crowded all around us, whispering their prayers.

'See how they are like fleas on a dog? Discover one, and a dozen more will follow. This place must be the very pit of hell,' Hopkins commented as if to a bystander. He was drawing leather gauntlets from his hands with a slow, luxurious movement. 'Witness the foul odour of these miserable creatures. I own that swine in the farmyard do smell sweeter than these abominations of womankind.'

You could see what he meant. Cringing back against the wall, I smelt it too. Stale sweat, the salt-fish scent of blood, human shit, urine. The ripe animal stench of fear itself.

Hopkins was flapping a square of white linen, as if to ward off contamination. Holding it to his long nose, he remarked that the stench of burning flesh would soon drive these other putrid odours out. 'There is nothing so efficacious as fire for cleansing the unclean spirit,' he mused. 'How sweetly the flesh doth sizzle. How it drizzles and spits. Especially when it be witch-flesh.'

Someone was reciting the Lord's Prayer. *Our Father, which art in Heaven, hallowed be Thy name* . . . but this was as far as it got. Over and over and over the prayer was muttered, as if repetition of the first part would bring the rest. Yet, when Hopkins lit the two candles, I could see no one. Only us three. Somehow we'd ended up in the furthest corner, by the iron grille. Lauren was hugging herself and weeping, a kind of fearful snivel like a kid waking from a nightmare.

'What ails the child? I wonder,' Hopkins said. He had the burr to his voice of a country farmer; down-to-earth, concerned with his crops. That was the chilling thing –

it was business as usual for Hopkins. A job to be done. Dirty work, but someone had to do it. He beckoned impatiently. 'Come forward, child, that I may see you. You have nothing to fear, unless the devil be your master.'

'Stay where you are,' Delilah all but growled from her corner. 'Don't move an inch.'

But just like I had the night before, Lauren seemed to glide across the space between herself and Hopkins as if sleepwalking.

Hopkins studied her. He sat at a rough table that surely hadn't been there when we came in? The great book was open in front of him again. The Devil's List.

'Lauren Alexander – is that not your name, child?' His pen scratched across the page as she nodded. Then he looked up into her face. I almost cried out. His face was yellow in the light, like old candle-wax.

'Now tell me true, my maid, Beelzebub and Finnegan are your familiars, are they not? You suckle them on all the numerous marks about your person, do you not? The devil's own grow fat upon your nourishment.'

The sighs again. Whispers. Faint fluttering vibrations all about me, as if the room were full of trapped birds. I fixed my gaze on Delilah, good old fuming flesh-and-blood Delilah, willing her to get us out of this. Alive. But she was strangely quiet, her face set, mask-like, in the shadow.

Lauren was protesting faintly, 'I don't know what you mean. I don't know any Finnegan. I haven't got any familiars.'

Poor Lauren. This sight of her cringing before Hopkins was too much for me. 'She can't keep pets anyway,' I blurted out. 'Not even a canary. She's allergic to fur. And feathers and stuff.'

'Silence, girl,' Hopkins said in that chilling, even tone. He tapped the book in front of him. 'I have *your* confession before me. Already your fate is sealed by your own tongue. The names of your familiars are here immortalized in print.'

'They are?' Vaguely I remembered, as if chasing a dream, the names I'd blurted out last night – any old rubbish that came into my head.

'You can't do this, you know.' Delilah was scathing. 'You can't scare us. You can't persecute us. And you're not going to stop me.'

Hopkins waved a hand for silence. Suddenly he was more interested in Delilah than me. '*Delilah* – how came you by that harlot's name, girl, hmmm?'

Delilah shrugged. 'My mum got it out of some book, I expect.'

'You are the leader of this most foul coven, are you not? I have heard with mine own ears, you speak in the devil's tongue. Such curses as would taint the very air.'

Delilah's breath was harsh, defiant. She folded her arms. 'Listen, I didn't come here to be interrogated by some old spook, right. Why don't you answer me a few questions for a change? Like how many innocent women did you murder? Hundreds? Thousands?' She made a spluttering sound of contempt, before waving her arm at him. 'Why don't you just go back to hell, where you belong? You can't hurt us. Didn't you know? Witchcraft – it's no longer a crime.'

'That's true,' I cried. 'It's just, like, this really cool hobby. There's no harm in it.'

'No harm, you say? Then what is this, I wonder, mistress?'

When Delilah waved her arm, I'd noticed something drop from her hand, as if she'd accidentally pulled something from her coat pocket. Now Hopkins seized it, held it in his palm. At first it was hard to make out in the dim light. It looked like a bit of old rag, or a scarf maybe. But the way the witchfinder was nodding, I knew it must be more than just any old rag. There was something special about it. Something incriminating.

'Truly, this is the devil's work,' Hopkins said.

'Give it back.' There was an edge of panic to Delilah's voice that I hadn't heard before. 'It's mine. Give it back now.'

'You think I would be so foolish, child? Here we have it – evidence. Proof of your diabolical tricks. You think you are special, is that it, hmmmm? You think yourself too clever to join the names upon the Devil's List?'

Then he began to name them – all those women we'd read about earlier in the museum: 'You think the devil favours you, child, above your sisters, Alice Nuttall, Eliza Dalton, Sarah Didlick . . .'

The horrible roll-call of names continued as if he were actually summoning them, those women, calling up their souls like birds from their perches. The lost souls crowded about us, weeping and wailing and denying their guilt. The very walls of the room seemed to drip with their tears. So overwhelming was this feeling of fear and despair that I had to clutch my hands to my head, as if to ward them off.

Delilah's voice was quietly menacing. 'That's *my* property. Give it back.'

Hopkins stood up slowly, as if his back were stiff. He walked a few steps away from us, slapping the rag-thing against his other palm as if keeping time. 'This poppet that is so important to you, this cloth you keep about your person – confess its uses, child. I tell thee, thy diabolical sorceries will not surprise me. I know the devil's works like the fingers of mine own hand.'

'Whatever.' Delilah actually took a step towards him. 'If that's what you want, me and Satan are an item, right. I admit, I'm Delilah, Bride of Satan. Now give me the rag!'

'Delilah! What on earth?'

Light rushed in on us suddenly, blindingly. Dazzled, I closed my eyes tight, then opened them again. The door hung open, and with the clean blast of air, the stench of fear and the whispers flew out, sucked up like feathers. No longer a cell but an old store room, smelling of rotten vegetables and sacking. Security lights beaming across the gravelled forecourt like the yellow brick road; two men flashing torches into our shocked faces.

'This is my stepdaughter,' Verne's voice said. 'What on earth is going on here?'

The gatekeeper began to gibber. 'I'm sorry, sir, I never knew you was related, like. She never told me. I caught her, like, scribbling on the wall. Foul language, sir. They wanted to see the cell. I thought they was snooping. I thought I'd teach them a lesson, like. I was gonna come and tell you, sir, straight away, like, but then I got called away to look at—'

'I'm not interested in your half-baked excuses, boy. You've got a radio, haven't you? Why didn't you contact me? At once?'

God knows what Delilah felt at that moment. Personally I never imagined I'd be so glad to see Verne, standing there, an overcoat hung over his black preacherman suit. I could have wept; kissed his shiny black thick-soled loafers. Next to the witchfinder, Verne was a pussycat. Well, he was human at least.

Lauren and I didn't hang about. We stumbled out into the air, too dazed to speak; just relieved to see the sky, stars, hear the reassuring rumble of traffic from the road.

'Where is that wretched girl now?' Verne said, exasperated.

'Delilah?' I glanced back over my shoulder. Unbelievably, she was still in there; in the cell. She looked like she was searching for something.

'Delilah, get out of there this minute!' Verne's voice hissed with suppressed rage. I sensed that every muscle was clenched tight to keep from hitting her. He took hold of her wrist, half dragging her across the courtyard to where his car was parked.

'Ow, my arm! You've twisted my arm!' Delilah blazed.

Burrowing into the back seat next to her, Lauren and I were subdued, like criminals. Or naughty girls. Naughty girls who needed to be punished. It struck me suddenly that this was just how the witchfinder made us feel.

'How dare you? How dare you come to my headquarters?' Verne hissed through his teeth. He accelerated through the arch, nearly flattening the cringing gatekeeper. 'What was your game, eh, Delilah? Some kind of joke, was it? Defacing religious property?'

'Religious property?' Delilah was still rubbing her arm. I could tell she was genuinely shocked. 'What are you on about? I didn't know this was your precious

HQ. I'd never have brought my friends here if I had.'

For someone so hot on the environment and fossil fuels and so on, Verne drove like a maniac. He hit the brake so hard on a sharp bend I thought I smelled burning. Hurtling along the spaghetti twist of lanes, trees looming in the headlights, he kept up his droning monologue.

How news of Delilah's delinquency would all be round the Brethren in no time, and didn't she know he had a reputation to think of? And what about her mother, a sick woman? Had she no regard for her? The trouble was, Verne said, her mother had been too soft and now the damage was done. Delilah was destined for a life of petty crime, whoredom and general no-goodness and there was not much to be done about it.

'I've done my best, God knows,' Verne said as we lurched to a halt outside Crud Cottage. 'But you and that wretched brother of yours are enough to try the patience of a saint.'

There was soup waiting for us inside. Delilah's mother had dragged herself out of bed to make it. Personally I would have preferred tomato, out of a tin, but this was more of a broth, yellow with veggie bits in it. We ate in silence, apart from the slurping, and went straight to bed like disgraced children, me with a scalded tongue and my legs aching like they were about to drop off any minute; Lauren vowing that she was leaving first thing in the morning.

'And don't try and stop me, Abbie.'

'Oh yeah, like I could stop anyone with this leg-ache. You're not the only one suffering, you know.' I nodded in the direction of the bathroom, where Delilah was brushing her teeth. 'Think of poor Lilah, stuck here with a ghoul, a religious nut and a sick mother. Think how she feels.'

Lauren tugged the bedclothes over to her side and turned her back on me. 'Don't ask me to be sympathetic, please. My sympathy reserves are dried up right now.'

'Yeah, well, Lauren, your compassion fatigue is, like, legendary.' I tugged a corner of blanket back, drawing my knees up to my chin and trying to massage my thigh. Just like the night before, I felt I like I'd been on some marathon walk, John o'Groats to Land's End, then back again.

Delilah came in from the bathroom. She had a strange gleam in her eye.

'Lilah, d'you mind if we just say goodnight?' I said. 'I mean, I'd rather we didn't talk about you know who. Not until daylight at least.'

Delilah said that was fine with her, we'd discuss it in the morning. In fact she sounded so cool, I was suspicious. You'd think she'd be a bit unhinged by now. Facing up to both the devil incarnate and the Loathsome Verne in one night was enough to de-rail anyone. Or maybe she felt like I did: too damn exhausted to be scared any more, wanting only to sleep.

Not quite yet, though. Just before she turned out the light and crawled into her sleeping bag, I noticed her holding something against her cheek. That cloth again. The manky old bit of rag that had so interested Hopkins; the one he'd actually held, caressed in his ghostly torturer's fingers. That was what she'd been scrabbling about for in the cell when Verne appeared. The precious rag. Maybe she really was finally losing her marbles?

I couldn't help murmuring in the darkness, 'Lilah, what *is* that thing?'

Silence. She was considering whether to tell me or not, I knew. Finally she croaked sleepily from the depths of her sleeping bag, 'What does it look like?'

'It looks . . .' I paused. 'It looks like your comfort-rag – you know, like little kids take to bed with them.'

Silence again. Then, 'I can assure you, this is no comfort-rag.'

I had to be content with that, because it was obvious from her breathing that she was asleep, out like a light. And I didn't take long to follow suit. I slept and dreamt that Verne and Hopkins were the same person and that I was in a dark wood, calling and calling for Joel. But Joel never came.

Chapter Eighteen

Christmas Spirit at Crud Cottage

Verne left Crud Cottage at first light.

'Busy time of year for old Verne,' Delilah said, over our breakfast of porridge. 'All that preaching – it could give a person a right sore throat.'

I didn't ask what she meant by this. Personally, after last night I didn't want to know. To say my nerves were, like, on edge, was an understatement. And as for Lauren's, they had gone over the edge already, and were lying on their backs with their legs in the air.

'We've got to get out of here,' were her first words to me the minute she opened her eyes. 'I can't stay another hour – no, another minute, in this place.'

The omens weren't good, I had to admit. Great inky blobs of cloud smudging the horizon. A solitary magpie chittering from the knackered old damson tree in the front garden. Also, consulting my handy star guide, I saw that the sun had just slipped out of fun-loving Sagittarius and into grouchy old Capricorn.

I mentioned this to Delilah, but she was busy heaving a pile of logs into the basket by the range and didn't hear me.

It was incredible. I mean, you'd have thought our incarceration in the black hole with the witchfinder and his poor tortured victims would have been a major topic of conversation. But, oh no. Delilah was raving on about Christmas decorations; holly and ivy and all that stuff.

'We're going to fill the house with it,' she said breathlessly. 'Verne won't like it. The Puritan Brethren are dead against such disgusting heathen excesses. Those are Verne's words, by the way. But what the hell. He won't have a lot to say about it; not by the time I've finished with him.'

Oh no? I felt it my duty to bring her back on track. 'Delilah?' I spread a thin layer of runny home-made marmalade on my toast. 'Delilah, about last night . . .'

'What about it?'

'What about it!?' Lauren and I chorused incredulously.

'I think we have to, like, discuss it.' I waved the knife at her. 'Because we have a major situation here. Being haunted is one thing, but haunted to death is another. Don't you think?'

Delilah scoffed. How could anyone be haunted to death? she wanted to know.

'I mean that he wants us dead. Delilah, he's after our blood.'

'Yes, and he's not getting mine,' Lauren wailed, pushing her porridge away in disgust.

Outnumbered, Delilah sat stubbornly twiddling her nose-ring. 'He's only as powerful as you want him to be. He's just a tormented soul, you know. I mean, imagine, still doing the day job after you're dead. He's what you might call a workaholic – hah!' She gave a rare burst of laughter at her own joke.

Actually this wasn't funny. Sometime in the early hours I'd woken up, and what I thought of was so scary, I couldn't sleep again. 'Yeah, workaholic. Lilah, you know the thing we saw in the museum, about the arrest of a dozen women?'

'What of it?'

'Well, it struck me suddenly last night. 'Isn't *thirteen* the number of people you need for a witch's coven?'

'So?'

'Well, just supposing it was, like, Hopkins's major ambition to uncover an entire coven. Say he was sick of all that riding around from town to town and only coming up with a measly two or three women a shot. OK, he got twenty shillings a town, but maybe he got some kind of major bonus for a whole coven, right?'

'You mean like targets.' Delilah squinted at me, like she was getting interested.

'Something like that. Some kind of efficiency target. Didn't you hear him say that thing about the fleas on a dog? "Find one," he said, "and a dozen more will follow, like the fleas on a dog."'

Lauren began to frantically scratch under her arm. 'Will you shut up about fleas, please?'

'So anyway, the last time he came to Ludlow in 1647, he managed to haul in a dozen women. What happened to the thirteenth? There had to be one more woman to complete the coven, don't you see? Wouldn't it be a major let-down for him, if he was one short? He'd have to come back, wouldn't he, to finish the job?'

'You mean –' Lauren left off scratching – 'he's looking for one more, as in one of *us*?'

I nodded. 'I think so, yes. That's what this list is all about: the questioning, the evidence. See, Delilah is the prime candidate – because of your spells, Lilah, obviously, and your fiendish plans for Verne. But now he's confused, because here we are, you and me, Lauren. You with your "marks", and me with my "stargazing", as he would call it.'

'Yes, but what about Northgate?' Lauren said. 'He was hanging around us in London. Why would Ludlow be such a big deal suddenly?'

This, I had to admit, gave me pause for thought. 'I'm not sure. It could be that your rituals attracted him in the first place, Lilah, and where you lived wouldn't have made any difference. Then he must have followed us all here, to Shropshire, to the very town where he'd nabbed a record amount of women. Ludlow could have been the highlight of his career, who knows? Twelve witches in one town must have been pretty good going.'

'So you mean, he's re-living his moment of glory?' Lauren said.

'Kind of. But he's just remembered about the missing thirteenth witch.' I began to feel really clever suddenly, as it all began to fit. 'I mean, why do ghosts exist in the first place? Why is any restless spirit, like, *restless*? Because they have unfinished business, that's why. Hopkins has unfinished business in this town.'

All the time I'd been talking, Delilah had been engrossed with twisting the rings on her fingers like she was trying to squeeze them over her knuckles. I knew what was wrong. She'd cast me in the role of faithful handmaiden, and handmaidens are not supposed to have theories of their own. It was kind of a power-thing.

'So,' she said in her 'I am not persuaded' voice, 'where does that leave us?'

I shrugged. 'In the shit, I guess. Unless . . .'

'Unless?' Her head went up, her eyes challenging me to state the obvious.

'Unless we renounce our wicked ways,' I snickered, trying to make light of it. I mean, who was I to preach to Delilah? She'd had enough preaching to put up with.

'Get this straight. I'm not renouncing anything, right?' Delilah took a couple of steps towards me, a mad look in her eye.

'Whatever – whatever you say.'

'If all this is too much for you, you and Lauren, if you want out, then who am I to keep you here?' She nodded meaningfully at the front door. 'Your choice.'

I almost panicked. I mean, what kind of choice was that, when later that day my made-in-heaven love-match would be walking right through that same door?

'You think we'd chicken out now?' Back-pedalling madly, I tried to reassure her. 'Lilah, what do you take us for? We're your buddies, right? You think we'd just sneak away like . . . like two sneaks, and leave you to become that girl-hating ghoul's thirteenth victim? Hah! As if! We wouldn't dream of it, would we, Lauren? I said, *Would we*, Lauren?'

No, said Lauren, we wouldn't. Not very convincingly, I might add.

But thankfully this seemed to placate Delilah. 'I'll admit you've got a point,' she said grudgingly, flicking bits of black nail polish from her nails over the kitchen floor. 'About the coven and that. But I've just got this hunch, and I know it might be hard for you two to get your heads around, but I think it's Verne who attracts him – you know, the original Creep. They're kindred spirits. I've got this gut feeling that once Verne is gone then Hopkins will follow.'

★ ★ ★

210

We didn't question her about the 'once Verne is gone' bit. It seemed best not to. However, the minute Delilah stomped upstairs with her mother's breakfast tray, Lauren was on her mobile, frantically dialling home. I only caught certain phrases, thanks to her pacing around the kitchen: 'She what? . . . She did what? . . . Oh God. This is so unfair! . . . Yeah, put her on . . . Hi, Mum . . . But how did you do that, for God's sake? Yeah . . . Yeah . . . Yeah, of course, but . . . Well, OK, but . . . OK, bye.'

'What was all that about?' I said when she'd finished.

Lauren clutched at the tiny silver cross about her neck. 'My bloody mother got carried away at the Muzbelle Christmas special. She only dislocated her pelvis! And now she's in bed, with Harv-wit waiting on her hand and foot. Then I tell her it's like Cold Comfort Farm here, and she says a bit of hardship won't hurt me for once. Can you believe that? My own mother! Be thankful your pelvis is in good shape, she says, and if I do come home, they'll probably just be having a takeaway or something, because Christmas is cancelled as far as she's concerned. Charming, don't you think? I mean, simply bloody awesome.'

'Lauren, can you, like, calm down?'

'Calm down?' She hugged herself, running her hands up and down her arms, 'How can I? I feel like I'm pricking all over; as if that thing last night is sticking great long invisible pins into me. I think I'm going to crack up, if—'

'OK, OK. Look, I'll check out my parents if it makes you feel better. If the worst comes to the worst, we can go home to my place.'

I was in two minds as I dialled my number. What about my pledge to Delilah? And what about Joel? I

211

desperately needed to see him, to explain. But just supposing Verne took a benny and went totally berserk with that giant axe on the woodpile? It might be wise to have an escape route lined up, just in case.

At first I thought I'd rung the wrong number. It was Mrs Croop who answered the call. 'Oooh, it's you, lovey. I'm just keeping an eye on the place, ducks, for your mum and dad. Your mum said to switch the gas fire on in case the pipes freeze.'

It turned out that my parents had decided to spend Christmas at my Aunty Christine's in Weston-super-Mare.

'They thought they might be a bit lonely here on their ownsomes, ducks. They tried to call you but they couldn't get through.' Mrs Croop went on cackling until I could stand it no more and pressed the OFF switch.

It was my turn to whinge at Lauren. 'I turn my back for five minutes and what happens?'

Lauren raised her eyebrows. 'Don't tell me your mother's dislocated her pelvis too?'

'My parents get a life, is what happens. They didn't waste any time, did they?'

'So,' Lauren said, looking like someone on a desert island watching the last ship sail over the horizon. 'Looks like we're stuck here then.'

'Looks like it. Unless you've got the dosh for a bed and brekky in town?'

It turned out that we had fifty pounds between us, but this we decided we should save for an emergency. And we weren't quite at the 'emergency' state yet. Were we?

★　★　★

Resigned now to staying with Delilah's dysfunctional family for Christmas, Lauren and I resolved to make the best of it. The afternoon we'd just spent tramping about the woods gathering holly and mistletoe had helped to chase away last night's shadows. Lauren even had a glow to her cheeks as she rolled out pastry for mince pies in the kitchen. Delilah handed me fir branches to hang above the fireplace – me, who even got vertigo wearing high heels, now stretching precariously from the top rung of the ladder.

'There, how does that look?'

'Tacky,' Delilah said. 'Just how I like it.'

I leant back to admire the luxuriant swags of greenery, hung with streamers, decked with fairy lights. The silver baubles, Delilah informed me, were really 'witch balls'.

'That's where the idea came from. They used to stuff them with herbs to scent the room and ward off germs and evil spirits and stuff.'

'Take care you don't fall,' Delilah's mother warned me from her armchair. She was actually out of bed at last, with a book and a shawl over her knees, but *up*; even laughing as Lilah and I roared along to the cheesy *Christmas Hits* CD, Lilah in her terrible off-key voice: '*And so this is Christmas, and what have you done?* Don't ask,' she added, cupping a hand to her mouth.

With the candles lit and the whole place smelling like a pine forest, Crud Cottage was almost cosy. What with this and the prospect of my heart's desire arriving any minute now, it was all too easy to forget what Delilah had said earlier, in the woods. All that stuff about it being 'a good night for her ritual'. 'You don't need to worry,' she'd told us, her eyes shining. 'I know how to do it. I know how to get rid of Verne and Hopkins, whoosh! In one fell swoop. Sorted!' And she drew her finger across her throat to demonstrate.

I wiped this unwholesome vision from my mind as Lauren popped her head round the door. 'I don't suppose there's any vegetarian mincemeat, is there? The other stuff has that disgusting animal suet in it.'

'It won't kill you, will it?' Delilah said, sweeping up evergreen debris from the quarry tiles.

'It might. I'd rather not take the risk actually.'

This one sentence sent Delilah and me off into such a spasm of giggles, I dropped a sprig of holly on Lauren's head.

Lauren removed it with a piqued expression. 'Did I say something funny?'

'No.' I hung onto the ladder with one hand, clasping my stomach with the other. 'No, you just *are* funny, Lauren. It's a gift. You should be proud.'

Serve me right really. There I was, guffawing at Lauren like an old donkey, holly wreaths swagged around my neck, when *he* walked in. Him. My heart throb! My sweet, my sexy, floppy-haired fittie in all his total gorgeousness!

The shock was so great, it was all I could do not to fall off the ladder and make a total ass of myself. It was bad enough as it was. If you've ever tried to descend a ladder with a degree of elegance you'll know what I mean. Coming backwards down a ladder is hardly a flattering view with which to greet your long-lost amour, and is guaranteed to make your bum look twice its normal size.

'I got the earlier train,' was all Joel said, frowning. 'Where shall I dump these then?'

The parcels, he meant. You could hardly see him for

parcels. Mostly food parcels, it looked like. My mouth filled with juices as I identified a cartwheel of Wensleydale cheese, a huge Christmas pudding.

But then he was lost to sight, what with all the hugging going on. His mother first, then Delilah, dancing him round the room in time to 'Here Comes Santa Claus'. Cheesy stuff. Yet I had to stifle an impulse to rush over and join in. Sidling tactfully out into the kitchen, I offered to help Lauren roll pastry instead.

'Let you loose with a rolling pin?' Lauren sniffed. 'You must be joking. You could do that washing up though,' she added graciously.

'Thanks.' I bent over the sink, sneaking shy glimpses of Joel through the half-open door. Joel, brown hair flopping in his face, eyes warm with laughter, scuffling with Delilah across a carpet of pine needles. 'Get off me, woman!' He winced painfully. 'Control yourself.'

Then suddenly, shooting me a glance across Delilah's dreadlocks, he said simply, 'Abbie.'

I stood foolishly holding the sieve. 'Joel.'

We held each other's gaze. I don't know how long for – time ceased to exist. Then Delilah scoffed impatiently, 'Well, give her a Chrissie kiss, you dork!'

She all but shoved him into the kitchen, where he stood, eyes flickering away from me. I tried out a smile, but it felt awkward on my face, like a curled-up cater-pillar. It was humiliating, waiting for him to kiss me, with everyone watching. I mean, a gentlemanly peck would have been something. But all he did was stick his finger in the mincemeat jar and lick it.

'How long before these are ready then?' he murmured vaguely in Lauren's direction.

About half an hour, Lauren estimated. Offering to make tea as well, she tactfully pushed the door to between us and Joel, so he could have his family reunion in privacy.

'You've got a blob of mincemeat on your chin,' she informed me kindly. 'No wonder he didn't kiss you.'

I bent over the pastry bowl, head swimming with misery. 'Thank you, Lauren, but it's not that. It's because he thinks I'm a cold-hearted bitch.' I looked up at her. 'Oh, how am I going to explain to him?'

'Love will find a way no doubt,' Lauren said with more than a touch of sourness, as she put the kettle on.

If love was going to find a way, it was taking its time about it. Later, as we had the tea and Lauren's mince pies together in the sitting room, Joel ignored me. He was sitting on the arm of his mother's chair, intent on some map. Australia probably. The Antipodes. Tracing out his proposed itinerary, his thoughts already miles away from me.

Being ignored like this was so painful, I was almost glad when Delilah rammed her red devil beanie over her head, and grabbed her greatcoat.

'We're off then, Mum. Won't be long. Got stuff to do.'

Her mother didn't have time to question this. I mean, what kind of 'stuff' could anyone find to do on a bone-freezing night in the wilds of nowhere, unless it was badger-watching or something? Joel didn't even glance up from the map, as Lauren and I struggled into our arctic explorer gear and followed Delilah out into the ice-gripped darkness.

'He hates me,' I moaned to Lauren. 'He hates the sight

of me. He wouldn't care if I was sucked into a black hole.'

'Well, you'll soon find out,' Lauren muttered from the depths of her scarf, 'because we're probably about to fall down one any minute now.'

Chapter Nineteen

A Ritual Too Far

It was hard to get used to how dark the dark actually is in the country. This was nothing like our gladiolus-planting in Bromfield Park, dim and dream-like under a yellow-lit city sky. The moon had dwindled to no more than a cheese-paring above the wood. An old waning moon, gripped in the icy stillness.

We made our way down the track, with only Delilah's iffy torch to keep us from falling down potholes and breaking our legs. Feeling through the thin soles of my pink boots, I negotiated rocks and ridges and lethal patches of ice.

'Are you sure this is a good idea, Lilah?' I called ahead, my voice mousy thin in the freezing air. 'I mean, whatever your idea *is*.'

I had a vague idea, of course. Something to do with Verne. And it wasn't good. My only hope was that the dodgy landscape, and the fact that icicles were forming on branches even as we looked, would curb her ambitions a bit. Maybe a quick curse or two in the direction of the moon would be all it took. But who was I kidding? Already, Delilah was clambering up the incline that twisted right into the trees. In daylight there was a sort of track visible that skirted the edge of a boggy field.

'If we follow her in there, we're done for,' Lauren

whimpered. 'Imagine if I had to go home with a broken neck, when my mother's pelvis is up the creek?'

'Just don't break it, OK? And watch out for cow-pats, and sheep's doo-doos, because I think I just trod in something.'

We held onto each other's arms as we turned into the trees. While Delilah blundered on ahead like an armoured tank, Lauren and I took small, mincing steps, following the wavering torchlight.

'Ow!' Lauren yelped as a branch attempted to scalp her, snatching from her head the Peruvian helmet which I'd begun to think was glued on. She clutched it back again. 'See that? I nearly lost an eye.'

'Yeah, but you didn't, did you?' I was having my own problems. The tree trunk I'd just grabbed to save myself from falling was covered with green, slimy stuff. 'Think yourself lucky. My hand is covered in frog snot or something.'

'Why do we have to come out here in the first place?' Lauren grumbled. 'Why couldn't we do it in her bedroom?'

'Because real, serious witches do their thing in the open air, don't they? Among all the natural elements and stuff. Stark naked usually,' I added, relieved that Delilah hadn't gone that far.

It was better to keep talking. When you stopped you heard the noises coming from the darker thickness of the wood. It sounded like it was all action in there – there were inexplicable rustlings and sighings and snappings. Badgers probably, snuffling in the leaf mould, or whatever it was badgers did in the dead of night. This was *their* element, not ours.

'What kind of sound do badgers make?' I asked Lauren.

'Badgers? How should I know?'

'Do they – I mean, do you think they might make a whispering sort of sound?'

It wasn't that I was imagining things. It was just that my ears were hearing things my brain would rather not know about. Like the voices I'd heard in that cell last night. That barely audible rush of whispers like the wind ruffling through long grasses.

Be warned, Abigail . . . He's coming . . . He's on your trail . . . He'll bind you . . . Prick you . . . He'll take you to the water . . .

'OK, this is far enough.' Delilah beckoned us on with her torch to where the trees thinned slightly. To one side of us, the wind whooped freely across the open expanse of fields. Somewhere in the darkness a solitary sheep was bleating uneasily, as if it sensed trouble.

'Are you two up for this?' Delilah wanted to know. She shone her torch over our faces, as if checking. As if she didn't trust us suddenly.

'Depends what it is.' Lauren blinked in the torchlight. 'I mean, you haven't really told us yet.'

'Told you what? You have to take what comes, understand? This is magic, not rocket science. You have to be ready for anything.' Delilah swung her arms wide as if to test the extent of the space about us. 'Listen, I'm going to cast the circle, like normal. Just remember, whatever happens, you stay inside it, right?'

'Whatever happens? You mean if . . .' I'd been going to say 'if he comes'. But there was no need. We all knew what the risks were.

'Just remember, the circle's for our protection.' Delilah passed me her torch before drawing the *athame* from its sheath. 'I'm telling you this in case. Nothing can harm us, right. Not when we've got the protection of the Ancient Ones.'

This didn't exactly fill me with confidence, because personally I doubted the Ancient Ones were up to the job. And frankly, I didn't think I could survive another visit from the man in the hat.

'Promise me one thing, Lilah, please,' I blurted, before she could go into ritual mode. 'I know that you have to see this through for your mum's sake, and that's why we're helping you. But it's just a one-off, OK? Whatever happens with your stepdad after this . . . please – no more rituals.'

'No problem,' Delilah said vaguely. She was making random patterns in the night air with the *athame*, as if she was warming up for the real thing, testing its blade. She added that there wouldn't be any need for more, anyway, 'because I intend to finish Verne for good.'

This time, when she drew the pentagram and cast the circle, she told Lauren and me to close our eyes. I'm not sure why. But deprived of sight, my imagination went into overdrive and filled in the blanks. For a start, there was something different about the Ancient Ones. Now, when Delilah called up the elements, her old wise-woman voice battling to make itself heard against the wind, you could almost *hear* them, like aged relatives dragging slippered feet.

With my eyes closed I also became more aware of the cold. The way it fingered its way inside my jacket. My internal organs were freezing like chunks of breaded fish.

My ears stung. The blobby tip of my nose, always a hazard in such weather, was surely purple by now.

Meanwhile Delilah was muttering what sounded like a demented prayer, which consisted mostly of names: Hecate, Cybele, Ceridwen . . . Blimey, who had she not called up? I whispered to Lauren, 'They're all here tonight. It's like a girls' night out for the moon goddesses.'

But my joke went down like a lead balloon. At least, Lauren didn't respond. I began to get restless and opened my eyes. Just a peek. Just enough to make out Delilah in her statue-like pose. Her head was flung back, arms outstretched. She was holding out her hands, cupping her palms as if making some sort of offering to the moon. There was something in them. My eyes, straining to penetrate the shield of darkness, made out shapes, but not the detail. That 'blob-shape' in her hands might be anything, but – wasn't it? Yes – my throat squeezed tight. That rag again! I realized now that the rag must somehow be connected to Verne. An old handkerchief maybe? He always had one, I'd noticed, when he went preaching, a crisp white triangle sticking out of his top suit pocket. Hadn't Delilah once sneered at how sick it made her feel, watching her mother ironing the Loathsome Verne's snot-rags.

'He's just leaving Gridford House,' Delilah was saying now, as if she could actually see her stepfather on a TV monitor. 'Now he's saying goodnight to the gatekeeper, but when he opens his mouth to speak, no words come. It's like they've dried up on his tongue. There are splinters of broken glass in his throat . . .' Delilah's commentary grew jerky here, as if she were

222

concentrating on something else at the same time; some physical activity, some performance.

'His throat is burning . . . It's closing up . . . tighter . . . tighter.' I watched as she tugged on the corners of the handkerchief. The loose knot was hardening into a taut ball, tighter and tighter. My own throat seemed to contract in fear. Just one more tug on those ends and Verne might be . . . he might be—

Then, 'Stay where you are!' Delilah commanded. It was a moment or two before I realized she was speaking to us, to Lauren and me. Then, as soon as I heard those four words, 'Stay in the circle!' my heart seemed to shrivel inside me. The words I'd dreaded hearing: *If anything happens, stay in the circle . . . the circle . . .*

The men had come out of nowhere, shouting, whooping; signalling with strange barks and whistles and hoots. Their fire-brands flamed yellow among the trees. I knew with a sick, sinking feeling who they were. Hunters. Witch-hunters. Thanks to Delilah's ritual, the ghostly mob had sniffed us out like carrion scenting blood. Bizarre as it seemed, they were hunting for us; for three silly girls from Northgate.

'Now we have them!'

'We catch them in their most foul employment.'

'Witches!'

'Creatures of the devil!'

Delilah's voice seemed to come from a long way off. 'Hold hands!' The torch fell to the ground as her rough, squarish hand with its pathetically short life line grasped my own, squeezing; Lauren's slender mittened hand trembled on my other side. 'Hold on and don't let go. Don't leave the circle.'

'Make way!' a voice barked out. 'Make way for the gentleman.'

Don't leave the circle, she'd said. It was hard not to, when my every instinct told me to run as fast as my tottery heels and sadly unfit carcass would carry me across the bog-field. But maybe Delilah was right. We could hear Hopkins clearly enough. The snorting of his horse, the thump of his weight as he slid from the animal seemed as real as the hands fastened on mine. Then came the slow crunch of his boots on frost-crisped leaves, the *chink-chink* of spurs. But would he actually touch us? Could he actually man-handle – or rather, ghost-handle us? Were such things possible?

'I think –' Lauren spoke as if she were choosing something from a menu – 'I think I'm probably going to faint.'

'Don't you dare.' Delilah's fingers must have bitten into her hand because she winced. 'Don't even think about it. We're safe, I told you. They can't touch us.'

It seemed she was right. Maybe the circle really did stop him and his rabble, because they held back from us, like animals kept at bay by a campfire. All I could see of Hopkins and his lynch party were eyes shining from a few metres away. The witchfinder himself was just an image, distorted, elongated, shimmering somehow as if through the skin of a bubble.

My heartbeat slowed slightly. Of course. I remembered Delilah once explaining that we should think of the circle as more than just a hoop of invisible energy; its perimeter went down below the earth and up over our heads, enclosing us thoroughly, like an egg.

Even Hopkins's voice sounded fainter than usual as he commanded, 'Thy poppet. Give me thy poppet, mistress.'

Delilah's eyes burned fiercely on mine and Lauren's. 'It's working,' she whispered. 'They can't get through.'

'Thy poppet ... thy poppet ... thy poppet...' Hopkins's voice repeated its request over and over, but it was distant, like a voice burbling from the bottom of a well.

'Hah!' Delilah's eyes shone with fanatical triumph. She shouted as if throwing her voice outside the circle, 'Fat chance, matey!'

I held my breath, waiting for a response. The voices muttered, frustrated, making no sense. Meeting Delilah's eyes, I giggled. This was our chance – our chance to give Hopkins a piece of our minds.

Unfortunately this was the moment when Lauren had to go and spoil everything. Her hand, which I thought I was hanging onto for dear life, just slipped out of mine. And she was gone, just like that. Bolted into the night. Lauren, that faint-hearted jellyfish, had done a runner on us.

'Trust Lauren,' I mumbled. 'You can always count on her in a crisis.'

At the same moment the implications of this sank in. I saw the look of triumph on Delilah's face falter, as the circle was broken. My own expression of horror matched hers. We were done for, weren't we? The Ancient Ones were scattered. The egg had cracked. And here we were, vulnerable as newly hatched chicks, while all around us shadowy figures armed with sticks and axes and fire-brands closed in.

'Oh – my – God.' I mouthed the words at Delilah. She had let go of my hand, and was busily stuffing the precious rag-thing inside her coat. Not a moment too soon, for the mob didn't waste any time.

'Take them to the water!'

'Give them a ducking!'

'Hanging's too good for them!'

'Prick them!'

'Burn them!'

'Walk them!'

'Have them confess . . . confess . . . confess . . .'

Mainly it was a babble of tongues. They didn't actually touch us. But without the protection of the circle, the force of their hatred whooshed at us like a gale-force wind. We staggered about, hands clasped to our ears, moaning. They didn't have to drag us off and hang us at the crossroads, like Sarah Didlick and her friends. They couldn't do this. Yet it seemed like my wrists and ankles were actually bound. I stumbled and *wham!* Attempting to save myself with my arms proved useless. My face slammed up against earth, cold, rock-hard, unforgiving earth. I lay awkwardly, stunned. My arms were flung out in a diving pose, clamped at the wrists. I could actually *feel* the rope nuzzling my chin, its hairy coarseness burning into my flesh.

So this was what it was like to be trussed up. You struggled to find things you could actually move, parts of you that still worked, no matter how ineffective they might be. Like my fingers, wagging uselessly, clawing at twigs and stone. Then something cold and plasticky. The torch! Snapping it on I craned my head back, snorting earth from my nose. In doing so, I noticed Delilah. She seemed to be crawling on all fours like an animal. Back and forth she shuffled, hemmed in by the witchfinder's boots.

'Hand over thy poppet, witch,' Hopkins said in his

reasonable, businesslike tone. 'Hand it over, or would you have me search for it, hmmm?'

I never heard Delilah's answer because someone was screaming. That kind of piercing, nerve-shattering scream that zaps through you like a thousand volts. The silence that followed made my skin creep. Lauren! They must have gone after her when she broke the circle, and now they were sticking her with pins. Torturing her. Slowly. Oh, Lauren. I closed my eyes. Much as I'd like to strangle her myself, she didn't deserve that.

Then, 'Can you move?' Delilah's voice said.

'What?'

'Can you move? Yeah, you can. Get up, quick. They've gone. I don't know why, but I don't think we should stick around to find out.' She was standing over me, holding out her hand.

'I can't,' I groaned. 'I'm tied up.'

'No you're not.'

'I am – I'm—' Then I realized she was right. My arms and legs were free. I reached up and allowed her to hoist me to my feet. She stood brushing leaves and earth from her coat and looking annoyed rather than scared.

'Are you all right?' I asked her.

'Yeah. Just. That wasn't supposed to happen. You never break the circle – I told her.'

'Yeah, but that's Lauren. She takes a lot of convincing.' I was leaning forwards, hands on knees, trying to clear the muzzy feeling from my head. Then, as if in delayed reaction, we both turned in the direction of the scream. 'Lauren, oh my God. Supposing they've taken her? Supposing they've taken Lauren for their thirteenth witch? We've got to find her – come on!'

We began to blunder back the way we'd come, towards the track. As we did so, the sound of voices reached us. 'Abbie! Are you OK, Abbie?'

I gasped with relief. I never thought I'd be so pleased to hear Lauren's shrill, whiny voice. Then, as a deeper voice joined in calling for Lilah, my breath caught in my throat. Joel. Joel sounding well pissed-off, like someone whose dog has run off once too often.

'Did you hear me screaming?' Lauren rushed at us, as we blundered out of the trees onto the track. 'I was running and running and then I slammed right into your brother, Lilah. And – oh, it was terrible – guess what, I knocked him flat, and we both fell over, didn't we –' she glanced coyly at Joel, who stood silent and fuming – 'like, on top of one another.'

On top of one another! My hands clenched. How dare she? How dare Lauren go throwing herself at my beloved in this wanton fashion?

'Did you have to screech like that?' I snarled at her. 'I thought you were being tortured or something.'

'Yeah, and thanks a bunch, Lauren, for breaking the circle,' Delilah joined in. 'What did I tell you about that? You just put Abbie and me in serious danger.'

At this, Joel let forth a contemptuous sigh. 'Jesus, Lilah, when will you ever grow up?'

'What's *your* problem?' She stuck out her chin as Joel turned his back and began walking along the track towards the house. 'What have I done to you?'

'It's not what you've done to me, it's what you've done to Mum. If you and your mates want to play Murder in the Dark or whatever it is, can't you do it when Verne's not at home? He's up at the house, losing his marbles.

228

He will have it that you lot are tarting it up in the town.'

'I wish,' Delilah said bitterly. 'I bloody wish we were.'

'Yeah, well I said I'd come and look for you. Now, for God's sake move it, before he bursts a blood vessel.'

He was striding ahead of us, like we were disgraced children who hadn't come home for our tea. This was too embarrassing. How could Joel possibly take me seriously as a romantic proposition when he thought I was out playing silly games with his sister? Pissed-off, he was even more fanciable, which made it worse. And Lauren, that no-good rat, must have thought so too, the way she was mincing along beside him, simpering, 'I hope I didn't hurt you, running into you like that?'

'What?'

'When we fell. You went flat on your back. I hope I didn't, like, damage anything?'

I'd damage something in a minute! For two pins I could have dragged her backwards by one of her silly plaits. I might have done, if I hadn't been feeling dazed from our run-in with Hopkins. I could still feel the imprint of the rope on my wrists and kept rubbing them, just to make sure it wasn't there. I was hardly in a fit state to prevent Lauren making a move on a guy who was rightfully mine. Obviously, the fact that he was eternally bound to me via the tangled roots of a gladiolus bulb and a few oaths to the goddess troubled her conscience not a jot. So it was just as well that Delilah was wedging herself between them and demanding, 'How does Verne *seem* though?'

'Seem? I just told you how he seems,' Joel said in a growly, uninterested voice.

'I mean, is he, like, OK?'

'No, he's a sodding freak, like always. In Verne's book that's normal. Listen, I'm not going to stay out here all night and discuss Verne's health with you. Just get a move on, OK. Mum's up there trying to keep a lid on things, and making him that herbal tea stuff that smells like vomit.'

'Herbal tea? What's she making that for?'

'I dunno.' He shrugged. 'Because it's good for colds or something. Poor old Verne, he's caught a cold standing around on doorsteps all day and lost his voice.'

Delilah stopped. 'He's lost his voice? Did you say he's lost his voice?' She glanced back at me and held up her thumb. 'Hear that, Abb? Success!'

'Yeah,' I said uncertainly. 'Congratulations.'

At which Joel turned and gave me a brief once-over with the hurt, mystified look that boys sometimes get when they just can't figure a girl out. Then he turned away, sighing. 'You girls,' he said (although I guessed he was referring specifically to me). 'You girls are on a totally different planet.'

Chapter Twenty

Confession

By now we'd rounded the bend in the track, and my heart sank at the sight of the feeble glimmer of light from Crud Cottage. Delilah might be congratulating herself on the supposed success of her spell, but as far as I was concerned, things could scarcely be worse. Just look at the facts. Up at the house, the Loathsome Verne (with or without his voice) was apparently flipping out big time, while somewhere out in the darker regions of hell, the Witchfinder General was signing our death warrants. If we sidled off back home, Lauren and I would have a dislocated pelvis and Mrs Croop to contend with. While my cosmically arranged love-match would hardly care if I disappeared into a time-warp this minute. Or would he?

I found myself falling behind, as Delilah began to lecture Lauren on the dos and don'ts of magic and ritual. 'What you did back there was like a major snub to the goddess,' she was saying. 'It's like sticking up two fingers to the Ancient Ones . . .'

Perhaps not liking the turn the conversation was taking, Joel let them walk on ahead. He stood shining the torch in my path, as if I were some old stray sheep he had to usher into the fold. Then, as I drew closer, he murmured unexpectedly, 'Hold on, you've got something in your hair.'

The brush of his hand as he extricated a twiggy bit from my mop made my scalp prickle so much, I imagined my head sparking like one of those fibre optic lamps. Had he forgiven me after all? Did this gesture mean something? Or would he remove twiggy bits for any old bat who harboured such things?

When I opened my eyes, he was tossing the twiggy bit into the hedge.

'Thanks.'

'S'all right.'

Funny, but wrestling with demons must clear the mind wonderfully. This was no time to cower modestly away in my crabby old shell, hoping the bulb would do its stuff, without my fluttering so much as an eyelash. I decided to go for it. 'Joel . . . did you, er, know I was going to be here?'

'In the woods?'

'No, here. Staying here at the cottage, for Christmas.'

'Yeah, Lilah mentioned something. Don't worry, I didn't come up here to see you. It was important to Mum, Christmas 'n' that, so I came.'

'No, no, I didn't mean . . .' I sighed. This was going to be harder than I'd thought. 'Joel, what I said, when I wrote you that letter, when I—'

'When you dumped me.'

'I didn't. I didn't *dump* you.'

'Funny, I could've sworn you said you never wanted to see me again.' His voice was flat, bored. If it hadn't been for the twig-removal I might not have had the courage to go on.

'Well, it wasn't a, like, "you are dumped" thing. There is an explanation.'

'Yeah?'

'I mean, it sounds like a mad explanation, but it's true.' My voice sounded jerky as I struggled not to slip on the ice or trip in a pothole.

'Listen, you don't have to explain anything, OK. I can take it.' He kicked at a stone with the toe of his baseball boot like he had far more important things on his mind.

'Don't be angry with me, Joel. I didn't want to write that letter. I just had to, like, *sacrifice* you.'

The word 'sacrifice' must have finally got through to him, because he shot a sideways glance at me.

'It was because of how we met,' I blurted out, deciding to come clean at last. 'By magic.'

'Magic?' The corners of his mouth twitched. 'My sister getting pissed as a newt was magic?'

'No – no, well, sort of. I mean, it was magic us coming together – how Lilah brought us together, kind of . . .' I trailed off feebly. Now he must think me a total loony. And there wasn't much time to correct this view, because Crud Cottage was looming horribly close.

'Lilah got sick deliberately, to bring you and me together?' he said, in this bitter, mocking sort of voice.

'No, it wasn't like that. See, things don't just *happen*,' I said. 'It might seem like they do, but they don't. Some things are *meant*, and there's, like, nothing you can do to stop them, and—' I broke off with a sigh. 'I'm not making much sense, am I?'

Joel kicked another stone, then he said grudgingly, 'You're a girl. End of story.'

I began to panic. In another few minutes we would have Verne to contend with; I might never get another chance. 'I've still got something to confess.'

Uh-oh, that word 'confess' again. For a second it felt like I'd pressed some button between this world and the next. As if the listeners had been waiting their chance. *Confess, confess . . . She confesses . . . She admits her most foul deceptions, her diabolical tricks . . . Confess, confess . . .*

'Joel! Please wait!' I hadn't meant to grab hold of his hand like that. The good thing was, he didn't snatch it away. He just said with a kind of sigh, 'Look, I don't understand you, Abbie. I don't know what your game is.'

'Joel, you thought you, like, really fancied me, right? That I was totally gorgeous and all that. The thing is, it was all a trick. Delilah and Lauren and me, well, one night we performed this special ritual. Lilah said I had to think of someone in particular; I had to come up with a boy's name, someone I really liked, and well –' I waited for him to drop my hand in disgust – 'I thought of you. See, I lured you to me with sorcery. You only thought I was hot stuff because of a spell. And then, when it actually seemed to work, I got scared. And that's why I tried to stop it.'

'You got scared of what? Of me?'

'No, no, it was . . .' I hesitated. The Witchfinder General was not a concept many sane people could take on board, face it. 'It was, like, dishonest,' I said. 'A cheat, kind of.'

'My sister's box of tricks, eh? What did you do? Don't tell me you slept with one of my old socks under your pillow.'

'Ha-ha. No. Does that work, by the way? It would have been a lot easier than the gladiolus bulb.'

'You slept with a bulb under your pillow? Or did you

234

slip it in my drink or something? What are they? Aphrodisiacs?'

I sensed, without seeing it, the twitch of a smile. For all his coolness, Joel was beginning to thaw. Seizing the moment, I told him about our nocturnal gardening stint in the Millennium Gardens.

'As far as I know it's still there, sprouting and budding and that. See, it's because of that bulb that you and me are . . . are . . . holding hands,' I finished feebly.

The next thing I knew, we were doing more than holding hands. Our bodies pressed up against the damson tree like we were rooted there. And Joel was kissing me, his breath warming my frozen ears, my cheeks. I'd forgotten how good he smelt, tasted. I'd forgotten how we kind of fitted together so well, as if it would take some kind of major earthquake to prise us apart. Or maybe Delilah's foghorn voice, screeching from the porch of Crud Cottage, 'Are you two coming, or what?!'

'Yeah, coming!' Joel shouted. Drawing back from each other a fraction, we stared into each other's faces like we were in shock. He said in a kind of fierce whisper, 'That wasn't the gladiolus bulb, right? That was nothing to do with my sister's daft spells. That was *me*, all right? Just you and me.'

And then we followed the others indoors.

I suppose that under normal circumstances watching someone else's dad, a grown-up, middle-aged man, throwing a fit would be mega-embarrassing at the very least. But when you've been interrogated by a sadistic ghost and passionately snogged by the love of your life, all in the same evening – well, let's just say it was a hard act to follow.

Lauren and I had to make out like we didn't notice a thing, while Verne rampaged through the cottage, tearing down all the decorations we'd arranged so artistically earlier that day.

'I will not have these pagan symbols in the house, you know that, you know very well, Delilah!' Hurling swags of holly and ivy about the room, he had the look of a parent who'd come across drugs or a porn mag under your mattress.

'This is the work of heathens, idolators. Hear me? Hear me, young lady?'

Actually it was pretty hard to hear him at all. Something had certainly happened to Verne's voice. He was shouting, yes; or trying to. But it was like turning the radio up full volume when the reception is dodgy. A string of words would blast out, only to die away in an unintelligible squeak. Words roared, then squeaked, then hissed out of Verne at every possible pitch.

'First you disgrace me in front of my colleagues. Then you fill my house with your satanic *trash*!' We caught this much, although 'trash' went off the scale a bit.

'Dear, I don't think . . .' Delilah's mother began wretchedly. 'I don't think Lilah meant any harm. It's only a few decorations. She did them for me, to cheer me up. It was my fault.'

'Calm down, Verne. It's only a bit of holly,' Joel put his arm around his mother.

'Who invited you anyway?' Verne's voice whistled, not unlike those disembodied voices in the wood earlier.

'We did,' Delilah said, eyes gleaming maliciously. 'Joel's

family. Something wrong with your voice by the way, Verne? You sound a bit croaky.'

Verne clutched at his throat and rolled his eyes pathetically. 'My throat is on fire, no thanks to you. It's hardly surprising, after the stress of yesterday – and now . . .'

'You should learn to chill out, Verne,' Joel said, coolly insulting. 'I reckon you're losing your voice.'

Perhaps his tantrum had worn him out, for Verne now collapsed into one of the comfortless armchairs, legs flung out. Sweat glistened on his scalp as he yanked the tie from his throat. Verne, it must be said, did not look like a well man.

Now that his fury was spent, Delilah's mother seemed to revive. Trying to sound as if everything was normal, she told Delilah to go and look for the honey. 'I think we've got some orange blossom somewhere, love. There's nothing like it for sore throats.'

Delilah went through the motions of looking in the kitchen cupboards, rolling her eyes at me secretly. 'Hah, it'll take more than honey to put him right.'

It was left to Lauren and me to sweep up the pine needles while Joel saw to the fire and Verne was shepherded off to bed. Lauren began muttering furiously about our escape money, and how we should leave tonight, this very moment.

'Define "emergency",' Lauren challenged me. 'Go on, define it. Because if this isn't an emergency, I don't know what is.'

'If you ask me, Lauren, it's your lucky night,' I said sarcastically. 'I mean, if Joel hadn't cushioned your fall like that earlier, you might have suffered a nasty accident.'

Oh, that got her! I saw the guilty look on her face as she crouched over the dustpan and brush.

'I mean, how fortunate for you that he just happened along and caught you in his manly arms.' Then I felt mean because, thanks to the bulb, Lauren had no chance with Joel. And anyway, you couldn't really blame her for trying.

'Anyway, don't worry,' I said more kindly. 'At least there'll be no more rituals, now Lilah's pulled this one off. And that means we've seen the last of Hopkins, so I wouldn't call it a real *emergency*-type emergency exactly.'

Lauren said she wasn't even thinking of Hopkins. Tipping the pine needles into the bin, she jerked her head towards the stairs. 'We might all be murdered in our beds, in my opinion. And if we are, don't say I didn't warn you.'

As it happened, Verne didn't murder anyone in their beds. I would have been ready for him if he had, for how was a person supposed to get a wink of sleep next to the snoring lump that was Lauren, when their soulmate lay cramped on the downstairs sofa?

Anyway, Verne was in no fit state for murder. Even preaching to the heathens of Flopshire was out of the question. This was one side-effect Delilah hadn't bargained for – that Verne would be confined to the house all day, dragging himself around in a checked granddad dressing gown, throat swaddled in a muffler, ponging of Vick. Losing his voice didn't stop him from hissing his orders. By the time we three got up Joel had already been set to chopping practically a year's supply of wood.

Not only was the woodpile low; the cupboards were

bare. Since it was only four days to go to Christmas, Verne handed Delilah a shopping list, along with the housekeeping money and a lecture about 'trust'.

'Personally I'd be happier if you stayed away from the town altogether after your previous escapade,' Verne squeaked. The result of the 'trust' lecture was a prolonged bout of coughing, which brought tears to his eyes and a painful wheezing sound from his chest. This paroxysm seemed to exhaust him: he lay back in his chair, gasping.

Oh dear. I scrutinized Delilah's face for the slightest hint of remorse, but there was none. Just that strange glitter of triumph in her eye as she counted the notes. Scanning the shopping list, she said innocently, 'Throat sweets? Any particular sort of throat sweets?'

Verne waved his arm imperiously at us, as if the very sight of us disgusted him. 'Anything,' he rasped. 'Just throat sweets. And Delilah . . .'

'Yep?'

'I shall expect you back here by three o'clock at the latest. Understand?'

'Sorry, didn't quite catch you,' Lilah said, although she had heard perfectly well.

Verne repeated this final order, at great cost to his throat, and lapsed into another paroxysm of coughing until he was red in the face.

'Yeah, got you, Verne.' Delilah was already out of the door. 'Heard you the first time!' she called out over her shoulder.

Outside, she doubled up laughing. 'Throat sweets, he says, throat sweets! Oh my God, what a joke, eh? If he thinks a packet of Tunes will put him right, he's got a shock coming.'

There was no spoiling Delilah's moment of triumph. She was jubilant, buzzing, like success had gone to her head.

'Delilah, this is just like a lesson, right? You're teaching Verne kind of a lesson?' I couldn't help asking her. She didn't answer, because at that minute Joel rounded the corner, pushing a barrow-load of logs.

'He got you working too then?' Delilah said.

Joel nodded at the logs. 'Don't worry. I'm doing it for Mum. Personally I don't care if the git freezes to death.' He lowered the barrow and wiped the hair out of his eyes with the back of his hand. I swallowed. In his baggy checked shirt he looked like one of those hunks you see toiling away in the background on the garden make-over programmes. I waited for a sign. A sign that the damson tree thing last night had meant something.

Delilah stood smirking wickedly, her eyes on my love-struck face. 'Quit drooling, Abbie, and kiss him goodbye.'

'That's if you can bear to be parted,' Lauren said. Obviously a sarcastic dig at my refusal to resort to our emergency fund.

'You can catch us up, OK?' Delilah turned and headed off down the track.

'Drooling,' I said, practically squirming with embarrassment. 'Hah! I don't know what she meant by that.'

'I don't mind you drooling,' Joel smiled. 'Drool all you like. As long as it's you doing the drooling and not that bulb.'

He came over to me, his hands finding my waist beneath my jacket, staring into my face with that worried, tender look that made my heart burst.

'If I was drooling, which I'm not, it would be *me*,

not the bulb. That lumberjack look suits you.'

'Yeah, well, may as well do my duty while I'm here. I won't be hanging around for long, Abbie. Don't know if I can take much more of him.' He jerked his head towards the house.

'I wish you were coming with us,' I said.

The words were out before I could stop them. Funny thing about this bulb spell – there was no way you could give the object of your desire the 'come and get me' treatment. It was such an overpowering feeling, this wanting to be together always, for ever, for the rest of our lives, like my mum and dad. No! Not like them, for God's sake! For the rest of our lives, OK, but in a permanent state of insatiable passion, like every day was the first.

'Your lips are all squelchy,' Joel decided, tasting them in puckered and drooling mode. 'Look, tell you what. I'll come and pick you all up in town, right, with the shopping? At the café opposite the castle – know it?'

I nodded, sniffing the cherry-wood scent of his skin.

At the same time Lauren's voice came piping up to us from the bend, 'We'll miss the bus, Abbie!'

'I'll be there at four, OK?' Joel said.

'OK.'

'And be good.' He stroked my chin with his forefinger. 'No more voodoo, right?'

'Right. Don't worry. Absolutely no more voodoo.'

That was one thing I *could* promise, I thought, as I called out to Delilah and Lauren, 'Hey, you two! Hang on. Wait for me.'

The time for spells was over. Or, as Delilah might have put it, we'd sown the seeds, and now – now it was time to reap the harvest.

Chapter Twenty-one

Web-Woman's Warning

This was going to be *my* day. I didn't know why exactly, it just was. There aren't many times in life (not in mine, anyway) when finally everything seems to be going *right* for a change. But now it felt like the planets were lined up in my favour; the goddesses were all twirling their flaming torches and chorusing, 'Yay! Way to go, Abigail Carter!'

This was how I felt as the bus dropped us off in the town square. Snow was starting to feather the rooftops of Ludlow white. The snow and the medieval fair which was on at the castle might have been ordered specially for me. Without the rituals, without Hopkins to worry about, and Joel crazy with love for me, suddenly everything was perfect.

Or it might have been, except that certain people were in a mysterious strop, and getting stroppier by the minute.

'We'll leave the shopping till last,' Delilah mumbled as we jumped from the bus. 'I'm not going to lug a load of parsnips around all day long.' She added that Verne must have forgotten the fair was on. 'All that hog-roast and beer-swilling and stuff would just about do his head in. Still, I reckon it's just what we need, right?'

I agreed. Why not? Good idea, I told Delilah, thinking it would at least take her mind off ill-wishing Verne for five minutes. Her gloating over wrecking his tonsils had turned out to be short-lived. On the bus she'd suddenly gone all quiet and gloomy. There was a brooding menace in her eyes that I was afraid to interpret too closely. It was as if she'd just realized she hadn't gone far enough; she hadn't quite finished the job she'd set out to do.

Still, I wasn't going to let Delilah's moodies spoil my perfect day. Or Lauren's whingeing, come to that. It was quite a task, though, convincing Lauren to pay our entrance money out of the emergency fund.

'Supposing we need it?' she grumbled, as we were separated from Delilah by a troupe of wandering minstrels.

'We won't. Think positive.'

'But supposing we do?'

'Supposing, Lauren, just supposing you shut up and enjoy yourself for a change – how about it?'

Inside the castle bailey was like a scene from an old Robin Hood movie, all jolly peasants in fetching little sackcloth numbers, hogs' heads rotating on spits, women hunched over spinning wheels and fat beardy types swilling beer. Outside the main marquee a man was showing kids how to make whistles out of apple wood; another careered around on stilts, while a bloke with a Gandalf beard carved faces out of bits of old tree trunk.

Delilah, pushing her way through the onlookers, remarked that the tree-face reminded her of Verne. 'It's got his mean, slitty eyes,' she said, urging us to agree on the likeness.

Lauren sighed. 'Lilah, couldn't we try to forget Verne, just for this morning?'

An innocent enough remark, I thought. But Delilah

just flipped, lashing out like a crocodile homing in for the kill. 'You can forget him. I can't, OK? He's still my problem.'

Lauren almost reeled from this attack, stunned. You couldn't blame her. Bolshie as Delilah was, she'd always reserved her temper for other people. Never us, her faithful handmaidens and partners-in-crime. Now I noticed something in her face that I'd never seen before. As we wandered around the stalls she would stop and admire the jewellery, or snigger at the dancers, but she wasn't really seeing them. She wasn't really with us at all, but miles away, back at Crud Cottage, I reckoned, with Verne.

It was freezing, just idly wandering about. We bought ourselves meat pasties, which Lauren swore were made from hog's head. Delilah devoured hers like she hadn't eaten for a week, and belched loudly.

'Well, that's what peasants do, isn't it?' she snapped when Lauren made a face. 'I suppose you're so refined, you don't have any bodily functions like the rest of us.'

Now this was a bit unfair. Seeing Lauren's eyes pricking with tears, I swallowed the rest of my pasty and dusted the crumbs off my jacket. 'Lilah, is something wrong? What's the matter?'

Her eyes widened, mocking. '*Is something wrong?* You ask me. Hah! What could possibly be wrong? Only my whole sodding life, is what's wrong.'

Lauren and I exchanged glances as Delilah slouched on ahead of us, hands in pockets, jiggling the chain that hung from her belt like she was planning to hit someone with it.

'Wait, Lilah,' I said, catching her up. 'What's up? Your

spell worked, didn't it? I mean, you know, the rag-thing? You were well chuffed about it last night.'

'Yeah, I was well chuffed. I was well stupid an' all. So he loses his voice for a couple of days. Big deal. Meanwhile my mum comes over all nursey and spoon-feeds him with Greek honey.'

'Orange blossom, I think it was,' Lauren put in.

'Greek, orange bloody blossom, what's the difference?'

'Well, actually—'

'Lilah, we understand how you feel, really,' I said quickly before Lauren, the world expert on honey, could enlighten her. 'It must be really hard for you living with him. But you can leave, you're old enough. You could get work abroad, become an au-pair, travel – I don't know . . .'

'Exactly,' Delilah said. 'You *don't* know.' She nicked an apple from a pedlar's tray, and bit into it. 'Spwah! It's sour!' Luckily the pedlar was looking the other way as she spat it out.

Somehow, without noticing, we'd moved away from the stalls. Now the outer walls of the castle reared around us, the ancient stone slabs sprouting whiskers of dead grass and frost-blackened creepers. Crows peered down on us from the battlements, shaking greasy black feathers and cawing at us like malicious gossips.

Leaning against the buttressed stone, Delilah fished in her coat pocket. My heart sank as she drew out the rag. 'Oh no, not that again.' I noticed how dark and greasy the knot looked, as she waggled it defiantly in our faces. The twisted folds of cotton seemed to have grown into their distorted shape, the way roots do, never to be separated.

'How much tighter d'you think I could pull it?' Her eyes glinted.

'For God's sake!' I cried, wanting to wrench it out of her hand. 'Can't you just burn the thing?'

She considered. 'Hey, that's an idea, Abb. Thanks. Burning – I never thought of that before. Imagine Verne spontaneously combusting while saying his prayers. That'd be a right laugh.'

'Lilah, you can't go on like this.' Lauren pushed her woolly helmet back. Her forehead puckered anxiously. 'How can you think of it after last night in the woods?'

'Yeah, well, if it hadn't been for a certain person behaving like a total wuss . . . Anyway, I told you, I can fix him.' She was toying with the rag, teasing us, whirling the ends until the knot spun. 'Ooooh . . . Verne's feeling a bit dizzy just now. Think he'll have to go and have a lie down.'

'Delilah, please, give me that thing,' I said, knowing there wasn't a chance in hell.

'What? Give it to you? You've got to be joking.' She looked from one to the other of us, her face darkening. 'What is it with you two? All of a sudden you care so much about the Loathsome Verne? All of a sudden you're sorry for the git?'

I shook my head. 'It's just wrong, that's all. No matter how bad a person is, you can't misuse your power in this way. You can't just . . . just . . . choke people to death. You know you can't. You'll only hurt yourself, bring God knows what on yourself.'

'If you won't give it up, just loosen the knot a bit,' Lauren pleaded.

A snowflake melted on Delilah's thick lashes. Or was it a tear? She folded her arms, refusing to meet our eyes. 'Maybe I should join the Puritan Brethren; how about that?'

'You could just pack your bags,' I suggested.

'Hah! Sure, pack my bags and go where? Tell me, Abbie, where?' She tugged the lining out of her pockets and wrenched open her purse. 'Look. Wouldn't get far on two pounds fifty, would I? I suppose I could always break into my lottery winnings and catch the next flight to Acapulco. Or perhaps I could come and stay with you and your nice little mummy and daddy, and we could be one big happy family. You two have no idea, do you? No bloody idea. Tell you what, just . . . just –' she waved an arm at us both – 'just bog off, will you, and leave me bloody alone!'

'Look what you've done,' Lauren said as we watched Delilah flouncing off in the direction of the stalls.

'Look what *I've* done?'

'Yeah, you've really upset her now. Where's she going?'

I ignored Lauren's accusation and hurried after Delilah. 'Lilah! Lilah, come back. Don't be daft, we only meant . . .'

But the twenty-first-century peasants kept getting in the way. Some idiot was juggling flaming torches right in our path. I caught a glimpse of Delilah passing the beer tent, and then she vanished.

I tugged Lauren's sleeve. 'She must've gone in the marquee – quick.'

But inside the huge marquee it was hopeless. A long, shuffling crocodile of people blocked the aisles. We found ourselves carried along as if on a conveyor belt. On either side of us the stalls glittered with silver, velvets, stained glass and sumptuous cushions fit for a desert prince.

'Stuff Delilah,' I murmured to Lauren. 'I'm sick of chasing after her. And I'm not going to get down and grovel to her – but hey, look at this . . .'

We detached ourselves from the crowd to examine some necklaces made from semi-precious stones, the jewelled colours of fruit drops. 'How much is left of that emergency fund?' I asked Lauren.

She looked at me. 'Not a chance. Ask your new boyfriend to buy you one.'

'He's skint,' I said, realizing that I loved him all the more for that. Distracted by the next stall, I moved on. 'Oh, my, Lauren – Lauren, look.'

There was something familiar about the next stall. It sold the usual New Age paraphernalia of candles, charms, books and dream-catchers. It also sold mirrors. Not just any old mirrors. These were clasped in webs of silver and bronze, decorated with minute spiders.

'Gorgeous, aren't they?' said the girl behind the stall. 'I've got two at home, myself.' She was a round-faced girl wearing a big cardie, unlike the rest of the stall-holders in their medieval costume. Lauren and I looked at each other.

'There can't be,' Lauren said faintly. 'There can't be two people making these things, can there?'

'Sorry I can't help you on the prices,' the girl apologized. 'I'm just minding the stall for Imelda. She'll be back any minute – oh, here she is. Speak of the devil!'

We stood there, Lauren and I, unable to move or speak as a horribly familiar face loomed out of the crowd.

'Lost your friend, have you?' Web-woman had taken

the medieval theme to the max. She was a vision in scarlet velvet adorned with furs. The cap had been replaced by one of those wimple things that women wore in the days when they sat doing cross-stitch in draughty castles.

'It's all right, Maggie.' She waved away the girl, who was asking anxiously about price lists. 'Go and get yourself a cup of tea, poppet, why don't you? I'll take over now.'

'Abbie – Abb!' Lauren nudged me hard. 'I think we should go.'

So did I. But those ice-blue eyes drilling into me kept me standing there. 'Yes, you might well stand there looking like butter wouldn't melt, both of you.' Web-woman began fussily rearranging crystals on her stall, as if our very breath might have contaminated them. Then she said in a voice that could cut steel, 'I've just *seen* him. She's brought him here, your friend, hasn't she?'

Seen him? I glanced around in panic, searching for signs of a black-brimmed hat among the bobbles and head scarves.

Amazingly, Lauren kept her cool. 'We don't know what you're talking about,' she said loftily.

Web-woman shook her head, and I noticed her strange earrings of drooping tail-feathers, the tigerish colour of the dead cock pheasant that Verne had left hanging in the back porch of the cottage.

'You girls should choose your pals more carefully,' she said, clicking her tongue. She wore green eye-shadow, I noticed as she leaned closer; her make-up was slapped on so thickly you could smell it, like wallflowers and antique velvet. She added confidentially, like she was doing us a favour, 'He's on her trail. He *shadows* her.'

She must have interpreted our silence as dumb insolence, because suddenly she hissed, 'You girlies make me sick. You think it's all a game. You play around with your spell books and your crystals and you seriously screw things up for us Old Ones. No one, I tell you, *no one*, has unleashed Hopkins on us before. And we don't want him here, see.'

'Well, thank you, we'll pass the message on,' Lauren said coldly.

Web-woman sighed, pretending to rearrange some charm bracelets that claimed to bring the wearer everlasting good luck. 'Tell your friend,' she said, very casual, like she was talking about the weather. 'Warn her. She shouldn't mess with things she can't handle. If Hopkins doesn't finish her, then we Old Ones are ready. We Old Ones are ready to do the job for him – Wait a minute, what's this?' Reaching out unexpectedly, she flicked a stray hair from Lauren's collar.

'What are you doing?' Lauren flinched as if Web-woman had actually struck her.

'Nervy little thing, aren't you, poppet? I'm only tidying you up a bit.' She was holding the hair in her palm, stroking it with an elegant finger. I can't say how painful this was to watch. It was just a hair, long and brown, still kinky from Lauren's tight plait, yet it might have been her heart beating in Web-woman's palm.

'You'd be surprised what the Old Ones can do with a hair or two,' Web-woman said in a chatty tone, as if she were giving us a recipe for sponge cake. 'I've already got one of your friend's, of course, and yours, poppet.' She winked at me. 'People are careless about what they leave behind in my shop. Stray hairs, bits of bitten nail, it all goes in the pot. We haven't used them yet, but we might. Any one of you girlies might take sick any minute.' She shook her head. 'Not a nice way to go, I might as well be honest. Slow. Painful. Nothing the doctors can put a name to—'

We were spared further gory details by a couple of customers enquiring about the mirrors. Lauren and I took our chance at once, melting back into the crowd.

'Oh my God, I feel sick already. She's got my hair, she's got my hair, Abbie!'

'OK, OK.' I had to admit it was scary. The idea that your health and well-being rested in Web-woman's hands.

'What's she *doing* here?' Lauren whispered.

'I don't know. I suppose she's as much right as anyone else – these craft people come from all over the country. Still, she's got a nerve raving on about "girlies and their spell books". That's how she makes her living, isn't it, out of girls like us.'

'True. And what does she mean about the Old Ones doing the job for Hopkins? Who *are* the Old Ones anyway?'

'Well, they're not the local old age pensioners' club, that's for sure.'

Lauren nudged me hard. 'Isn't that Delilah – look, just going out of the exit?'

If it was, we were too late to catch her. By the time we'd wiggled our way through a solid wall of people, she was gone. No Delilah, even though we searched the entire outer bailey, including the Portakabin loos and the souvenir shop.

I looked at my watch. It was just gone two. We had two hours to find Delilah and make our peace before Joel appeared.

'Damn her!' I said; then, seeing Lauren bent double, 'Lauren, what's wrong?'

'I think I'm coming on,' Lauren said in her woeful voice. 'I've got this awful cramp in my tummy. It's her, isn't it? It's Web-woman. She's affected my menstrual cycle already.'

'That's all we need. Don't do this to me, Lauren, please,' I said.

'Do what?'

'Have one of your period-from-hell days.' It had been known for Lauren to lie in a darkened room cuddling a hot-water bottle, doped up on paracetamol for twenty-four hours.

At this Lauren recovered enough to gripe sarcastically, 'Sorry, I'm sure, to put you to such inconvenience. But if I don't get in the warm for five minutes and have some kind of nourishment, I may just drop dead on you.'

The café was across the road from the castle. Not exactly a gourmet hot-spot, but a tea and fry-up kind of place. Lauren and I sat at a table next to a group of elderly Americans with maps and souvenir booklets spread out between them. I stirred the dollop of cream into my hot chocolate. Comfort food – just what we needed. It was too bad about Delilah, but we could hardly chase her all over town, just to tell her she'd got the Old Ones as well as Hopkins to look out for.

'I wonder if the Old Ones are the same as the Ancient Ones,' I mused. 'Only not so, like, *ancient*. Imagine some bunch of old crones like Web-woman hanging around through the centuries. D'you think a real, genuine, in-league-with-Satan-type witch could live for hundreds of years?'

'Do me a favour, don't talk about them, please. Did you say you were meeting Joel in here later?' Lauren changed the subject.

'Yeah, not till four though.'

'You'd better get rid of your moustache then,' Lauren suggested, making a miraculous recovery from her cramps. The cream, she meant, of course.

We sat there bickering enjoyably for a bit, and it struck me how good it was to get away from Delilah. Just for a while. 'She's been a bit hard to take just lately,' I confessed, feeling disloyal as I did so. 'I mean, I know she's got problems and that, but—'

'Haven't we all?' Lauren said.

'Yeah, haven't we all. Anyway, it's so nice to be, you know, *normal*, for a change: just two normal girls drinking hot chocolate with a whole lot of normal old tourists and yokels and stuff.'

Lauren agreed that it was. Especially since last night, when her nerves were just about strained to bursting point. 'And now Web-woman's threatening us, it wouldn't take much to make me snap.'

'A minute ago you were about to drop dead,' I said. 'You can't do both.'

Lauren didn't see why not. In fact we might have gone on sipping our chocolate and discussing her nerves snapping for ever, if the conversation on the next table hadn't grabbed our attention.

The American woman was talking to her husband

about the fair – and how authentic it was and everything. 'And the historical re-enactments are so convincing. Did you see that girl being dragged away by a mob? Well, I don't know what the story was, I missed the beginning, but that guy in black gave me the shivers, I can tell you. And the girl. What an actress! Screaming enough to wake the dead. Just like it was, you know, for real . . .'

Lauren's mug of chocolate halted halfway to her mouth. So did mine. Our eyes met through the steam.

The husband was commenting that it would have worked better had the girl dressed up too. 'She looked like some kind of punk,' he muttered.

Lauren and I lowered our mugs. The chocolate inside looked sickly suddenly. I leaned across to the next-door table. 'Excuse me – that, um, spectacle you just mentioned: the girl, was she actually dragged away, did you say? You didn't see where to exactly? I mean, which direction?'

The woman waved a blue-veined hand at the window, where snow was now falling so thickly you could barely see the castle. The girl had been dragged right out of the castle gates and down the hill, as far as she could tell. 'I think they were headed for that cute stone bridge that crosses the river. Some kind of street theatre, I guess. You Brits do that stuff so well, don't they, Raymond?'

Raymond supposed they did, but he didn't know they had punks in medieval times. His wife laughed. 'Excuse my husband, he's such an old purist. Haven't you ever heard of audience participation, Raymond – honestly!'

They turned back to their map, and I looked at Lauren. 'You know what this means?'

She nodded.

254

'How's your period pain?'

Lauren said she felt like she was giving birth to triplets actually but not to worry. 'I'm sure I'll live.'

'You'd better. I'm not sure about Delilah though,' I said, pulling back my chair. 'Living, I mean.'

Chapter Twenty-two

Deep Waters

This wasn't how I'd planned it. I mean, Lauren and I setting off on a totally absurd rescue mission in sub-zero temperatures. As we negotiated the rugged track which spiralled down behind the castle, I couldn't help silently cursing Delilah. Why did she have to go and get herself dragged off, just when things were going so well?

'What are we going to do if we find them anyway?' Lauren said, echoing my own thoughts.

'God knows. But we can't just leave her to get pricked and tortured and ducked, can we?'

Lauren looked at me fearfully through a whirl of snowflakes. 'Maybe he wants her for his thirteenth witch, like you said.'

'Maybe. If only Delilah had ditched that stupid rag, this might never have happened.'

As we reached the bridge, we paused for a moment. The river guzzled beneath us, foaming over the weir. Snowflakes whirled like a white bee swarm, stinging our faces raw. There was no one about. Not even a besotted tourist would fancy a riverside walk on an afternoon like this.

'Imagine if you fell into that, you wouldn't stand a chance.' Lauren, who wouldn't even dip her big toe in the shallow end of Bromfield baths, was hanging over the bridge wall. She was right. Used as we were to the tranquillity of Bromfield Park lake with its over-fed ducks, the sheer force of this water took our breath away. It gushed below us, sludge-coloured, flecked with froth, wrenching up twigs and branches and debris on its way.

'It looks like the jacuzzi from hell,' I murmured. 'If you fell in there, you'd get rid of your cellulite and be pulverized into the bargain.'

Lauren didn't even smile, and I couldn't blame her. This wasn't funny. I closed my eyes against the sting of the blizzard and imagined slithering from this bridge, down into darkness. My breath caught in my throat. What would it feel like, to have that ice-cold water dragging you down – the tombstone weight of it over your head? Think how it would slosh about in your nose, in your fish-gulping mouth, the taste of clay vile on your tongue. The blood would pound in your ears as the shapeless great beast of the river swallowed you whole.

'Abbie? Are you listening? I said, 'we can't just stand here all day. Abbie?'

Lauren's voice sounded strange, muffled. Or was it my ears? I was clutching onto the slippery stone rim of the bridge as if for my life. Crows cawed from the opposite bank like hardened smokers.

'What's wrong with you?' Lauren said, in the peevish tone of one who does not like her role as invalid usurped.

I shook my head, as if to shake water from my ears. 'Don't know. I think I just had a *déjà vu.*'

'A *déjà* what?'

'You know, it's when you get that feeling you've been here before, in the exact same place, saying the same thing to the same person. Like you've lived this very same moment before. Like us looking at this river, with the snow falling, and knowing . . .' I swallowed.

'Knowing what, for heaven's sake?'

'Knowing that any minute now something really, really awesomely terrible is going to happen.'

Lauren groaned. 'Huh. And here's you always telling me that *I'm* the pessimist.' Still, the fear showed in her face as she spoke. I knew she could feel it too. As if something foul and dark were sweeping towards us in the current itself. Something we'd rather not see. Not know about.

I looked at her. 'Lauren, I've just had this awful feeling about Delilah.'

'What about her?'

'That's just it, I don't know. It's just a bad feeling. Look, I think we'd better go on, just a little way along the opposite bank.'

The riverside walk led to the bridge we'd crossed the other day with Delilah. Upstream you could just see the faint hump of Gridford Bridge − the bridge which led to Gridford House and its ghost-ridden holding cell. Was Delilah there now? Was that where my instincts were leading me?

We stumbled blindly on along the towpath, wrapped up in our scarves and hunched like old peasant women, Lauren protesting all the way. 'This is crazy. We're not going to find her. Maybe what that tourist saw had nothing to do with Lilah, and she's up there in the café, stuffing herself with sausage and chips.' Then, 'Abbie . . . Abbie, I don't think . . . we should go any further . . . Abbie . . .' Lauren's monologue slowed to a halt, like an old record. 'Oh my God . . .'

We froze, right where we were. It was a bit like that party game you play as kids. When the music stops you have to turn yourself into a statue. One twitch, one wink out of place and that's it, they've got you! Out!

Had he seen us? Hopkins stood some way off along the bank, just where the towpath narrowed and the trees thickened. Squinting through the blizzard, I could see that he was standing beneath a giant oak, its roots dug in like clenched toes, as if to stop itself toppling into the torrent.

I don't know how Lauren and I could hear the whispers above the roar of the water. Maybe the wind carried them to us.

'Duck her! . . . See if she floats! . . . Drown the witch!'

It was then I noticed the package-like bundle laid out on the platform of tree roots. Bound up. Trussed. Tied.

My hand found Lauren's wrist. 'Delilah . . . they're going to duck her. They're going to drown Delilah!'

'Please don't notice us,' Lauren pleaded selfishly. 'Please.'

Hopkins stood back a bit, like a princely observer at some rough sport. Any minute now he *would* notice Lauren and me, surely. But he didn't even turn his head in our direction. Maybe he just wasn't interested in us any more? Maybe he was too intent upon that package at his feet?

'My God,' I whispered. 'What have they done to her?'

Now, as the wind nudged the snowstorm in another direction, I was able to see more clearly. Delilah was lying face down, in the very same pose we'd seen in *A Discoverie of Witchcraft*. The victim's toes were bound to her thumbs from behind, until the body contorted in the shape of a bow. This was the classic posture of witch-ducking, old women and young girls alike, bound and trussed like chickens before being lowered into their watery graves.

The voices began their hideous chorus: 'Give her the ducking! . . . See if she doth float like her accursed sisters! . . . Give her the ducking, ducking, ducking, ducking . . .'

Beside me, Lauren whispered that she thought she might possibly faint.

'Oh, not that again! Don't you dare bloody faint. You've got to think. How are we going to save her? How—?'

But already, the package was moving. Some invisible force seemed to be rolling Delilah's body towards the water's edge. Hopkins stood well back, as if he were afraid of being dragged down with her. I even saw him examine his boot fastidiously as if he'd just trodden in something horrible; as if the girl at his feet were a nasty smell under his nose. Then he began mumbling and crossing himself. He was saying his prayers! He was saying his prayers while his henchmen, whoever they were, rolled Delilah to her death.

This was too much.

'Stop! Stop in the name of—' I paused even as I broke cover, charging at the shadows. In the name of who? Not God, because Hopkins obviously thought that God had given him the nod and the wink to hound all womenkind to death. A goddess then? 'Stop in the name of Hecate!' I shrieked. Then stopped as the shadows recoiled, before hissing in my direction, 'They come! She brings her accomplices by her devilish code!'

I froze, too horrified to be scared for myself any more:

the bundle at Hopkins's feet was continuing to roll towards the water's edge. There was a kind of horrible inevitability about it, as if it were a natural phenomenon, a landslide. Only this was a girl-slide. Nine stone of tattooed, henna-decorated, pierced and studded girl-flesh hitting the surface like some old rock. The displaced water whooshed up in a shimmering fountain, like a grand finale, a farewell. Then, nothing. Just the river as before, rushing carelessly on, swallowing those bits the land no longer wanted – dead birds, shards of animal bone, leaves, litter . . . and our friend Delilah.

What would I tell her mother? This was all I could think of suddenly, breaking the news to the bed-ridden woman. Her only daughter, drowned.

'Help me, will you, Abb-eeeee! Abb-eee, don't just stand there!'

Lauren was yelling at me from upstream. Upstream? How did she get up there? Blinking snowflakes out of my eyes, I found it hard to believe what I actually saw: dozy, dithering Lauren turned into action girl, her long loopy scarf swirling like a great rainbow into the waters. 'Abbie, help me pull, will you!'

I lumbered wretchedly towards her, cupping my hand to my mouth, shouting against the wind, 'You can't save her, you'll only drown yourself. Lauren, you . . .' I trailed off, not really believing what I saw. For incredibly, there was Delilah, bobbing to the surface like a piece of drift-wood. It was as if the river itself had taken charge, and decided to be merciful, nudging her into the crook of a great tree root. She must have broken free of her bonds: she grabbed hold of Lauren's scarf, groping her way up the bank while retching up half the river. Once clear of the water, she lay face downwards like she'd never get up again. She (or rather *they*) must have removed her great-coat, for she was only wearing her old combats and T-shirt. Her dreadlocks streamed down her back like that dark, oily seaweed you find washed up on the beach, hiding her face from view. Her bare feet looked almost blue with cold.

'We ought to cover her,' Lauren said, nobly sacrificing her Afghan coat and tucking it around the sodden Delilah. 'I don't think she needs the kiss of life or anything, because she's spewed up all the water.'

'Blimey, Lauren, did you learn all this for your Deep Sea Rescuer's badge?'

Not funny. But this is what I do when I'm terrified – make stupid jokes. It's kind of like whistling in the dark. At the same time I began to shiver – that uncontrollable shivering you get with the flu, like you're never ever going to be warm again your whole life. Stupid of me. I mean, what had I expected: that Hopkins would just assume Delilah had drowned? That he'd call it a day and conveniently melt away back to his hellhole like before?

Hopkins, it seemed, had no intention of giving up on us. His boots left no footprints as he loped slowly along the water's edge towards us, his staff tapping softly in the snow. As he moved closer, I could hear him muttering his incomprehensible prayers, full of threats and curses and unspeakable tortures. It was as if he had 'right' on his side. As if *we* and not he were the true demons. He moved so slowly. Well, what was the hurry? One thing a spirit has plenty of is time. A whole eternity of it.

'Here he comes again,' I said, aware that we were all

shivering now, as we huddled beneath the trees. I looked at Lauren. 'What does he want, blood?'

Actually Lauren looked like she didn't have any blood in her veins. Her skin had gone an odd cheesy colour, like those triangles of Dairylea my mother kept in the fridge. She muttered, 'Thirteen, you said. He's come for his thirteenth witch. He won't be happy until he's made up the coven.'

Even as she spoke, he was there, looming over us. I knew this without looking up. Being in the witchfinder's presence was like some horrible illness where you lie helpless. I felt physically sick as he removed his hat to brush snowflakes from the brim.

'So —' he spoke in a reasonable, kindly-uncle tone that didn't match his words — 'what strange fish is this, I wonder?'

At once, those wretched voices supplied the answer.

'The witch lives!'

'She survives the drowning!'

'The witch floats like a cork!'

'Truly she is a child of Satan!'

'The witch must die!'

'Hang the witch!'

Hopkins frowned. He still seemed more intent on his hat than on us, brushing and smoothing it before settling it back upon the greasy coils of his hair. Finally he delivered his verdict: 'We shall hold this female at Gridford House this night. But do not think to call your master to help you, witch. Tomorrow at noon justice will take its course. Tomorrow, witch, you hang.'

Delilah didn't respond to this death sentence, except

to groan slightly beneath Lauren's coat, as if she no longer cared what happened to her. Maybe she didn't care, but *I* did.

'She's not going anywhere.' I plonked my bum firmly on a corner of Lauren's coat, thus pinning Delilah down. 'You can't have her.'

Another voice echoed unexpectedly in my head. A female voice. A voice that twanged like a fork scraping in a saucepan. 'If Hopkins doesn't finish her,' the voice said, 'we will. The Old Ones will.'

Web-woman! All at once I could feel the life seeping back into my fingertips, the blood flowing. Of course! If Hopkins wanted his thirteenth witch, let him have her. But let him have the real thing.

'We could do a deal!' Maybe my idea made me un-usually brave, I don't know. Even so, just getting to my feet took all my strength. My knees felt wobbly. I couldn't look Hopkins in the eye, but addressed the dark vacuum about him, where even the snow dare not fall. 'Did you hear me, Hopkins? I'm making you an offer you can't refuse.'

I could feel Lauren's restraining hand upon my ankle, but shook her off. 'It's OK,' I whispered. 'I know what I'm doing.' At least, I hoped I did.

'A pact, you mean, child? Your pact is with the evil one, I think. I make no "deals", as you do call them, with a child of Satan.'

I swallowed hard. 'Wouldn't you like to have more names? For your list? Wouldn't you like another name for your Devil's List?'

'What trick is this?'

'No trick, really. I'd just like to point out that none of

264

us three are actually real witches. We're fakes. It's like I said before, a fashion thing.'

'Fakes? Fashion?' Hopkins frowned, suspicious, as if my unrecognizable works were a sly trick to conjure demons out of the air. After all, what did he know about fashion? The drab, white-collared Puritans were hardly the fashionistas of their time.

'What I mean is . . .' I blathered, desperate not to lose my nerve. 'What I mean is, it's a trend. In our time, see, all the girls are at it. You'd have to murder the lot of us if you lived in our time, and then you wouldn't have any girls left.'

'You speak the devil's language, mistress,' Hopkins decided, obviously not caring about there not being any females left. 'The proof doth lie before us. A witch cannot drown. 'Tis well known. A witch floats, aided by her master the devil.'

I sighed. Hopkins had his own spook's agenda after all, his mission, his reason for living on in this world. Still, now that I'd started I had to go on, my voice piping pathetically into the void.

'OK, suit yourself. If you want to mess about with a bunch of kids it's up to you.' I pointed back down river, towards the town, where the castle walls were still just visible, rising out of a clutch of ancient pines. 'If you want us kids when up at the castle there's a real live witch, wicked as they come and an adept in the black satanic arts, selling her diabolical wares to innocent young girls like us, right this very minute. Right under your nose.'

Behind me, Delilah finally seemed to revive – enough to mumble blearily to Lauren, 'Why did you pull me out? You should've bloody left me there. Why bother . . . ?'

265

Somehow, Delilah saying this was even more scary than the figure of Hopkins looming over us. What did she mean leave her in there? As if she wanted to drown. To die.

'Right under your nose she's doing it,' I ploughed on, hardly knowing what I was gibbering about any more. 'She even has a shop where she sells her tarot cards and spell books and stuff. And she makes these mirrors,' I continued, 'like spider webs, to trap your reflection when you look into them. And this morning I actually heard her talk about her coven—'

'Coven, you say?' Hopkins pricked up his flappy old ears.

'Yeah, the Old Ones, she calls them.'

'The Old Ones! You speak of the Old Ones, child!' Did I imagine it, or did Hopkins actually shudder? He wrapped his cloak more tightly around him, as the voices chorused again:

'Do not heed the witch, sire.'

'She mocks you.'

'She tricks you.'

'Bind her wrists.'

'Bind her ankles.'

'Give her the ducking.'

'See if she doth float like her accursed sister.'

Surely, though, the voices were growing weaker? Now you could hardly hear them above the roar of the river. The realization gave me new courage. 'Why don't you try ducking a real witch, instead of persecuting young schoolgirls? She's up there this minute, drawing children into her web, trapping their souls and feeding them to the devil.'

'Her name!' Hopkins spluttered. 'I would have her name, child. I order you to tell me her name. Now!'

I hesitated, mainly to whet his appetite. Also because, at that moment, Web-woman's name slipped entirely from my mind. Just like that. Oh, come on! I scolded myself. How could I forget? My mind groped for something to fill the vacuum. What was it? Miranda? Esmeralda? The more I chased it, the more the name eluded me.

'Do not think to play with me, child.' Hopkins was holding the Devil's List, pen poised to add this new potential victim. 'If you knowest this name, say it. Now!' His head swivelled slowly towards the river. 'Or else face the ducking like your friend.'

Still my mind fumbled, searched . . . Im— Im-something. Imogen? Immaculata? Immerse, Imitate, Im-Im-Im . . .

'IMELDA!' Where did it come from? I don't know. The name just burst out of me like a curse. 'Imelda! That's her name. Did you get that? Do you want me to spell it out?'

He didn't. There was no need for spelling. Hopkins had gone. And with him the voices. There was only the hiss and roar of water in full flood, rushing on past us to the sea.

Chapter Twenty-three
The Thirteenth Witch

The effort of thinking up Web-woman's name had wiped me out. Only when Hopkins had disappeared did I notice that my knees were shaking. I collapsed onto a nearby bench, which was slimy with melted snowflakes, and leaned forward, head in hands. Would my ploy really work? Would Web-woman really become the thirteenth witch? It seemed too much to hope for.

Lauren stood gaping at the empty space where Hopkins had been. 'You know, Abbie, I never thought I'd say this, but you – are – a – genius!'

Delilah roused herself enough to mumble hoarsely, 'Web-woman? What did you bring *her* up for?'

I lifted my head, taking in her bedraggled crow looks and river smell. 'Imelda,' I explained. 'We bumped into her at the marquee, up at the castle. She's got a stall there.' I waited for the significance of this to sink in. When it didn't, I added, 'The thirteenth witch, you know? The coven? Hopkins's great mission? Hopkins wanted *you* to make the numbers up. We gave him Imelda instead.'

'Imelda, right . . .' Delilah nodded dumbly. 'Cunning.'

Cunning? Was that the best she could do when I'd rescued her from the jaws of death! Still, I forgave her. You could hardly expect her to jump up and down, hailing me as a saviour, when she'd been fighting for breath only a few moments ago.

'You look awful,' I managed to say, as she joined me shivering on the bench. 'Like you've just been dragged out of a river or something.'

She snorted, wiping away some greenish river gunk with the back of her hand. 'Yeah, very funny.'

Lauren began to twitter, partly on her own account, I reckoned. 'Delilah, we should get you home. Get you dried out.'

'Oh yeah,' Delilah croaked. 'A nice mug of Horlicks in front of the blazing fire is just what I need. Then Verne can preach hell and damnation at me.'

Lauren and I exchanged glances over her head. Delilah's attitude was puzzling. My experience of people being hauled back to life from the brink wasn't great, but you would expect them to be grateful at least. Or if not grateful, reborn, kind of. Delilah sounded defeated. Her whole body oozed despair, anger, contempt.

'But Lilah, you could catch pneumonia out here. You're soaked through,' Lauren fussed.

I laid my hand on Delilah's shoulder. 'Are you — I mean, you're not injured, are you? It must have been so painful, what they did to you. Before you rolled into the water, I mean.'

'What d'you mean, painful? I went for a swim, that's all.'

'A swim? But . . .'

Delilah lifted her head, briefly meeting my eye, 'It's no big deal, is it? I fancied a swim, OK?'

Lauren raised her eyebrows at me and tapped the side of her head. She whispered, 'Maybe she hit her head on something while she was in there; a branch or something?'

Warily, I tried again. 'Lilah, we saw you. Lauren and I, we saw how they tied you – your wrists, ankles. The ducking. Remember?'

'Yes, no – whatever. I just went for a swim. I like swimming; nothing wrong with that, is there?'

I tugged at her sleeve. 'In your clothes? Lilah, are you trying to tell us you decided to go for a swim fully clothed in the middle of winter?'

'In a raging torrent?' Lauren shook her head. 'Delilah that would be—' I don't know what stopped Lauren from actually finishing her sentence. Some kind of gut instinct perhaps. Still the unspoken word hung there in the air in screaming blood-red letters: SUICIDE.

My brain whirred, confused. Hadn't we seen her, trussed and bound, while Hopkins decided her fate? Hadn't we heard the ghostly chorus of *Duck the witch! Give her the ducking*?

'Lilah, we heard, up in the café . . .' I began. 'How did you get here?'

'How d'you think?' Delilah raked her fingers through her wet hair. 'I flew here on my broomstick of course.' She met our eyes properly for the first time.

'Look, I walked, OK. I got sick of all that racket up at the castle. I wanted to be on my own. Then, when I got to the river, I just fancied a swim. Don't look at me like that – it was an impulse. I just felt like it. Or I thought I did. Look, just leave it now, will you?'

Her eyes slid away from us to her hand. A deep scratch ran diagonally across the palm. In her battle to reach the bank she must have scraped it on something.

'Nasty scratch,' I murmured, tracing it with my own forefinger. In doing so, I checked out the life line, that

270

way-too-short-for-comfort life line. It was funny, but from where I sat it didn't seem so short any more. Maybe the lines on your hand can change, disappear, tangle, sprout off-shoots and strike out in new directions. What did this say about fate then? Was it cast in stone? Or could you actually change it, control it, be mistress of it? Had Delilah tried to do that this afternoon? Had the Loathsome Verne finally proved too much for her?

If this was the case, then Lauren and I must have been hallucinating back there. Seeing things. Hearing stuff that only mad people heard. Whispering voices. Shadows. Snow-blindness.

I hadn't much chance to ponder this, because my mobile was bleeping. I read the text:

DID WE SAY 4? OR AM I DUMPED? TELL D GOOD NEWS.
JOEL XXX

'Good news?' Delilah said sarcastically, when I told her. 'Well, I can't wait to hear that ... unless...' Suddenly she seemed to remember something. She rummaged frantically in her trouser pocket, but whatever she was looking for wasn't there.

We all knew what it was, of course. The knotted rag, swept along by the current to lie tangled in undergrowth until it simply rotted away to nothing.

'How do I look?' I asked Lauren as we climbed the hill back into town.

This is a rule of life, when you're female: you're supposed to look jaw-droppingly gorgeous at all times, no matter what. I'd spent the afternoon in an arctic blizzard, wrestling demons and dragging an ungrateful friend from a raging torrent, but this was no excuse for looking like an old boot. (As anyone who's watched an immaculate Buffy kick vampire-ass will tell you.)

'Do you want me to be totally honest?' Lauren whipped out the mirror she was always using to check on her eczema patches and held it in front of my face. '*Voilà!*' she crowed a little smugly. 'The mirror never lies.'

I almost gasped as my reflection gawped back at me. Joel might be blinded by love thanks to a certain bulb, but surely he wasn't that blind. What with cracked lips and a splodge of river-sludge on my cheekbone, I'd seen better-looking creatures on Sainsbury's fresh-fish counter. And there was no time for a make-up renewal job. For here was Joel, dragging an obscenely large Christmas tree over to the car and trying to wedge it in the boot.

Wait a minute. Something was wrong here. Christmas trees?

'I thought Verne hated Christmas trees,' I said to Delilah.

As Joel spotted us, I knew that something amazing, something momentous had happened. At first he just stood there by the car, arms folded, looking all strong and mysterious in that hunky old flying-jacket of his, like one of those blokes from a Levi ad. Or was love blinding me too? I didn't care. I just wanted to be close to him as we crossed the square, Delilah shivering between us like a drowned rat.

'She slipped,' I explained quickly as we drew near. 'On the river bank. That's why we're late. She fell right in.'

'We really should get her home and dried out before

pneumonia sets in,' Lauren warned. 'Or even arthritis. Young people can get it, you know. It's not just a disease of old people.'

'For chrissake, stop fussing. I'm not a baby,' Delilah growled. 'Anyway, what's going on? What's with the tree? Has Verne had a brainstorm or something?'

Joel shook his head. He had a teasing look on his face, like he knew something we didn't. Something amazing. Something he could barely contain. Something so fantastic he hardly registered his sister's sorry state as he opened the car doors for us. 'Get in, then,' was all he said. 'Hurry up. You need to be sitting down for this one.'

I expected Delilah to sit in the front beside him, but she didn't. She and Lauren huddled in the back with the Christmas tree, Lauren mumbling something about her evergreen allergies, although that was a new one on me. As I slipped in beside Joel, he gave me a quick sideways look. 'All right?'

'Yeah, all right.'

'You should dress up warmer.' He took off his scarf and looped it around my neck. It might have been a mink stole the way it made me feel. Kind of special and loved, in spite of the splodge on my cheek and my red nose and everything.

Behind us, Delilah groaned. 'Well don't mind us, freezing to death back here. When you two have finished gazing into each other's eyes, d'you think you could tell us what's going on? What's happened to Verne? He'll go berserk if he sees that tree, or has something . . . I mean, is he . . . ?'

Delilah couldn't finish her sentence. I knew what she

was thinking. But then Joel swivelled round in his seat and told her.

'Verne's not at home,' he said, really cool, like Verne had just popped out to buy a newspaper. 'He's, er . . . he's been arrested.'

We sat in silence as the incredible story followed. Joel had been stacking the logs when a car screeched up the track and three plain clothes officers jumped out, wanting to speak to Verne.

They had gone inside Crud Cottage, where Verne was still padding about in his dressing gown, in no fit state to speak to anyone. When they asked him about the young women who claimed to have been abducted by his religious sect and locked up in Gridford House, Verne could only squeak in reply. There was no need to warn him, Joel said, unable to resist a wry smile, that 'anything he said could be used in evidence', because by that time Verne had totally lost his voice.

'He locked them up?' Delilah's own voice was pretty croaky, or maybe that was just the pneumonia setting in. 'In Gridford House? You're kidding. You're having us on, right? This is all some joke . . .'

Joel just raised his eyebrows, Delilah's own thick brown brows. A look that said, Come on, some things are not for joking about.

'These girls, though,' I couldn't help asking. 'What did he do to them exactly?'

Joel laughed. It seemed Verne preached to them half the night. 'Kept one girl awake until she was dizzy. Can you believe it? Probably just bored them to death. Although they were on about drugs too.'

'Drugs?' Delilah snorted. 'Don't tell me they've laid

some kind of drugs charge on Verne. The man whose favourite tipple is Adam's Ale; who never takes a paracetamol unless he's dying – oh, this is just a joke. I—'

'Shut up a minute and listen,' Joel told her. 'I told you, I heard this through the door. They were just shooting questions at him, bang bang, hardly giving him time to answer, even supposing he hadn't lost the power of speech. It seems this girl is accusing him of shooting her up with something. She's been examined by the police doctor and she's got needle marks all over. She's being tested for Aids.' Here Joel's smile became a grimace of disgust, contempt. 'The lengths some people will go to to make converts.'

As we all stayed silent, he added, 'Some religion, when you have to drag people off the streets and spike them with dope to get them to get them to see the light. I mean –' reserve finally crumbling, he slapped his head incredulously – 'we knew he was a head-case, but . . .'

We three girls looked at each other. Nobody spoke. There was no need. We were all thinking the same thing: that maybe, just maybe, Hopkins had been even more zealous than we'd thought. That Hopkins had been pursuing his thirteenth witch all over town. He'd been spiriting likely females to his favourite haunt, the holding cell, where he searched for the mark with his sticking pin. Since Gridford House was the headquarters of the Puritan Brethren, it was obvious that Verne, as leader, would have fallen under suspicion.

'Supposing he gets bail though.' Delilah's own voice was hardly more than a whisper. 'Suppose he turns up on the doorstep again. They can't keep him without evidence.'

'Yeah, well, if he does, he's got a shock coming. You think Mum would let him in after that lot? His stuff's already out in the shed. She told me to dump it there.'

'But Mum . . .' Delilah shrugged, totally perplexed by now. 'You mean Mum isn't siding with Verne? She's not down at the station, mopping his brow and raving about his good character?'

Joel sucked in his cheek and said that their mother wasn't such a fool. 'It's been on the cards that they'd split up for ages. She told me. The country was meant to be a new start. It was bad enough when Verne went and trashed your Christmas decorations, but she was scared. Now she's talking about going back to London— Hey, Lilah.' Joel broke off, confused. 'This is not how you're supposed to react. This is meant to be *good* news, right?'

Because Delilah was crying – that kind of noisy, gulping crying you do when you don't care who sees, who knows; when you've given up trying to be tough. When you don't have to be some kind of hard case any more.

When Lauren put her arm round her and said we should get her home, Delilah didn't even shake her off. Her teeth were chattering like a funky skeleton-person, as a perplexed Joel turned the ignition and Verne's car stuttered into life. I laid my hand on his wrist. 'Hold on just a sec, will you? Look, what's going on over there?'

Through the castle gates, the torchlight procession had begun to unwind. Undeterred by the weather, tourists stood, cameras clicking, as the pipers, weavers and wood carvers emerged, holding their lighted torches aloft, marching to the beat of kettle drums.

'Very picturesque,' Lauren grumbled. 'Now can we—?'
She was about to say 'leave'. But she stopped. Just to

276

the right of the gates, where the castle gardens lead down to the river, some sort of theatrical sideshow was going on. A woman in a fur-lined robe and wimple was being arrested by a mob dressed in tall hats and breeches.

As far as I could see – the closeness of Joel and the snow falling make me an unreliable witness – she was being dragged screaming onto the back of a waiting horse. The horse took off at a gallop, the sound of its hooves soft in the snow.

Chapter Twenty-four

Aura Angora

Guess what? Six whole months later and Joel and I are still together. And I mean 'together'. *In every sense of the word*. Lauren says the very sight of Joel and me holding hands and gazing into each other's eyes makes her feel sick.

'Face it, Lauren,' I say. 'It doesn't take much to make you feel sick, does it?'

Actually this isn't strictly true. Now that the moon-dew is in full production again, Lauren's sneezing and scratching days are gone for ever. In fact, she and Delilah are even thinking of setting up a little business when school is finished; sort of 'moon-dew by mail order'.

'My sister,' Joel shakes his head with that puzzled frown that never fails to make my knees go weak. 'She just doesn't get any better.'

'Mmmm . . .' I say. I don't tell him he's wrong; that Lilah is a whole lot better. For a start, she doesn't do the dark stuff any more. She doesn't need to, with Verne behind bars for about a thousand years.

'A danger to decent womenfolk everywhere,' the judge decided (and who are we to contradict him?).

Not long after that day when Verne was arrested, Delilah and her mum moved back to London and rented a flat not far from Smedhurst Road. Delilah's mum underwent a miraculous recovery from that nerve-thing she had, and now she's got this stall at Camden Lock Market, where she makes and sells her knitwear under the Aura Angora label. The angle is that Lilah sits there with her mother and reads the customers' auras, and then they get a matching scarf or hat or whatever, which is a pretty neat business idea when you think about it!

As for *you know who*, well . . . we never mention him. As far as we're concerned, that snowy afternoon when Delilah almost drowned never happened.

I tell a lie: we did sort of mention it a couple of weeks back, when the three of us were cruising around The Gates one Saturday afternoon.

There we were, standing right by the escalator outside Dixons, and Delilah just looked at us and said, 'Shall we?' Then we snuck down the escalator to the bottom level. Just to look. Except there was nothing to look at. Imelda's Web is gone. Totally. Not even a closing down sale. Just the whitewashed windows and a sign saying, QUALITY LINEN AT FACTORY PRICES OPENING SOON.

We didn't say anything. We didn't need to. It was obvious we were all seeing the same thing: Web-woman, dragged, kicking and screaming, onto the back of a horse. Hopkins's thirteenth witch.

As for me and Joel, hardly a day goes by when we don't see each other. He's still got this look, like he's trying to solve the world's problems, and we go to so many museums and exhibits and stuff that I know more about Ancient Man than I do about the modern sort. Still, that's all part of his Capricorn charm.

Only one thing worries me – that blessed gladiolus. The other day I crept into the Millennium Gardens just to check it out, and there among the tulips, right in the middle of the bed, were these strange, sword-like leaves thrusting up. Perhaps no one's noticed them yet. But what happens when they do? What happens when they rip out my offending stray glad; even if they leave it, what happens in September when its petals go brown and shrivel up like old onion skins? Will Joel just shoulder his backpack and tootle off on that Aussie trip he's been saving up for since God knows when?

Who knows? If Joel's right, and our love for each other has nothing whatsoever to do with stupid old bulbs and magic rituals, then it won't matter, will it?

September. I kind of long for it and dread it all at once. September will be the true test of our love.